PRAISE FOR
AUDREY CARLAN

"FIVE STAR REVIEW! I recommend this book to anyone looking for a sweet, fierce love story. It takes a lot to write an original story that takes twists and turns you won't see coming."
~Abibliophobia Anonymous Book Reviews Blog

"DAMN! Audrey did it again! Made me smile, made me laugh & made me cry with her beautiful words! I am in love with these books."
~Hooks & Books Book Blog

"A sensual spiritual journey of two people meant for each other, heart and soul. Well-crafted and beautifully written."
~Carly Phillips, *New York Times* Bestselling Author

Intimate Intuition

A LOTUS HOUSE NOVEL: BOOK SIX

Intimate Intuition

A LOTUS HOUSE NOVEL: BOOK SIX

WATERHOUSE PRESS

DEDICATION

Ceej Chargualaf

*No person on this earth will be able to feel the connection to
Silas and Dara the way you have.*

*I dedicate them, their journey,
and their love to you.*

*Always remember...
happiness and loneliness are choices.*

With sisterhood and love.

NOTE TO THE READER

Everything in the Lotus House series has been gleaned from years of personal practice and the study of yoga. The yoga positions, meditation practices, and chakra teachings were part of my official schooling with The Art of Yoga through Village Yoga Center in Northern California. Every chakra and meditation listed has been personally written by me and comes from my perspective as a Registered Yoga Teacher and follows the guidelines set forth by the National Yoga Alliance and the Art of Yoga. If you want to attempt any standard yoga positions detailed in any of the Lotus House novels, please consult a Registered Yoga Teacher.

The meditation and aura learnings listed in this particular book have been from taking classes and hours of research.

I suggest everyone take a yoga and meditation class. When the mind is still...you are free.

Love and light,

Audrey

CHAPTER ONE

THIRD EYE
C H A K R A

The third eye chakra is the sixth chakra in the body. It is located in the brain at the brow, above the top of the nose. In Sanskrit, it's called Ajna. This chakra is considered the part of the body that can transcend time.

D A R A

Positive. Plus sign. In the modern world, the addition symbol is literally *positive*. As in *more*.

More quantity.

More happiness.

The white stick with the pink plus symbol glaring at me evokes the exact opposite of more. Next to the plus is a second window with two lines—in dramatic opposition to the glaring addition symbol I so desperately want to be a *subtract* symbol.

A negative.

The two lines infuse everything with glaring, unavoidable clarity—and mean only one thing.

Pregnant.

I close my eyes, sigh, and lean back against the bathroom wall. It's been three weeks since I laid eyes on him. Two weeks since I'd given up hope he'd call and explain himself. One week since I missed my cycle. Now here I am, knocked up with the product of a one-night stand. Only this isn't just any one-night stand. We have mutual friends. Several of them. Of course, they have no idea we spent a drunken night of carnal delights with one another. No, they are none the wiser.

Technically, my friend Nick did ask how "drinks" went with his buddy. As usual, I played it off like it was just another night. Nothing special. Definitely nothing to talk about.

As if I would discuss the feel of his lips trailing down my neck.

The way his hands curved perfectly around my naked breasts.

Our endless worshipping of one another.

Except how can they all not know?

We couldn't get enough of each other's bodies. We were careful, using condoms every single time. Completely on top of it. Literally. Went through a half dozen of them throughout the night. But one round...the condom broke. At the time, it wasn't a big deal. We were drunk as skunks and feeding on flesh and booze. It took a lot of meditation and thinking back through the haziness to even remember the incident, as inebriated as I was. By the time I recalled the slip, it was too late. The day-after pill wouldn't have worked. I know—I asked the pharmacist. Three of them. At different locations. And my gynecologist.

Until this moment, I had been banking on my good luck.

Except I've never been lucky. Not in love and not in life. At least not in my formative years. I started out in foster care and a girls' home for orphaned kids, no family to speak of, until I was eight years old. Then out of nowhere, a round black woman with big cheeks, dark eyes, and an easy smile picked me out of a lineup of children in my age group to sit and talk with. I knew from the other kids, when one of us was pulled out and talked to, it could mean ending up in a home. It was all any of us ever wanted. Still, one of the scariest days of my life was meeting Darren and Vanessa Jackson.

Until now.

For a week, the Jacksons came back to the home to visit with me. I guess they were making sure we were a good fit. I clung to Mrs. Jackson during our visits. I'd always wanted a mother, someone to look at me with soft eyes and a smile. Once our week was up, the Jacksons both held my hands and asked me if I wanted to come home with them. *Live* with them. I couldn't have known then it would be the best thing that ever happened to me.

I distinctly remember looking up into Mrs. Jackson's eyes and then Mr. Jackson's, trying to discern the significance of what was happening. All I could do in that moment was ask an awe-filled question.

"You want me?"

They assured me that, yes indeed, they very much wanted me to be their child. They took me to their expansive home in Berkeley, California, and showed me a room painted in a soft yellow with sunflowers scattered throughout. I was in heaven. Two human beings who wanted me, craved having me as their daughter. They worked, fought, and paid through the nose to adopt me officially. I had a family.

As I stare down at the three positive pregnancy tests, I cup my hand over my belly and cry. Big, heaping sobs. I've wanted nothing more in life than to be a baker and a mother just like my adopted mother, Vanessa Jackson. To show my child from the second it took its first breath I would always want her and do right by her—or him. Unlike my biological parents, I would *want* to give a child the love and family the Jacksons gave me.

And while the tears fall down my cheeks, I vow to my unborn child I will do exactly that. Regardless of whether or not Silas McKnight wants any part of his child's life, I'll be everything our child needs and more.

Positive.

Plus...one.

★ ★ ★

Three weeks earlier...

Harmony Jack's is packed to the gills with bodies as I enter and push past a beefy, handsy fellow. Mentally, I chastise myself for my choice of attire, but the sparkly blue, micro-mini dress called to me. So the hem sits just below my ass...big deal. I work hard in the studio to keep my shit tight. Aside from my ba-donk-a-donk. It seems there is nothing I can do about the size of my ass. Squats, leg lifts, and an endless circuit of yoga poses with an emphasis on slimming the glutes does absolutely nothing but make my bum higher and tighter. I've since given up on trying to slim it down and now focus on flaunting the hell out of it. If a man doesn't want tits and ass, they can get to steppin'. *Ain't nobody got time for that noise.*

I see my crew at the back of the bar. They look like they are hugging Honor, Nick's woman, for some reason. As I wiggle my way through the dancers and partygoers, I see Nick and wave. He pulls me into a hug. I turn around and snuggle Dash and his wife, Amber, and then Atlas before Nick hooks his arm with mine and leads me toward where Honor is standing next to a fine-as-fuck black man. His mocha-colored skin positively gleams under the flashing lights of the bar as I give him the once-over. He's dressed to impress: black slacks, a royal-blue dress shirt tucked in, with a thin leather belt around his trim waist. I can tell by the V shape of his upper body he's likely packing some seriously tight muscles under those threads. When I make my way up his form and my gaze lands on his face, his bright smile positively blinds me.

"Lordy..." I whisper under my breath as Honor leans into the fine man's space and says something I can't hear.

Still, I watch as he nods and does his once-over of my body, from my spiked silver heels up my bare legs to my cleavage-bearing chest, before landing on my face. He licks his lips and bites the bottom one. I'm positive my panties have dampened from one damn perusal.

I lift my hand to push my suddenly heavy locks off my neck so I can get a little air on my overly heated skin.

"Hey, babe, you know Dara Jackson from Lotus House." Nick lets me go and loops his arm around Honor.

She smiles softly and glances at me. "I do. Good to see you again."

I glance at Nick and note his rather possessive hold on the blonde and can't help but offer encouragement. I want to see my friend settled and happy. Honor seems to give him that. And I know for a fact she needs him. Shy, sweet, and naïve. Plus, her aura is starting to shimmer with a glowing pink, meaning these two are about to have some serious fun!

"Glad you scooped up your man. I'm sure there are yogis everywhere crying into their soy chai latte over the resident hottie being off the market." I laugh and wink at Nick.

"Absolutely off the market," Nick confirms and then curves his head toward Honor's and kisses her. "We're living together now too," he says with pride and another peck of his woman's mouth.

I sigh. I love seeing Nick so taken with this woman. It gives me hope the right man is out there for me too. Not that I've had a good one yet.

The man standing next to Honor clears his throat, reminding me of his presence. Not that I could forget. He's ridiculously attractive, and his light eyes have not left me since I arrived. Hell, I could feel those hazel gems running all over me while I greeted my friends a few minutes ago. Now, it's no different. He's not even trying to act cool. Confidence. I like that in a man. Almost as much as I like a body that won't quit and a smile that could melt the panties off any sista in here.

"Righteous." I grin at Nick before turning my attention lazily to hot stuff. "And who is this tall, dark drink of heaven?" I extend my hand.

He takes hold of my hand. The instant our palms touch, a sizzle of magnetism starts my hand chakras spinning in the opposite direction, my body's way of trying to pair instantly with his energy. *Interesting.* More interesting is when he lifts my hand to his mouth and kisses my knuckles. I swoon in my spiked heels, nearly falling over, but his tight grip won't allow that, and I sway toward him.

"I'm Silas McKnight. I work with Atlas." He gestures over to our friends behind me.

Right then, Atlas claps Silas on the back. "Don't let him

fool you, Dara. He's my boss. The dude is rich, available, and a hard worker." He clocks Silas on the arm. "Don't say I never did nuthin' for ya, buddy, but I've got to get home. Mila says Aria is awake with a fever and calling for her daddy. My girls call, I'm out. Bye, guys. Great job tonight, Honor. Really killer voice. Hope to hear it again soon."

I frown. Honor sang? I would have liked to see and hear that side of the sweet woman.

Silas ruffles Atlas's hair, making me smile. There's a brotherhood there. If Atlas let Silas touch him in such a casual and friendly manner, he must be well-liked. "Catch ya Monday. Don't be late...again!" Silas warns, and Atlas chuckles, lifts a hand above his head, and waves as he exits. Dash and Amber are quick to follow.

"We've, um, got plans tomorrow. We should, uh..." Amber twists her lips in a pensive gesture, but her aura is spiking red-hot, readying for a romp with our resident Tantric yoga teacher who also happens to be her husband.

Dash chuckles and hooks her around the waist. "I promised my wife a handful of orgasms tonight," he says with absolutely no concern for decency or etiquette. Such an endearing quality in my friend. "It's been a long week for her." He nods to his wife. "Means we're headed out."

Amber widens her eyes to the size of dinner plates. "My goodness. I can't believe you just said that! Dash!" She smacks his arm with righteous indignation.

He nuzzles her temple. "Little bird, everyone here tonight is going to go home and fuck like rabbits. We're no different. Am I right?" he asks our group. I'm not touching that statement with a ten-foot pole, because it has been too damn long for me. My dry spell is closing in on ten months, and I need to get me some. I glance up at Mr. Tall, Black, and Handsome, assessing my chances of a sexy romp with a stranger. It's not the first time—although, I don't make a habit of sharing my body without strings attached—but something about this man has me squeezing my thighs and fanning my face. I'd like so very much to take a bite right out of him. Plus, he must be solid if my friends like him so much.

Nick coughs into his hand. "I'm hitting my girl for sure." He twists his head so his lips rest against Honor's ear where he whispers something I can't hear in the overly loud bar.

"Yes, please," Honor murmurs, and her pink energy starts changing to the same bright red Amber's was a moment ago. Nick, on the other hand, is a straight fireball of energy. Always is. Everything he does is accomplished with a thirst for life and an unmatched exuberance.

"I think we all need to head home." Nick sets down his beer and grabs his girl's glass, adding it to the ones on the table.

"Guys, I just got here!" I offer my best pout, knowing it's going to be useless with this much sexual energy bouncing between my two friends.

That's when Silas offers his hand. "I'm happy to keep you company." He grins, and I place my hand into his once more. Again, the hand chakras start buzzing. I briefly wonder if he can feel it. "Come on." He leads me over to a quieter area with a hand to my lower back. I glance over my shoulder and realize all of my friends have left me high and dry.

Brats. Really, I can't blame them, and at least I get a hottie out of the exchange.

Silas offers me a corner booth seat. I grab the hem of my micro skirt and sit down, situating my legs so they don't show too much but leave very little to the imagination. His gaze takes in my bare thigh as he settles into the booth next to me, sitting so close, our knees touch.

"You work with Atlas?" I start off the conversation, wanting to get the basics out of the way. It's not as though I want to jump him straight away...but I kind of want to get to the good part a lot faster. Figure out if he's a psycho or not before I jump his bones.

He lifts a hand up and flicks his fingers at the bartender. Within what feels like seconds, she comes over with a glass of champagne, which he hands to me, and a full pint glass for him.

"Sorry, the women were all having champagne earlier, and I figured you looked a little parched. Champagne okay?" he asks. His voice is a low rumble, which sends my earlier arousal from a five out of ten to a nine out of ten.

"Uh, yeah. Never heard of anyone turning down the bubbly before." I take a sip, allowing the sweet taste to permeate my dry mouth.

He sips his beer and then licks his upper lip. I'm instantly fascinated by the small movement, wanting so much to lick that same lip myself but knowing it's far too aggressive at this stage of the evening.

"Ah, back to your question. Atlas and I work together, yes." He leans back into the booth.

"He said you were his boss."

He nods. "True. Really we're all part of a big team at Knight & Day Productions."

I smile. "You own the company, don't you?" I cock an eyebrow, waiting to see if he'll start to boast and fall all over himself telling me how amazing he is, how much money he makes, blah blah, like every other successful man I've dated in the past.

19

Silas lifts his hand and rubs at his bottom lip with his thumb before glancing away momentarily. "Guilty. But only because my father retired and I'm the eldest son. Couple of my siblings work the business too. Then we've got incredible talent like Atlas Powers. He and the team as a whole are why we're so successful."

Now that response I did not expect. To downplay his status in the company...

I shake my head and smile into my drink as I take a sip.

"Tell me about you."

I swallow the rest of my bubbly before answering. "For that, we're going to need a bit more alcohol. As in shots."

His eyebrows rise nearly into his hairline. "Shots?"

"Yep."

Silas leans closer, placing his arm on the back of the booth so his face is near enough for me to hear him whisper into my ear, even over the boisterous chatter and music. "You planning to get me drunk and take advantage of me, Ms. Jackson?"

Feeling bold and brave, I turn my head so our cheeks are touching, and I know he can catch a long whiff of my perfume. I lift my hand and link it around his neck, holding him in place.

"You can't take advantage of the willing, Mr. McKnight."

His body trembles as I scratch my nails lightly along the back of his neck.

"No, I guess not. You offerin' up a night of bliss?"

I grin against his cheek and use my patented sexy lilt, the tone that usually gets me what I want with the opposite sex. And right now, it's a hot night with one Silas McKnight. "Order up the shots and we'll find out."

"Anything you say, my queen."

★ ★ ★

I'm floating, lost in the plane between pleasure and then pain, as my back slams against a picture frame. We didn't make it three feet into his home before we were attacking one another. Silas's lips are on mine, his hands gliding along my thighs. He hikes my dress up to my waist and hoists me up until my bare ass hits cold, lacquered wood. I flail my arms out, knocking over a vase. It crashes to the floor, but he doesn't stop kissing me. I lock my legs around his trim waist and grip his shoulders like my life depends on it. He maneuvers his hand in between our bodies until he's cupping me possessively. A whimper slips past my lips, and he grins, running his mouth along my neck, sucking the parts that particularly interest him.

It *all* interests me. I'm so gone for this man. Drunk as a skunk and feeling damn fine, every kiss and touch making the evening even better.

I lift my legs, allowing my stilettos to drop to the floor before I dig my heels into his backside. "Please," I beg. The festivities haven't even started yet, and I'm already begging.

Hussy, I think to myself but can't find the wherewithal in my drunken mind to care. All I care about is getting this man naked and him pounding me into oblivion.

"*Jeez-us* woman! So damn wet." He moans, feeling me up with his talented fingers. "No underwear, baby girl. You trying to drive me out of my mind?" He licks a path between my breasts. "Shit. I'm going in," he warns before he sinks two long fingers inside me.

I arch my back and press against him, wanting more. "Deep." I gasp, bracing my hands on the flat surface and curling my fingers around the edge of what I think is a side table near the entryway.

"My queen wants it deeper, I give her deeper." He urges my legs wider, tips his head back, and watches as he presses those digits in as far as they can go. Then he blesses me with a thumb roll over my clit.

I cry out and start to pant, my eyes rolling, my head falling back against the picture or mirror or whatever it is behind me as he expertly works his fingers inside.

"You are so beautiful. Laid open, offering up your beauty. I'm going to watch you come all over my fingers, and then I'm going to get on my knees and lick you all up and down."

He thrusts in and out at a faster rate, my body reacting to every filthy promise. A litany of incoherent words spill from my lips as I climb to the pinnacle of my pleasure. I lock my internal muscles around his fingers and cry out in ecstasy. Wanting a deeper connection, I tug the back of his neck, forcing our mouths to crash together in a hot, wet kiss.

"Can't wait to feel that when I'm inside you, Dara. Now ride the feelin', babe. Take yourself there while I watch you fall apart."

I raise my hands and lock my fingers around his biceps. "Don't stop," I demand. As my arousal hits the peak, everything within me tightens, and I fall over the edge into nothing but pure heaven. He continues his pace for a long time, making sure every last wave of my release is gone before he pulls his fingers out of me and grips my hips, his lips falling to mine.

Silas is panting almost as heavily as I am as I come back down. I can feel his sizable length pressed against my thigh. With a renewed surge of energy from my free-fall, I slide my hand down his hard chest to his waist and below, where I palm his erection. Thank the good Lord above—he's a big boy!

AUDREY CARLAN

He grips my wrists and locks my hands to his chest. "Woman, I thought I told you the plan."

I blink stupidly and purse my lips, trying to figure out what he's talking about. I got mine and am damn ready to return the favor.

And then he floors me and starts my heart going to a jungle beat as he lowers before me. He lets my hands go and locks his to my knees, where he spreads me wide, this time with his face at eye level with my throbbing center. I squirm and attempt to close my legs, my body heating beyond what is a normal temp.

"Silas..." I attempt as he shakes his head but doesn't speak a word.

His eyes are a pale hazel but not quite. More like a startling green amethyst. People say my eyes are haunting, being an aquamarine color with my caramel-colored skin, but his are ethereal. Even more so now as his gaze shifts from mine to between my legs. His nostrils flare and he inhales.

"You smell sweet and earthy at the same time." Instead of going straight for gold, he turns his head to my inner thigh and inhales deeply. "Like coconuts and trees." He runs his nose along my thigh until he reaches my wetness. He closes his eyes briefly before opening them and glancing up at me one last time. "And sex. Let's see if we can't make that last one a bit more potent." He grins devilishly before licking straight up my seam with the flat of his tongue.

My hands fly to his head as if they were separate from my body. "Oh, my God!" I cry out when he swirls his tongue around the tight bundle of nerves and flicks it repeatedly, driving me crazy. Swirling my hips, I lose track of time, focused only on the warm, wet heat of his tongue, the grip of his hands on my thighs, and the incredible feeling of being worshipped by this man.

Soon, I'm gyrating against his face, gripping his head and forcing him to give me more pressure. He growls his appreciation, and before too long, he's got my ass in both hands, his face plastered between my thighs, and his tongue driving deep.

I ride the wave as my second orgasm of the night crashes over me, hot and heavy. He moans, licking up every ounce of my release.

"Jesus, you're a prince!" A cunnilingus god is more like it, but I don't want to stroke his ego too much. The brotha might get a big head. Not that he wouldn't have earned it. *Sweet Jesus.*

As he brings me down, he stands up abruptly, pulls his wallet out of his pants, and fingers a foil packet. "Not gonna wait, baby girl. After tasting heaven, I need to get inside." He rips the packet with his teeth while I make quick work of his belt, unzipping his pants enough to see the tip of his cock poking out of his black silk boxers.

"Sweet man, you're a big one." I shimmy his pants and boxers down far enough that his considerable length springs free.

He wraps his dick, making a show out of rolling the condom on. My mouth waters, imagining wrapping something else around those hard inches. His gaze shoots to mine as I lick my lips, practically panting with desire.

Silas grins, and his eyes darken. "We'll have more time for that later. Don't you worry." He lines up his cock to my center, dips his hips, and eases the crown inside.

Holy shit! Just the tip is in and he's stretching me.

"Damn, baby, you are *tight.*" His voice strains on the last word, and he blows out a breath. Easing in and out on slow strokes, he takes his time. Once he's wedged to the hilt, we both let out a long, drawn-out breath. I roll my shoulders and cringe at the discomfort of being propped against a piece of furniture for two big Os.

Silas must have read my mind when he says, "Need you in my bed. Hold on." He wraps his arms around my back, keeping one on my ass, holding us smashed together. The second I'm in his arms, I fall farther onto his cock. Speared and in motion. My mind swirls with the pleasure and pain of each of his steps as he makes his way down a hall. Then he's leaning over me and laying me on a cloud of red. A crimson comforter greets me when I turn my head to the side to capture my surroundings. And then it all just disappears into darkness when Silas, who's standing at the edge of the bed, grips my hips, retreats from my passage, and then slams back home.

"Jeez-us, woman. You'll break my dick with that grip!" he barks. "I fuckin' love it!"

For the next several hours, we fuck in his bed, on the floor, in his shower, in his kitchen, and in between more rounds of shots extricated from his liquor cabinet.

Never in my life have I had such a life-changing experience...until I wake up close to dawn, cuddled up to his side, so thirsty I think I'll die. I crawl out of bed and make my way into his kitchen to search his cabinets before finding a glass, turning on the tap, and glugging down two full glasses before I stop midgulp and take in the space. The room is strange. Not the normal bachelor pad. This is a home. A *real* home. Something a man and a woman share together.

The more I look, the more freaked out I become. Until I walk over to the mantle and see all of the pictures displayed proudly there. Silas with a beautiful blonde. Years' worth of pictures scattered all around the living room, dining area, and kitchen.

The fire in my gut, telling me to run, gets worse as I make my way down the hallway toward his bedroom and spy two doors that are unopened. One is a bathroom. The other...a fucking nursery. Pink. Butterflies everywhere.

Silas McKnight has a family.

Fuck my life.

CHAPTER TWO

The human aura is a bioenergy field, which exists in an egg shape around the physical body unlike the chakras that lie inside the body. The average person is not typically in tune with their spiritual self to see or feel the energy surrounding their body or that of the individuals around them, but this doesn't mean it's not there. One must be open to viewing such things.

SILAS

My head is pounding alongside the base drum as I watch Mallory belt out the chorus on what is sure to be her next hit single. As much as the woman drives me absolutely insane, she's making Knight & Day Productions a mint with her success. Every song we release for her hits the top of the charts.

The only problem is the spoiled broad thinks she can have whatever she wants, namely *me*. And I'm not on the market. Not for her.

Instantly caramel-colored skin and Caribbean blue eyes enter my mind.

Dara.

I can't seem to get the vixen out of my mind. It has been three weeks since that night, and I still can't get her taste off my tongue. Nor do I want to. It was pure hedonistic magic. Even though we both knew the score, wanted one thing, which we fulfilled many times over, I still felt my heart ache when I woke to an empty bed. Dara had sneaked out during the wee hours of the morning, with me none the wiser. I can't deny it was a hit to my ego. I'd given my all to the woman.

The last time I'd felt that good was with...

I shake my head. No thoughts of Sarah tonight. Thoughts of her have to be kept to the confines of my house. Letting her out into the open will ruin me. It's part of why my father threw me into heading the business. I needed the distraction. Three years ago, I was sinking into a hole of oblivion. I wanted nothing but the calm blackness of my loneliness to keep me company. My father, known far and wide as Daddy McKnight, wouldn't have any of it. And barely a year later, I didn't have him either. The need for me to take the reins of Knight & Day Productions became even more important, for my mother, my siblings, and my broken heart. The day I lost my father, I promised myself I'd never allow a person to hurt me so deeply, and I lost sight of everything else that mattered.

For two years, I've kept that promise. One-night stands, an empty bed, cooking for one, this is my life now. I'm alive, and the business is doing better than ever. My family is settled financially, the way my father would have wanted, and I...well, I'm alive. For now, that has to be enough.

I rub at my temples, wishing I had a few pain killers to knock out this headache.

A hand claps down on my shoulder. "Hey, bro, you okay?" My best talent scout and music writer, Atlas Powers, shoots me a concerned look. His mismatched eyes—one brown and one blue—are focused on me, and I can't help thinking how cool it is the dude has different-colored eyes. At first, it was discombobulating, but over time it's become unique and special, just like the guy. The past year with Atlas in the company has made an incredible difference. He has a knack for writing songs and pairing them with the right talent.

I smile brokenly. "Yeah, man. Headache."

Atlas lifts his chin toward Mallory, the current pop queen singing her heart out. "Doesn't take a leap to figure out it's probably a tiny blonde who's prodding at you?"

I sigh and nod.

"Man, why don't you let me take on her sessions? I'd do you a solid in a minute, and I'm a happily married man. Besides, you know Mila. My tiny wildcat would rip her to shreds if she so much as hit on me."

A laugh bubbles up my throat, and I let it out, trying not to do so while facing the glass window where our current topic of conversation is working. "Another reason why you can't take on Mallory. Mila would have my balls."

Atlas grins and toes the carpet. "That is no joke. She's a hellion, but I love the fuck out of her."

I clap him on the shoulder. "I know. Hold on to her tight. You never know when it can all disappear within an instant."

My buddy frowns and tips his head. "You act like you're

speaking from experience."

I offer a sad smile, sit in the chair, and press the call button. "That was excellent, Mallory. Let's give it one more go so we have some dubbing options. Maybe do it all one octave higher."

She smiles widely and fluffs her wild blond locks. "Anything for you, baby." She runs her hand seductively down the side of her chest, puffing out her breasts in all their medically enhanced glory.

I grit my teeth and force a flat-lipped smile. "Thanks. From the top." I press the button that starts the music Atlas wrote for her.

"Good idea to go an octave higher. It will sound sweet in the second and fourth verse." Atlas leans his back against the wall near where I'm pretending to consider tweaking the treble and bass as necessary. There's nothing needed. I've already dialed everything in for this particular song.

"Thanks."

Atlas groans. "Okay, I've got to say it."

I cringe and turn my chair fully toward my friend. "Spit it out."

"You're stressed out to the max, dude. You've got tension headaches almost every day, worse when Barbie pop star Mallory is in the studio, and I haven't seen you leave before me in weeks. You need to chill out. When was the last time you went out to let off some steam?"

Flashes of the night three weeks ago with his friend Dara come barreling through my mind.

Her lips surrounding my cock.

My face in her neck, mouth sucking on sugary skin.

Impaling myself deep inside her tight heat.

I rub furiously at my forehead, trying to obliterate those

memories before my dick gets hard. It's bad enough I've been wanking off to visions of her and memories of my time with her every night since it happened. I haven't even wanted to go out and find a new woman. Dara's possessed all of my carnal thoughts, and no matter what I do, those thoughts are not abating.

"Uh, we all went out and saw Honor sing, remember?"

His shoulders drop and his head follows, falling forward. "Dude, that was three weeks ago! You haven't so much as taken a break from work since then?"

I roll my shoulders and crack my neck. "Nah, it's fine. There's a lot to do anyway."

Atlas runs his hands through his mop of curls. "There's always a lot to do. But there's also a lot to live, and being in the studio day in and day out isn't living."

I want so badly to tell him how very wrong he is. It's practically the only reason I roll out of bed every morning. Making sure my father's legacy is intact and my entire family is set financially is the only thing I live for these days. The one and only thing that matters.

Another spike of pain pierces through my temple when Mallory's voice rises to insane heights. I grip my head and squeeze. "Fuck," I growl.

Atlas comes over to me and kneels, resting his elbow on the table where the sound system is. "Dude, you are too stressed out."

His concern rankles, but I know he means well. "You're just as bad as me. You work your ass off, maybe not the hours I have, but you also have a baby at home and a wife. Plus, you're always writing new songs. How do you manage the stress?"

My buddy grins wickedly. "I have the perfect stress

release."

"Don't you dare say it's bending your wife over on the regular." I grimace.

He laughs. "Nah, man. Though, not gonna lie, that helps. A lot." He waggles his eyebrows.

"You gonna share with me your magic stress relief or what?" I desperately try to change the subject. Thinking of his spitfire Latina wife bent over a couch being pounded from behind is hot but not something a brotha should be thinking about when it's his best friend's woman.

Atlas presses back onto his heels. "It's easy. I meditate."

I sigh and roll my eyes. "Fuckin' yogi bastard. You meditate."

Atlas grins widely. "I'm not joking. I take a class at Lotus House at least once a week. Does wonders for me. I'll take you tomorrow. It's Saturday. You don't have a wife and kids at home. You've got nothing better to do."

Without him knowing about my past, his comment sends a spear slicing right through my chest, obliterating my heart. "No, you're right. I don't have a wife and kid at home." I grit the words through my teeth, hating the sour taste that comes with them.

It's not his fault. He doesn't know. No one does.

"Great. Then I'll meet you at Lotus House tomorrow morning. Eight o'clock."

I widen my eyes. "Eight in the freakin' morning on a Saturday? You've got to be kidding me."

He chuckles. Always full of laughs, my friend. "Best way to start your day. Promise me you won't leave me hanging. I'll never let you live it down if you do. And there's no escape. I know where you work." He winks.

Mallory's voice rips through the sound room. "Silas, baby, I'm done. Were you listening?"

Ugh. I look at Atlas, who never loses that snarky grin, and press the talk button. "It was great, honey. Magic."

"Dude, you are so in for it with that chick. She is bad fuckin' news." He grimaces.

"I know," I respond, defeated. I haven't been able to shake off this client in a year of working with her.

"Tomorrow, then?" Atlas confirms as he walks to the door and grabs the handle.

The pain throbs around my temples and shifts to the back of my neck. I rub at it furiously, trying to stave off a migraine. "Yeah, I'm in."

Atlas opens the door just as Mallory bounces in with the exuberance only a twenty-year-old girl can have.

She runs the extra few feet, slams into my chest, and hugs me. I don't wrap my arms around her. Instead I put them on her biceps and push her the couple feet back.

"That was so awesome, right? Did you love it, Silas baby?" She blinks pretty brown eyes up at me. Her hair has the beach wave women are so fond of now, and her smile is wide on her glossy pink lips.

"Mallory, I'm not your baby. I'm your producer. I've been telling you that for a year."

Atlas coughs and stands near the door with his arms crossed. He knows I don't like to be alone with her, and I appreciate him staying when I know he wants to get home to his wife and daughter.

Mallory pouts, puffing out her perfect cherub lips. It would be a sin to deny the girl is beautiful. She is. Part of the reason she's so damn popular. Though it's the pipes on her that speak to me. Regardless of what Atlas and I throw at her, she can sing the shit out of it. I just wish her mother had taught her some freakin' manners about clinging on to men who aren't interested.

She runs a finger down my chest and toys with my belt. "Silas, you know we could have so much fun together. I've made it clear I'm yours for the taking."

I step back as she attempts to dig into the front of my pants.

"Mal, honey, that is an incredible offer, but I'm your producer, and I'm too old for you. By a decade. And I'm unavailable." A vision of Dara's beautiful honey-colored skin skitters through my mind. The waves of her soft brown and gold hair spilling through my fingers.

"Since when?" Her voice takes on a panicked, almost maniacal tone, her eyes going dark as she stares at me.

Danger! Danger! Danger!

An alarm bell rings inside my head.

Atlas, thank the good Lord above, comes to my rescue. "Mallory, sweetheart, he's been seeing a friend of mine, one his mama loves." He grabs her arm and leads her toward the door. Her purse and jacket are in a chair beside it. With his free hand, he lifts the jacket and purse and hands them to her. She takes them as if on autopilot.

"But, but, I'm perfect for him." Her chin trembles.

Atlas shakes his head. "He's too old for you. Besides, he never goes out, doesn't have any fun, and spends all of his time in the studio and church."

Church? Where the fuck is he coming up with this shit?

"I can go to church. I can." Her voice shakes.

Atlas places a hand to her lower back and leads her out.

"Sorry, sweetheart. He's very devout. And his mama's already in love with his new girl. We just need to keep this relationship professional. Okay?" I hear his voice teeter off the farther away they get.

I sigh and slump back into my chair. I'm going to owe Atlas for that one.

Oh yeah, I'll be paying up by attending meditation class. Whatever the hell that is.

Fuck my life.

★ ★ ★

The small Berkeley street is teaming with people at seven forty-five in the morning. I lean against the side of my gunmetal-gray BMW 5 Series Gran Turismo, aka the bullet, aka my pretty baby, while I wait for Atlas to arrive. He better not leave me hangin', or I'm not going in. I've never taken a yoga class, let alone a meditation class. I wouldn't know where to start. I didn't even know what to wear, so I threw on my couch-potato garb of a pair of gray sweats and a white T-shirt. The latest pair of Nike Janoski Max kicks in gray, red, and white on my size twelves completed the bum look.

Cinnamon and sugar wafts through the air from the Sunflower Bakery next to the Lotus House. My mouth waters at the idea of skipping meditation and just going straight for a gooey treat and an espresso. The bakery is hopping too. Patrons going in and out nonstop since I've been here. I glance around and notice a used bookstore called Tattered Pages, as well as the Rainy Day Café, both on the same side as the bakery and yoga studio. Across the street, there's New To You thrift store, Up In Smoke paraphernalia store, Amanda & Anna's

Antiques, and an empty lot with a metal fence and a sign that says Winters Group with a sold sign over it.

Winters Group. I know the name. I'm pretty sure that's the young, rich fella who's buying out old neighborhoods and building high-profile condos and high-rises. Claims he's gentrifying the area, but in reality, he's tearing down all the mom-and-pop businesses like the ones on this street and replacing them with multimillion-dollar skyscrapers or luxury condos for San Francisco executives.

I shake my head and look around. This neighborhood is beautiful. Quaint. Something you'd find in a small college town, kind of like Telegraph Avenue. Which is not far from here, now that I think about it.

"Hey, man, glad you came!" Atlas exits the front door of the yoga studio.

"What? Hey... I've been waiting. I didn't see you go in."

He laughs. "Cuz I parked in the back. I still teach here once a week."

My eyes practically bug out of my head. "You're kidding."

He shakes his head. "Nope. Mila and I met here. She teaches Vinyasa once a week too."

"Between running her gallery and having a baby?"

"Gotta keep in shape somehow, right? Plus, yoga is a calling. It's something we need to feel balanced mentally and physically. And the owners haven't found anyone who wants to teach naked yoga on a regular basis, so I keep it up."

"Naked yoga?" I sputter.

He grins. "Yep. Naked as the day you were born."

"I don't... I can't... Not sure I have anything to say about that."

Atlas opens the door for me, and I enter. The scent of spice and trees enters my nostrils. It's not unpleasant but definitely something I'd need to get used to.

"Hey, Luna. I'm bringing a guest with me to meditation. He's going to try it out before committing. Cool?"

A stunning redhead with snow-white skin and clear blue eyes waves. "No problem, Atlas. He'll be hooked after one session. I'm not worried."

I chuckle. "Confident, eh?"

Luna places her elbows on the counter, putting her head into her hands. "I'm confident in the teachers here, yes."

Atlas pushes me forward toward an inner door. "Luna is taking over the business. One of the co-owners, Jewel Marigold, is her mother. The other is Crystal Nightingale. They both want to retire and travel the world in their sixties and hang out at the studio when the mood hits them. Luna's our go-to yogi for all things. If you ever want to talk to someone about the other classes available or anything spiritual, she'd be a great resource."

Not wanting to sound like an asshole, I keep my thoughts and opinions to myself. Nothing spiritual has never done a lick of good for me. Sarah loved yoga, though. Toward the end, she went a couple times a week and said she never felt better than when she was doing yoga.

My heart suddenly feels like someone is squeezing it. Thoughts of Sarah always do that. I clutch at my chest and rub circles over the skin.

Atlas notices the move and stops in the hall. "What's going on?"

"Heartburn. Hits sometimes. No biggie," I lie.

He frowns and assesses my face with knowing, intelligent eyes. "If that's how you want to play it, fine. I'll give you that.

Eventually, your ass is going to talk to me about the shadows behind your eyes. I'm not stupid. I know when a friend of mine is hurting, and I'm pretty sure you've been hurting since the day we met. One day, I hope you'll trust me enough to share those burdens."

I purse my lips, rub a hand over the back of my neck, and squeeze the frustration building there. "It's not that I don't want to. It's just..." I let out a slow, frustrated breath. "Shit, man, I can't. Not today."

Atlas nods, puts both of his hands on my shoulders, and dips his head close. He's always been tactile. He seems to want people to feel his words as much as hear them.

"I'm here for you, when the time comes. Yeah?"

I grip one of his wrists. "Yeah, man."

"You're my brother." His tone is earnest and kind.

"From another mother?" I joke, and he smiles.

"Preach. Now let's go get you relaxed. Your shoulders are tense, you've got your 'heartburn' shit happening, and you need to fuckin' relax. I'm going to show you what that looks like, and man...it's going to be beautiful. Trust me."

I turn and hook my arm around his shoulder. "I trust you, bro. Let's get meditated."

He shakes his head. "Mark my words. This class is going to change your life."

"I'll believe it when I see it." I laugh as we walk into a cool, darkened room. Individuals are dotted around the room in random patterns. There is no rhyme or reason to their locations. One person is lying flat on a yoga mat in the center of the room. Another off to the side, cross-legged against a column, eyes closed, hands on her knees, facing up. A big man is settled in a cocoon of rolled pillows, one placed under every limb strategically.

"For your first class, we'll sit up against a wall, keeping your back flat. It helps you relax from the pressure of your back getting tired."

"I can't lie down?" I gesture to the person lying comfortably.

He grins. "She is a regular. She comes two, three times a week. If I let you lie down like that, you'd fall asleep. This is not nap time. It's quiet time for the mind."

"Whatever that means," I grumble.

Atlas leads me over to a wall close to the raised platform at the front of the room.

"We'll want to be close so you can hear her words. The first few times, it helps to focus on the guided meditation Dara offers."

Dara.

That name is not common, and yet, there's no way this is her class. Before I can question what he said, my skin heats, and prickles of recognition shimmer down my spine, prodding at my lower back. I look up, and there she is. The woman I've thought about every night for the last three weeks.

She's a vision.

Her hair is lifted off her neck in a mess of braids pinned up into a bun shape. She's wearing a turquoise flowing tank top and a pair of skintight black exercise pants. They have these cut outs in the thighs and calves where black sheer mesh offers a sexy swath of skin. Her wrists are loaded with bracelets, and a large crystal hangs down between her breasts, sparkling in the track lighting above. I watch, fascinated, as she lays out a dark-blue mat, sits down, places two bolsters on the ground, one under each knee, before she closes her eyes, places her hands together between her breasts, and bows her head.

I can't breathe.

Her beauty slams into my being like a wall of warm light.

Enshrouding me.

Protecting me.

Loving me.

Her eyes open, and I swallow at the heavenly blues.

"Welcome, class. Today we're going to focus on letting go. A lot of the time, we spend minutes, hours, days, and weeks wanting what we can no longer have or mourning something we have lost. It's time for you to let that go. Whatever may be plaguing your mind, your being, your soul..." She blinks slowly and glances around the room until her eyes find mine. I can tell the moment recognition crosses her vision.

It's like a wave of energy or two magnets reaching for the other when our gazes meet. Still, she doesn't falter in her words.

"If it's not meant to be yours, let it go." Her eyes stay locked on me. "Perhaps it was never meant to be yours in the first place."

I can't help but think she's speaking just to me. Every word, every utterance of her breath seeps deep into my psyche.

My heart squeezes for an entirely different reason when she says four words that could very well change my life.

"Set your loss free."

CHAPTER THREE

THIRD EYE
CHAKRA

The energy of the sixth chakra allows us to access our guiding voice, deep within. When this chakra is active, especially during meditation, it can cut through the noise of our busy minds. This is where we can find our true selves. The truths beyond the mind.

DARA

When the air around me changes, suddenly getting warmer and filling with a magnetic energy that seems to throb against the surface of my skin, I should know why.

He is here.

"Welcome, class. Today we're going to focus on letting go. A lot of the time, we spend minutes, hours, days, and weeks wanting what we can no longer have, or mourning something we have lost. It's time for you to let that go. Whatever may be plaguing your mind, your being, your soul..." I blink and glance around the room, my gaze settling on his, locking into place, the most natural thing in the world. And yet, it can't be. Shouldn't be.

He's not meant for me. Though the child I'm carrying has other rights. Our living proof of a night I'll never forget. Don't want to. Still, the energy weaving around his form, flickering a bright sunflower yellow is calling to me. It speaks of his curiosity, playfulness, awareness of self, and the power he holds firmly within his muscled form. I swear it's a siren's call, battering against my mushy heart. I want nothing more than to jump off this platform, wrap my arms around him, and burrow into his light, but that's not possible.

He has a family, and I have a *secret*. One I'm not ready to lay at his feet.

Silas smiles softly, the furrowed brow he had moments before now smoothing out as my presence registers. For a few long moments, I give my eyes the gift of taking in his masculine beauty. Sitting cross-legged, in a simple pair of sweats and a white tee, he may as well have been in a three-piece suit, because the casual attire takes nothing away from his sexiness. His hair is shorter than the last time, buzzed tight to his skull so only the shading of hair covers his round head. Those kissable lips are a force, even from this distance. Like two perfectly soft pillows that form into a breathtaking smile when he offers one. Though none of that holds my attention the way those pale-green gems do, perfect jewels against his mocha-colored skin, piercing me with their glory and honesty. But it's a farce, a smokescreen of glass and mirrors. Tricks of the eyes I can't fall prey to again.

With extreme effort, I break his gaze and glance at Atlas, who's beaming his pearly whites at me, a curl of unruly hair flopping into his eyes. A kelly-green aura shows my friend is balanced, full of love and contentment today. Just what I want to see surrounding my friends. He's fought hard to get to this place, and I'm thrilled that he has.

"As I was saying...if the thing plaguing you is not meant to be yours, let it go." I stare at Silas, trying to force myself to believe the words I'm speaking. Today, I need them just as much as my class.

I continue, breaking my own heart. "Perhaps it was never meant to be yours in the first place."

Silas frowns and rubs his hands over his thighs, gripping his knees like he's uncomfortable. Right before my eyes his aura changes, going from the playful yellow to a muddy brown. A disquiet ripples through my body.

He's insecure.

Silas closes his eyes, almost as if he's pained to hear my request for the class to let go. I carry on, committed to healing everyone in this room, including the man who holds my attention. He's been on my mind during my every waking hour, my consciousness invaded with thoughts of him and our single night together.

Knowing that nothing is going to change the outcome of what we shared, especially now that I'm carrying his child, I say my piece.

"Set your loss free."

I close my eyes and hold that thought within myself.

You must set the loss of him free. He's not yours.

Never was.

Never will be.

When I open my eyes, I'm shocked to see Silas now has a blackness pressing down around him. The only time I routinely experience an aura this color in such alarming detail is at a funeral. Straightening my back and my resolve, I inhale long and slow. I'm going to make that blackness disappear. I want to see the sun surrounding his form again. Something I said changed his energy so severely, I can almost feel the despair dripping off him, even fifteen feet away.

"Class, please close your eyes. I want you to inhale fully, counting to five while you fill your lungs. At the top of the breath, hold it in, experiencing your lungs full of life-sustaining air. Then slowly let it out, counting down from five. When you get to one, allow every ounce of air to leave your lungs before you inhale another full breath, filling your lungs to capacity before you once again hold and release. I want you to do this until I say otherwise."

I watch the class follow my instructions. It's amazing how simple breathing, feeding your life source, can change the energy reacting on the outside of the body. After five full minutes of doing nothing but breathing, I flick on the stereo, preprogrammed to one of my favorite meditation and chanting songs.

"We're going to listen to this song with a call and response chant. Listen to how it says Om Nama Shivaya. Break it down slowly. Let the ego go, and focus on your life force when you say the Om. Allow your voice to extend, rising and falling with the song."

Ohhh...ohhh...ohhh...ohhhh.
Naaa...aaah...aaahh...maaaa.
Shiiii...vaaa...aaaah...yaaaaa.

"Over and over. Let your mind still. Breathe. Inhale long

and slow. Taking in full breaths, exhaling full breaths. Chant. Let the singer's words soak into your being, then respond in song."

The entire class follows, and I'm filled with the beauty of each person's ego being destroyed. The egos dissipate, and white, pure auras pop up all over the room.

Until I settle on Silas. The blackness is fading but not quickly enough for my liking. There's a dirty gray overlay, which speaks of his skepticism, and it's guarding his energy.

Not being able to help myself, I pad bare-footed over to where he's resting. His beautiful eyes are closed, but his brow is still furrowed, showing his unrest and discomfort. Without thinking, I sit before him. His head twitches, probably sensing my energy, but he hasn't opened his eyes. That's a start. Means he trusts he's safe.

He has his hands palms up on his knees. Knowing I shouldn't, I lay both of my hands into his. Our hand chakras spin like a vortex of magnetic energy between us, sending sparks of recognition and delight through my arms. His eyes open in a flash, and he stares at me, not speaking. I close my eyes and settle in. Sometimes a person needs to be shown how to focus and chant so the mind can be free.

With my hands in his, our energy intermingling, dancing around us, I start to chant along with the song. Letting my voice rise and fall along with the singers. By the third time, he's following along. Silas has a lovely voice: rich, low in timbre, and devastating on my senses.

I should unlace our fingers, allow him to continue alone, but the feeling of fluttering in my heart and the rightness in my soul is forcing my hands to hold on. Giving myself this one time, I fall into true meditation bliss, holding the hands of the man I want but can't have.

My monkey mind stops thinking about the hurdles between us, the loss of what could have been, and the family unit we'll never have. There's nothing left, just simple, unending peacefulness. The plane of existence where worries disappear, love surrounds my being, and my soul is open and safe.

For a long time, I stay in this place, until a squeeze of my hands brings me back. I open my eyes to stare into the curious gaze of Silas McKnight.

"Your CD has ended," he whispers.

Ended. There's no music playing, which means forty-five minutes have gone by without me noticing.

Silas smiles, and it burns right through my body, settling like a lump alongside where his unborn child rests. I shake off the haze of contentment and stand up.

"Sorry about that, class. Looks like I went deep into my own meditation." I glance around, and everyone I look at is full of smiles and positive colors pinging all over the place. From blue, green, purple, to white, the happy auras fill me with joy. I turn around to check out Silas. He's back to a brilliant yellow aura, the same as when he arrived. Looks like the meditation finally worked, though I'd give anything to know what harshness he brought in with him today. There's definitely something he's holding close to the chest, which needs to come out or it's going to continue to plague him. Though I'm not sure why I care so much.

The man has a family. You were a fling. A one-night stand.

Of course, nothing changes the fact that I'm carrying his baby.

Silas and Atlas walk up as the rest of the class starts to leave.

"Great class as usual, Dara." Atlas pulls me in for a hug.

I inhale his musk and spice scent with a hint of baby powder. I chuckle into his neck and squeeze him tight, loving that I can smell his daughter on him. Means he's been holding his girl. The way I hear it from Mila, however, he never lets her go when he's home. The baby girl has her daddy wrapped around her pudgy finger, which is exactly how it should be.

"Thank you, Atlas. How're the girls?"

"Aria is perfect. And Mila...perfect for me."

I grin widely. "Yes, she is. You're the only man who could ever tame a fireball like her."

"Tame?" He tips his head back and laughs, hard. "Damn, girl, that's funny." He chortles a few more times before Silas pulls up behind him and taps his arm. "You remember meeting my boss and friend, Silas, a few weeks ago, right?"

I bite into my bottom lip and nod, not wanting to give too much away. I guess Mr. McKnight isn't a kiss-and-tell kind of guy. Good to know.

"Hello, Dara. I didn't know you were the teacher for this class," he offers rather shyly. The exact opposite of how he reacted the night we hooked up.

I tip my head. "Well, how was it when you opened your eyes?" I purse my lips, trying to make him remember the last time he opened his eyes after seeing me. I wasn't there. Because he's a cheating dirt bag, regardless of how innocent he seems right now.

He opens his mouth, swallows, and then rubs at his bottom lip with his thumb. God, that's sexy.

"Lonely," he mutters.

Atlas frowns. "Dude, she was asking how you liked the class, not your personal relationship status."

Wait, what? Atlas doesn't know?

I widen my gaze, cross my arms, and cock a hip. Now Silas McKnight is not only a cheating dirt bag, he's a lying, cheating, dirt bag.

"Oh, better than I expected."

I huff. "Glad you could make it." I refrain from suggesting he come again. That's the last thing I need. Seeing him for the first time in three weeks is already a punch to the gut, reminding me of the place on my body I've already lost to this man.

My Apple watch goes off on my wrist. "Shoot. I gotta get. It was nice seeing you again, Silas." *Not.* I want to gag but hold off. I've got to go. "Atlas, say hi to the girls for me. I'll call Mila for some chick time in the future."

I grab my bag and toss it onto my shoulder.

"She'd love that. I'll tell her." Atlas nods before going back over to his stuff.

Just as I think I've made my escape and I'm home free, long, mocha-colored fingers wrap around my bicep. "Dara, where are you going? We need to talk." He lowers his voice. "You just left. Without a word."

"Figured that was probably a good idea, since your wife could have come home at any minute," I fire back just as fast.

"What?" he gasps.

I shake off his hold and keep moving down the hall. He follows me at a short clip. "Dara, you don't know what you're saying."

Sick laugher leaves my mouth. "What? Was she on vacation? Girls' night out? Visiting a friend?" I continue hurling options his way before I stop, my flip-flops making a rubbery squeak against the wooden floor. Turning around, I walk right up into his chest until my breasts touch his wall of muscle and he can feel my breath fan his face. "I'm not stupid. I saw the pictures all over your house," I rumble through my irritation.

"Dara..." He runs a hand over his almost-bald head. I can practically hear the abrasions of each coarse hair prickling against his palm. I want so badly to wrap my hands around it like I did before, let it tickle my fingers as I kiss him.

With a mighty finger, I point at his chest. "We had a great night. Best I ever had. Ever. And that's saying something. You definitely know what to do with a woman's body."

"Thank you...but let me explain—"

I cut him off. "No, no, no. I've got one word for you. One thing you cannot deny. Something you did not think to bring up when you were balls-deep inside a woman who was—"

I jab my finger into his chest.

"Not."

Another jab.

"Your."

This time a flat hand against his chest, forcing him to back up a step.

"Wife."

"What?" He growls. "Tell me this magical word that changes everything we had, everything we shared. You've got it all figured out. At least you think you do. Enlighten me." His pale eyes have turned a mossy, murky green, and his aura has morphed from a startling yellow to a fiery red. He's pissed, and the energy surrounding him is flaring hot.

I glare at him, take a step closer, and get up in his face.

"Nursery," I practically spit.

He gasps, clutching at his heart as he backs up and shakes his head repeatedly.

"Yeah, that's what I thought." I spin on my foot and dash down the hall and through the doors, turning sharply to my left where I can already smell the scent of home surrounding me.

I open the door to the bakery and look for the one thing that will make this all better.

She enters from the back of the bakery, her round body, giant smile, and perfectly rosy cheeks a beacon to my battered heart.

Her eyes lock on mine, and she frowns. As I approach, her arms open wide. Everything I am and could ever be sits within the hopes and dreams of this woman.

I choke out the most blessed of titles. "Mama."

"My baby!" She wraps her arms around me as my tears fall onto her large bosom. "What is wrong with my dear child?"

I shake my head and hold her tight, clinging to the one person who can make everything better. She did when I was eight, and I know she can now, even though I'm twenty-five.

My mother puts the lockdown on me, shrouding me in the safety of her love. She doesn't care about any onlookers or patrons who may be seeing this sudden display between mother and daughter. She's only worried about me. My health. My happiness. Because she's my mother. Everything I could ever wish to be for my own child.

"Okay, baby, you're going to come with me."

I nod, tears running down my cheeks as she holds me close, never letting me get too far away from the safety and sanctity of her love. We make our way up the back stairs to my apartment. My parents gave me the apartment when I turned twenty and had made no plans to go to college. Sure, I'd gotten straight As in school, tried my best, but I didn't want a fancy education. I wanted to be a baker. Work behind the counter like my mother and father have.

This bakery is one of ten in the state of California. The flagship store, the beginning of it all, and I want to work in this store until the day I die. Raise my family with a man who comes home from work and eats the special treats I bring home for him every night.

My mother brings me straight through to my fluffy, purple couch. She sits me there and tuts. "I'm going to make some tea."

"Decaf," I say automatically.

"Okay, baby. Mama's going to make some tea, and then you're going to tell me what has put sadness in those eyes. You may be able to read auras, but I know when my daughter is hurting. And you are hurting. Me and you are going to get to the bottom of this, you hear?"

"Yes, Mama." I snuggle into the side of the couch and sigh, chilled to the bone.

My mother futzes around in my kitchen, making tea from a kettle, not the microwave, because that's sacrilege to her. Tea is freshly made from a hot kettle or not at all. Something about the impurities from the microwave. Mom has always been a purist.

While I wait, my thoughts start to wander back to what occurred moments ago in the hallway with Silas. He genuinely seemed like he wanted to explain something about his family. Maybe I should have let him speak. What if he's divorced, and I assumed incorrectly he was a cheating dirt bag?

No, then the pictures of a happy couple wouldn't have still been up all over the house. Plus, wouldn't he have denied it instantly?

Then again, he was surprised at what I said. Why, though? *Ugh*. I'm so stupid. I should have let him explain.

So he could lie to me some more? No way.

I kick off the blanket and sit back up, placing my hands in my hair and my elbows on my knees. An unsettled sensation slithers up my spine as I rock back and forth.

My mother comes back into the room, her round belly and large bosom leading the charge. She has her special apron on that says Best Mama in the World and has sunflowers embroidered all over it. Dad helped me make it when I was ten years old. She's worn it in the bakery every day for fifteen years. *God, I love her.*

"I love you so much, Mama."

"Child..." She taps my knee. "No need to spout things I already know. Get to what the problem is. I don't like seeing my beautiful girl with sad eyes."

I lick my lips and think about my options. Tell her. Don't tell her. Then again, I've never kept anything from her since the day she brought me home seventeen years ago. Besides, if I lie, she'll know. Even fibs don't work on Vanessa Jackson.

"What if what I have to tell you will make you think poorly of me?" I mutter, miserable but needing to get this out.

Her hand clasps mine, and she brings it up to her heart. "Child, since the day you were eight years old and I looked into your eyes, I knew two things. One, you were going to be my daughter. Two, I'd love you until the day I took my last breath and even beyond."

Chills ripple across my body and more tears fall. "Mama..." I choke out.

She pulls me into her arms and cradles me. "Baby, you're scaring me. Now tell me what's the matter before I have a heart attack."

I sniffle and cry for a long time, waiting for the sobbing

to stop. She pets my hair and hums me through the worst of it. Eventually, I'm able to suck in a few breaths.

"That's it, child. Breathe with me. It's all going to be okay. Whatever it is, me and your dad are going to be here for you. Always, baby. You never have to be afraid when you have us."

Pushing back far enough so I can consider the face that has only ever brought me joy and happiness, I offer up my greatest secret.

"Mama, I'm pregnant."

Her eyes widen, and she comes forward and lays her lips to my forehead. "Oh my, Lord in Heaven." She kisses me over and over. "No matter what the circumstances, a child is a blessing. You want this blessing, Dara? This gift?"

I swallow and nod. "So much it hurts."

"That's my girl." She pulls me into her embrace again and pats my back. "We'll handle this one day at a time. Your mama's here."

Breathing in and out, I pair my breath to hers, our heartbeats synchronizing naturally as they always do when she holds me.

Mama runs her fingers through my hair for a long time, humming and kissing me wherever she can reach in our cuddled-up position.

"Don't you worry, Dara. I'll show you the way to motherhood." She lifts my chin so that I'm looking into her dark eyes. "You, my sweet girl, are my gift." A tear slips down her dark cheek. "And this baby, this baby is your gift."

CHAPTER FOUR

It is thought that the human aura is made of fifteen different layers of energy, which present in a wide variety of colors. These colors determine where your mental, emotional, and physical embodiment is at any given time. For example, if you are happy and healthy, your aura may be a fresh-cut-grass green tone.

SILAS

"Damn infuriating woman!" I roar when I make my way outside to my car. Checking the street left and right, I don't see her anywhere, and yet it's only been a minute since she walked out of the door, *the* word dripping like acid off her lips.

Nursery.

Fuck! She saw the baby's room.

I palm my nonexistent hair, tip my head back, and groan. "Fuck!"

"Dude! What the hell is going on?" Atlas walks up to me, eyes wide, mouth tight. "I heard the little spat you had with Dara. I had no idea there was something between you two."

"It's nothing. None of your fucking business," I growl between clenched teeth. "I have to find her, but she's gone. Vanished into thin air."

Atlas chuckles, placing his hand over his mouth when I scowl and shoot a pair of invisible daggers at his laughing face. "Relax." He holds up his hands in a placating gesture.

"How can I relax? You don't understand."

"No, I don't, but you're going to sit down with me over an early lunch and tell me all about it. Then I'll tell you where Dara is."

I bum rush him, gripping his shirt between my curled fingers and get up into his face. "Tell me now." The words come out of my mouth like the lashing of a whip against bare skin.

He shakes his head and shoves me off him. "No fuckin' way. Not when you're a few shoulder bites away from being admitted to the loony bin. I protect my friends. Jesus, Si-Dog. What's gotten into you?"

A five-foot-five, sassy meditation teacher, apparently, but I keep my grill shut, not wanting to prevent him from giving me the information I need.

Atlas loops an arm around my shoulders. "Dude, you need to chill. Let's go have some lunch at Rainy Day. They have the best sandwiches. It will be like tasting heaven."

I scoff. He doesn't know, but I've already tasted heaven. Several times as a matter of fact.

Dara's plump lips.

The wetness between her thighs.

Every inch of her brown, smooth skin.

Sucking in a lungful of air does not dispel the images from pounding through my mind. "Fuck!" I growl again. "Just tell me where she is! I've got to clear the air. She has it all wrong about me."

"Does she now?" He blinks lamely, and I want to smash my fist into his stupid, goofy face. The first time I've ever wanted to hit my friend. Hell, one of my only friends. And it's over a woman. Course it is.

Atlas leads me down the street, past the bakery and bookstore, to the busy shop. Plants hang over the ceiling, vines sprawling all over the place, reminding me of an actual rain forest. A long wooden bar made from a halved tree log makes up the counter. A strawberry blonde works the counter as we approach.

"Hey, Atlas. How's it going? You teaching nakey yoga today?" She waggles her eyebrows and laughs to herself.

"Nah, we just came back from Dara's class."

She nods. "Did she soothe the savage beast within?" Her tone carries a joking lilt to it.

Atlas leans forward and winks at the waitress with the nametag that says Coree on it. "You know only Mrs. Powers can do that."

She smacks his bicep. "Totally! Crazy man."

They both laugh at whatever running joke they obviously have going. Me, I'm about ready to crawl out of my skin with the need to hunt down a frustratingly gorgeous woman with a sharp tongue and claws that dig deep.

"My friend and I will each have whatever sandwich is on special and a cup of the daily soup as well as two iced teas."

Frankly, I don't give a damn what he orders, because I'm not in the frame of mind to make any rational decisions anyway. Food included.

Atlas pays the woman and moseys over to a corner table away from the bulk of the customers. He pulls out a chair and gestures for me to sit. I do because, at this point, I have no choice. He's holding hostage information I need, and this is the only way I'm going to get what I want from him.

He sits opposite me and leans forward, clasping his hands into a prayer pose before resting the tips of his fingers against his mouth. "I'm ready whenever you are."

"Atlas..." I warn.

"You're going to sit here and tell me what happened between you and Dara that made her so pissed she screamed at you and ran off. I've never seen her anything but put together, man, and I've known the woman for a long time. She's one of my wife's best friends. Hell, she's one of mine. As are you. We're brothers. Right?"

His eyes are pleading. I know his background. His father left him when he was a kid to go live the life of an artist. He worked his ass off to pay bills and make something of himself in the music industry until he met his wife. With his wife's support, and since he came to work for me, Atlas has made a name for himself. As a couple they are doing great, and he has a small family. Blood-wise, he only has his mother and his daughter. The rest are the family he chooses, and he's chosen me. As I have him.

"Yes, brothers."

"Then share your burden." He crosses his arms on the table as though he's prepared to wait all day.

I shake my head and run my hand over my prickly dome.

"Dude, you don't want the burden I carry. Your life is beautiful. The last thing you need is my shit piling on top of your hard-earned goodness."

He scowls. "Shut the fuck up. Your shit is my shit."

I raise my eyebrows.

"You know what I mean. What happened with Dara? I'm guessing something happened after the night we saw Honor sing?"

"Yeah," I admit and lean back into the chair. "We hooked up."

The shock on his face is honest. Looks like Dara is as tightlipped as I am about sexual escapades. That's good. I guess.

"Okay. You hooked up. And..."

God, this is embarrassing. I shrug and glance out across the café. Everyone is happily eating, chatting, enjoying their Saturday morning brunch. "She took a runner." I purse my lips and rip at the edge of my napkin.

"Meaning she bailed before you woke up the next morning?"

"Yeah, that's what I mean."

He lets out a low hiss. "Ouch."

"Exactly." I rub across the back of my neck, working the tension there. "To find out she was teaching the class today was a bit of a shock to say the least. Then she sat in front of me, grabbed my hands, and chanted with me so I would get into the right headspace, and for a while I had nothing but peace. Brother, I haven't had peace in longer than I can remember."

"Why?" Atlas asks instantly.

"Because my wife and daughter were fucking murdered... all right!" The words fly out of my mouth, tasting like vomit on my tongue.

Of course, as with anything serious, that's when the server brings over the food. Turns out the day's special is ham and cheese on rye with a side of tomato soup. Neither of us speak as Coree drops off the food and drinks.

The second she walks out of earshot, Atlas is speaking. "I had no idea," he whispers.

"No one does. I mean my family knows, but out of respect, we don't talk about it."

Just like Atlas, always wanting to help, he reaches an arm out and grips my bicep. "Brother..." His eyes are filled with sympathy and concern.

I shake off his hold. "It's been three years. I'm over it."

He huffs loudly, sits back in his chair, and crosses his arms over the other. "Bull. Fucking. Shit."

"It was a long time ago," I manage, barely holding back the scowl that comes with talking about Sarah.

He frowns. "You don't just get over something like that. Tell me about her...your wife," he says softly, almost as though if he speaks too loudly, he'll spook me and I'll stop talking.

"She was beautiful. White. Blonde. Big blue eyes. And I loved her. More than anything or anyone on earth."

Atlas nods, grabs his tea and sips at it. "What happened?"

"Car-jacking gone really bad."

"I see. And the thing with Dara, the misunderstanding?" He switches gears so fast I get whiplash and yet, I'm grateful. Talking about Sarah, about what happened, is too much to take right now. As it is, I feel dirty and useless. Unclean.

I take a deep breath in and let it out before responding. "Apparently she got up in the middle of the night and looked around my house."

He shrugs and takes a bite of his sandwich. With nothing better to do, I follow suit. The minute the meat, cheese, and mayo hit my mouth, I'm in sandwich love. "Jeez-us, this is good."

Atlas nods around a mouthful before sipping from his drink and finishing his bite. "Told you, dude. Best sandwiches ever."

"I'll have to remember that." I shovel in another bite.

He stirs his soup before pinning me with his brown/blue-eyed gaze. "Continue. She saw your house. What's the big deal about that?"

I sigh and finish chewing before speaking. "I haven't exactly changed much since Sarah died."

His eyebrows rise into his hairline. "And..."

"She probably saw pictures of us. A happy couple. Man, she thinks I'm married with a daughter, when in reality, I'm a widower who lost his pregnant wife one horrible night three years ago." The next bite I take suddenly tastes of sawdust in my mouth, and I toss the sandwich aside and rub at my eyes.

"Dude, that's fucked up."

I nod. "Yeah, it is. But I need to set it straight. I can't have her thinking I'm some bastard who cheats on his wife. I'd never do that. If Sarah was still here, my life would be very different. But she's not, and there's nothing I can ever do to change that."

Atlas pushes his half-eaten lunch to the side. Apparently, I'm good at ruining other people's appetites too. *Awesome. Go me.*

"She works at the bakery," he says softly.

"What?"

"Dara. She teaches meditation at Lotus House every other morning at eight o'clock but works at Sunflower Bakery the rest of the time. Her family owns the entire chain."

"Really?"

He smiles widely. "Yeah. She's just two doors down. That's how she could disappear...as you put it. She just walked next door."

"Fuck me!" I stand up, my chair pushing back and falling to the floor with a loud clang.

Atlas stands up. "Easy there, fella. She's not going anywhere. She usually works the bakery until it closes at six p.m."

I tip my chin and place my hands on my hips. "I should go to her."

He shakes his head. "No, you should go home. Shower, chill out, get a good night's sleep, and then approach her when you're fresh...physically and mentally."

"Are you telling me I stink?"

He puts his hand under his nose. "You may be a bit ripe. Did you forget your deodorant today?"

I punch him in the arm and then loop my supposedly stinky arm around his neck. "How's that smell? Fresh as a daisy, right?"

"No, man, no. Stop! You're killing me with your pit funk!"

After a series of noogies that mess up Atlas's already wild hair, I let him go.

He lifts his hands up in supplication. "Truce!"

I laugh, surprised at how this man can make me laugh through an emotionally driven morning. Clapping him on the back, I lean close. "Hey, thanks. For, you know, everything."

Atlas hooks me around the back and walks with me out to the street. "Brothers. No matter what. I take my family very seriously, and you're family, bro, like it or not."

"I can dig it." I grin.

"Course you can. I'm a loveable guy."

"Says your mama!" I fire back and start jogging down the street. When I get to Sunflower Bakery, I glance into the windows hoping for a glimpse of Dara. Unfortunately, I'm not that lucky.

Atlas follows me to my car. He puckers his lips and looks down the street, a pensive expression stealing across his normally jovial face. "You gonna be okay?"

He's worried about me. Such a good guy and an even better friend.

"Yeah, man. Tomorrow's a new day," I offer quietly and tap the top of my pretty baby.

"You gonna take my advice?" He cocks one brow and smirks.

"I am. There are some things I need to do at home anyway."

He nods. "Call me if you need a friend. I'm there. Two shakes of my dick."

I tip my head back and focus on the white clouds passing by. "Powers, it's two shakes of a lamb's tail."

He cringes. "I don't have a fucking lamb, but I've got a dick. A big one. And I can shake it. Sounds better like that anyway."

"Only to you, numbnuts."

He shrugs. "Catch you on the flip?"

"Peace out."

"Peace out."

★ ★ ★

My home is cold and silent when I enter. No surprise there. It's been that way every day since Sarah was taken from me. Three long years I've grieved, held on to her memory. I walk past the entry table, noticing the red vase we'd gotten as a wedding present from my uncle is gone, smashed during the throes of passion between Dara and me. That was the first time I'd ever brought another woman home.

I never really liked the vase anyway. Sarah had thought we needed to display it in case my uncle ever came for a visit. She was worried about what he'd think if he didn't see it out. I couldn't care less, but that's how Sarah is. *Was.* Her entire being existed to make others happy.

Her family.

My family.

Me.

From the day we met, she exuded kindness and concern for others. She never wanted for much, always giving everything she had to others, whether to charity, her friends, or me.

God, I loved her.

I worshipped the ground she walked on. Worked my ass off day in and day out to give her the best possible life. And all she wanted was a baby. Took us five years of trying to get pregnant after our wedding, but that timeline didn't come without considerable loss. We'd lost two babies before we became pregnant with our little girl. Each loss brought with it a deep depression. Until the last pregnancy when we passed the twelve-week mark. The air around Sarah started to lighten, her mood improved, and she began to have a renewed sense of self.

We had the perfect life.

And then it was gone. *Poof.* Just like that. A single piece of metal killed my wife, my unborn child, and every hope and dream I had for the future.

All the hurt, anger, and anguish came rushing back today when Dara accused me of having a family. I couldn't utter the words fast enough.

They're dead.

Gone.

She wouldn't have listened anyway. She was furious, filled with indignation. Me? I was at a loss for words. I wanted to tell her something, make her see I'm not the man she thinks I am...

I sigh and make my way over to the mantle, where picture after picture of my life with Sarah is given a place of honor in my home. The home we built together, where we planned to raise our daughter. She chose every picture as a timeline of our lives. From high school prom, through my college graduation, our wedding, first anniversary, and the day we found out we were having a daughter. Five photos showing a young, happy couple.

Lying next to the last picture is the program her mother had made for her funeral. My beautiful wife, relegated to a folded piece of paper and a handful of typed sentences.

I grab the piece of paper and each one of the framed photos and take them down. I haven't so much as changed a single thing in this house since she passed. As much as I don't want to let her go, having all our happy times staring me in the face every day is not helping me heal. I know that. I've always known it, but I didn't care...before.

Now, it feels right. Making this small change.

My front door eases open, and my mother enters, holding up her key. "The door wasn't even locked. Boy, have you lost your damn mind?" she chastises as she bustles inside, placing her coat on the tree before assessing me. Her eyes scan my entire form, and her lips purse. Then she sees the empty mantle and the stack of frames in my hands.

She places her hands on her hips. "You ready to do this? To let Sarah rest in peace?"

My dead wife's name on my mother's sweet lips cracks my chest wide open. I stumble where I stand, grabbing on to the mantle as tears fill my eyes. "I need to try."

"What's changed?" Her words are soft yet direct.

I move forward and set the stack of frames on the oversize chair's cushion.

"The chair made for two," Sarah said, a twinkle in her eyes, her hands clasped to her chest. "Perfect for a couple in love."

Flashes of that day in the furniture store hit me like a wrecking ball to a broken-down building in Oakland.

"Ma, I don't know..."

She shakes her head, her black bob moving with her. One of her hands comes up, and she points to me, my own personal judge, jury, and executioner. It's not possible to hide anything from her. My siblings and I never could. "You've met someone."

I close my eyes and drop my shoulders along with my head. Shame filters through my frame.

"I can't live like this anymore."

My mother moves fast, coming over to my side and dipping her head, which forces me to look her in the eyes. She clasps my cheeks in her soft hands. Tears fall as I let it all go, just like Dara said.

"Sarah needs to be set free," I mutter, wishing it wasn't the truth.

"Mmmhmm, you can no longer live in the shadow of your old life," she croons.

"But it feels wrong, boxing up our memories, putting them all away." I clutch at my chest, worrying my heart will implode with the overwhelming emotions tearing through me.

She shakes her head and gets close enough that I can smell her sweet-smelling perfume. Chanel No. 5. It's been the same scent my whole life.

"Son, it's not wrong. It's part of the healing process. It hurt so bad when I boxed up your father's clothes and donated them to charity. I couldn't see them hanging in the closet, expecting him to come home and riffle through his dresser, toss his clothes on the floor *near* the basket, never in it. Those clothes were a constant reminder he was no longer there, baby. Look around." She gestures to the room.

"You've been living in the past. Sarah's been gone three years. You still have a pink nursery for a child who will never sleep in there."

I choke on a sob and grip my mother around the waist, allowing her to hold me up while I cry into her neck. Me, a grown-ass man, and my mother, a small, thin woman, but no one is more mighty than her.

"It's time to let Sarah and that sweet baby free. Time for you to live again."

"But the guilt, Ma. It's eating me alive." I shudder in her arms, and she holds me up.

"Don't you dare feel guilty. You've been dealt a rough hand. We all have, losing Sarah, the baby, and then a year later, your father. None of it is fair, but neither one of them would want us to live without joy. To mourn them day in and day out. We must move on. Find happiness in something else. Otherwise, baby, we're just dying on the inside."

I nod against her neck, allowing her words to sink in like they never have before. Pulling back, I wipe at my eyes and cough, trying to expel the emotions running rampant through my system.

Shame.

Guilt.

Sorrow.

Hope.

That last one shocks me as I find my place on the couch. My mother sits next to me, tall and straight, always the brave warrior, ready to take on any battle, especially when it comes to her children.

"Now tell me her name."

I swallow and glance at the empty mantle.

"You can't fool me, son. The only way my boy would have such a reaction is if a woman is involved. I'll ask one more time, and I expect an answer. What is her name?"

I lick my lips and focus on my mother's beautiful face. Her bright-red lipstick perfectly matches her flowing pants and tunic-style blouse.

"Dara. Her name is Dara."

CHAPTER FIVE

THIRD EYE
CHAKRA

*The "way of the third eye" is seeing life in moments. We are
a witness or an observer, being mindful of our surroundings
and all that graces us with its presence.*

DARA

Saturday and Sunday came and went with my mother fussing
over me like I was a small child again, making sure I ate well,
laughed plenty, and rested in my apartment. Usually I work
weekends so they can rest, but not this time.

Monday, the start of a new week, with brand-new
opportunities to enjoy all that life has to offer. I lay my hand
over my bare belly in front of the bathroom mirror.

"It's going to be you and me, kiddo. And Mama and Papa
too. The three of us are going to make sure you are so loved,"

I promise, cupping my belly and sending thoughts of love, happiness, and good health to my growing fetus.

Yesterday, I pulled up some websites with pregnancy information and ordered a pregnancy guide. Technically, I ordered two. Mama was adamant she would take every step alongside me because she never got this opportunity herself. I like having something special with my mom, a little secret between the two of us. Though I'm certain the second she got home the other night she told my father, I commend him on not barreling through my apartment door and checking on me.

The websites I reviewed had a lot of great information. Based on what I read, and when I know I had sex, I'm only a couple days past three weeks. It's still really early, and I've got a long way to go until I know for sure this little ball of cells will turn into a baby. Still, I plan to make an appointment with my gynecologist for three to four weeks from now. By then, I'll know if the baby has a heartbeat and is proceeding along well. I had no idea the amount of fear and concern being pregnant would bring with it.

There is a living entity growing inside me.

A baby.

My child.

Mine and Silas's child.

I run my hands over my completely flat stomach and up to my breasts. Squeezing them, I note a new sensitivity, a bit of a painful twinge. The websites I searched say they might start feeling sore as I progress through my first trimester.

Turning on the hot water, I quickly run through my shower routine and am out within ten minutes. I've picked a funky sports bra top today with a fun lotus design on the front and several crisscrossing straps in the back. I want to wear my skin-baring items while I'm still able. I throw a loose tank over the top and pair it with a teal pair of fitted yoga pants. My hair dries naturally as I head downstairs and flick on the lights of the bakery. My staff prepped everything needed for this morning's first round of freshly baked treats. I fire up the wall of ovens, set the right temperatures for the first five items, pull the trays one at a time from the fridges, and set them cooking.

While the first set takes approximately thirty to forty minutes, I tug on my apron, put my hair into a net, and start on the cupcake batter. Before the first ding goes off, I've got six pans of twelve cupcakes each ready to be put in. Nice thing about our ovens, I can cook in all six at once.

Walking over to the stereo, I put on an upbeat soundtrack from Muse, my current favorite band, and shimmy my way around the bakery, setting up the next set of bowls and utensils.

The timer for the first set of pastries goes off, and I pull that one out, set it on the countertop, and place the cupcakes in a line to cook away.

A buzzer goes off, signaling the back door is opening. I glance up at the clock and note it's six a.m. Dancing his way into my kitchen, Ricardo, my bisexual BFF, strikes a pose and flings his jacket at the hook, where it clings perfectly. He spins in a circle, grabs my wrist—attached to the hand still holding a wooden spoon—and twirls me around the middle of the kitchen. When the song is done, the second pastry alarm goes off.

Ricardo brings me close and places a flurry of kisses on my neck before spinning me back to my workstation. He puts on a mitt and removes the next item, going straight to work.

"How was your weekend?" I ask, shaking some powdered sugar over a tray of Greek butter cookies and the next tray of

Pizzelle, the Italian pinwheel-looking cookies I'm trying this week. I've found if I cook things with powdered sugar, people gravitate toward the items. Add in a funky shape, and they are intrigued. Explaining our new treats of the week makes my day more fun.

Ricardo shimmies as he squirts custard into a set of pastries. He finishes his task and then turns around. "Not like you really care...hmm?" He lifts his chin to the sky and wiggles his way over to the oven to get the apple fritters out so he can glaze them.

"I so care!" I frown and work on the éclairs the night team completed, which were chilling in the fridge.

He passes me the filling for the éclairs, and I hand him the cherry mixture for the cherry tarts. We're a well-oiled machine and the only two who work this early in the morning. That's why my parents hired the night crew. Two people work from seven to eleven every night, prepping anything we need for the next day that can be chilled or needs to chill overnight.

"You didn't call me all weekend to check on my date with Esteban," he tuts and then walks out of the room with the first tray of the day to load into the displays.

The cupcake buzzer goes off as he comes in, so he starts pulling them out and laying them on the sideboard we use so they can cool before we frost.

He comes over to my side, bumping shoulders as he gets the new pumpkin spice mix I just made, already knowing they are for another batch of three dozen cupcakes. He sniffs the bowl. "Festive. Pumpkin?"

I smile and nod. He walks over to the wall of cupcake sleeves. I'm dead set on having a variety of wrappers for our cupcakes. He picks the falling leaves with gold swirls, the exact ones I would have picked, and proceeds to get them ready for cooking.

"This weekend was weird. I ran into a man I had a one-nighter with..."

"Oh, Silas?"

"You remember his name?"

"Girl, you don't recall giving me all the dirty deets the following weekend when we drank our weight in tequila and I crashed out in bed with you?"

I frown. "That's right. You cover hog!" I laugh and set about taking the next tray to the front. He follows with his own tray of tarts.

"What happened?"

For a brief moment, I think about telling him my secret. I'm not the best at keeping secrets on a good day, let alone something so monumental, but I'm only three weeks. I need to be smart about this. The fewer who know until I've seen a doctor and can confirm I'm going to carry to term, the better. Still, I've got to give him something. It would do me good to talk about it.

"He came to meditation class with Atlas on Saturday."

Ricardo places the treats in the case and lifts up the empty tray. "You're kidding?"

"Nope."

"Was it weird?" He grabs for my hand and holds it, wanting to give me support immediately.

"Not at first. I mean, he's so good-looking. It was hard not to stare. And then he had this weird aura change during class. I don't know; something's up with him. He's got some demons, I think."

Ricardo scowls and puts a finger up. "Then stay away from

him, honey. You do not need a creepy clinger." His Latin accent rolls off his tongue when he's feeling feisty, which is most days.

I chuckle as we both go back to work. "I can't deny the attraction is still there, even more so after seeing him again."

"What you're saying is the crazy is worth the sexy time?" He lifts his eyebrows and twists his mouth into a smirk.

I shrug. "Maybe..." I admit begrudgingly.

He knocks my shoulder and sets up the next tray of cookies with the dough that was left out. He hands me a ball of dough to work on my batch. The mornings are always like this. For the first two hours of the workday, I get one-on-one time with my best friend, and there is nothing better, no conversation off-limits, just him and me, shooting the breeze and doing what we love. Baking.

"Are you going to see him again?" he asks, breaking the silence of a moment ago.

Again, I think about the whopping secret I have. I've already decided I'm not going to say anything to Silas until I know everything is okay. My plan is to tell him after the twelve-week mark. Which means I've got a little more than two months before dropping the bomb on him. I'm just not looking forward to the ordeal of dealing with a scorned wife on top of an unhappy baby daddy.

"Not sure," I fire off to Ricardo. "We had some pretty heated words the other day. I guess if he comes to class again, I'll know he's still interested." I finish laying out my batch and wash my hands before taking off my apron.

Ricardo snorts and makes a big show of looking me up and down in my yoga gear. "He'll show up again. I'd bet every last dollar in my bank account. Ain't no hetero man going to give up seconds of tapping that bubblicious ass. If I wasn't your best friend, I'd be riding you all day, *every day* like it was my job, sugar pie!"

I ball up my apron and toss it at him. "Shut up!"

He grins wickedly. "Just promise me you'll be careful. Your heart is so big and pure. I'd hate to see a creeper walk all over it."

I go over to him and kiss him on his perfectly smooth cheek. My best friend is a knockout. Amber eyes with skin a similar color to mine, not exactly dark, not exactly light. More in the middle like a toasted brown. He's tall with an athletic build and a full head of thick, layered, black hair he slicks back with some product. It always looks absolutely perfect. "I'll be careful. Off to teach people how to chill out. Be back in ninety minutes." I remove my hair net and toss it at him. "Namaste!"

"Nah, I'ma stay right here." He laughs at his own joke while I roll my eyes.

Just as I'm leaving, my ma unlocks the front door and bustles her body in. "How you doin' this morning, baby?" she asks.

"Right as rain. See you in ninety!"

I dash out the door and turn right toward Lotus House. My feet falter the second I hit the sidewalk because standing against a sleek gunmetal-gray BMW is none other than the man who was featured solely in my dreams and waking fantasies all weekend.

Silas McKnight.

He pushes off his car, a white hoodie covering his head, hands tucked into his pockets. A pair of black track pants offer a stark contrast to the bright white of his Nikes. I'd swear the shoes were brand-new, but this is the second pair of Nike's I've seen him in, and those looked new too. I sense a bit of a shoe fetish. Which I totally understand, since I have more flip-flops than Berkeley has hippies—and that's a crap-ton.

"Hey, I thought I could catch you before class, but it looks like you're cutting it right down to the minute."

"I can do that. I'm close." I gesture to the bakery.

"Atlas told me you work at the bakery too."

"Yep. Family-owned and run. We have a handful of staff to help, but this store's mostly mine."

"I'd like to try it after class, maybe sit down with you and talk?" He bites down on his bottom lip, but it's not his face that shows his nervousness. It's his aura. A cherry red hue with the undercurrents of his normal sunny yellow.

He follows me inside.

"You know eventually you're going to have to sign up as a paying customer." I deflect from his question, not sure I want to sit and have a dessert with him and talk. Even though I know I need to, for more reasons than to get his betrayal off my chest.

"Already done. I was early. Paid for ten sessions up front and made sure they took off the one from Saturday."

"Hmm. That was mighty decent of you."

"I'm a decent guy," he fires back instantly, and I cringe.

"Yeah...that'll be the day."

Before I reach my room, Silas grabs me by the arm and spins me around until I'm backed against the hallway wall. He cages me in with his big body.

Talk about sensory overload. My body remembers exactly what it feels like to be pressed against a wall by this man. In perfect detail. I squirm, placing my hands at his sides. I'm not sure if I'm holding him close, trying to get distance, or just touching what's available to my eager fingers.

"Silas...I have to work," I grit through my teeth. It's better than panting, and right now, breathing isn't an option. His crisp fresh-soap smell alongside the musk of the apple, oak, and leather cologne he wears is a lethal concoction when paired together. I could sniff him all day. It's absolutely intoxicating. Better than any sugary treat in my bakery, that's for sure. But I must fight it.

Don't fall into his sexy trap, Dara. You've already been down that road.

He leans forward, close enough I can feel the warmth of his breath on my lips. "You've got the wrong idea about me."

I huff in his pretty boy face.

"I'm not married." He grinds the words out as the nervous flare of red that once sat on the edge of his aura flickers with an additional hint of black at the tips.

Regardless of the change in his aura, I can't help but push against his form, needing space. "I saw the pictures. You and the happy blonde. Your wedding photo! You think I'm blind?"

He shakes his head and inhales harshly. "No. Not blind. Coming to inaccurate conclusions."

I snort a laugh, letting the hilarity of the situation get the best of me. He curls his hand around my cheek and traces my smile with his thumb. "You're so goddamned beautiful..." His eyes glaze over with a lustful, smoky green.

"Silas, what we did was wrong. It shouldn't have happened," I attempt, the words tasting foul on my tongue even as I push forward. "Just let it go. I'm not going to be someone's mistress."

He groans and leans his forehead against mine. "Why is this so fucking hard to say?" He clenches his jaw, a muscle ticking against his cheek, proving how hard this conversation is hitting him, but I have no idea why.

"Look, we had a good time. Let's leave it at that. We have mutual friends..." I try.

"Jeez-us, woman." He smacks the wall at the opposite side of my head, grabbing my attention. I close my mouth and watch as his eyes swirl with frustration. "This is hard enough to say without you yapping your nonsense. Now, you're going to give me a minute to gather my thoughts, keep your mouth shut, and just listen."

He widens his eyes as I hold my breath and stay perfectly still and, more importantly, silent.

Silas closes his eyes on a slow blink. They are a startling green when he opens them and takes in every feature of my face. He lifts his hand and runs his fingers through my long hair. I swallow back a whimper at how good his touch feels. It's as if every inch of skin he touches becomes energized, waking from a darkened sleep.

"I'm new to talking about this." He frowns. "Please understand. I *was* married. I'm not now."

I narrow my eyes and wait for him to continue.

"My wife...she uh..."

Oh, this ought to be good. He's about to lie through his teeth. Except I'm an expert at knowing when people lie. Auras always tell the truth.

"Dara, I'm a widower."

He lets out a long slow breath, his eyes closing. The word bounces around in my mind like a pinball.

Widower.

Widower.

Widower.

"My God...I'm so stupid!" I gasp, throw my arms around him, and sink my face into his neck. He wraps his arms around me and holds on tightly. So much so that I can barely breathe, but I don't care. He's not a cheater; he's a *griever*.

That's why the black suffuses around his energy sometimes. It's why the pictures are still all over his house. He's still grieving the loss of his wife.

But what about the nursery? He didn't say anything about his daughter. Was she at a family member's for the night? Maybe her grandparents?

For some reason, I hold off on asking about his daughter, especially in light of the information he just shared.

"See, I'm not a scumbag," he whispers in my ear, sending chills throughout my body.

"I never thought you were a scumbag."

"No?" He nuzzles the side of my face and inhales.

"No. I had you down as a dirtbag cheater."

He chuckles into my hair. "Never. I'd never cheat on my woman. I don't have it in me." He pets my hair and lets me lean back against the wall.

"Can we finish this conversation after class? I think I'm already a few minutes late."

Silas smiles, the yellow scintillating around his form like a ray of sunshine, its magnificence burning the black away with every passing second. "Treat on me, after?"

I grin and grab ahold of his hand. Our hand chakras activate the moment our palms touch, energy buzzing in the same circular motion on contact. He squeezes my hand, letting me know he feels it too, though there's still darkness behind his eyes. A shadow he keeps to himself. I have nothing to say about that because I've got my own secret, and now that I know he's not cheating on his wife but grieving her loss, my timetable for telling him about our baby just increased. When I thought he was a lying dirtbag, it didn't matter when I told him the truth. Now it just seems wrong.

We walk in holding hands, and I break the connection to step up on the riser.

"Sorry I'm a few minutes late, class. Thank you for waiting and being ready. We'll start with some gentle breathing exercises. In for five, out for five. Holding the breath at the top and then releasing fully. I'm going to come around and offer you some essential oils I want you to breathe during your meditation."

I grab the small brown bottle, open it up, and shake a drop onto my finger. I start with a new client and kneel in front of her seated position. She's in the lotus yoga pose with her legs crossed and the soles of her feet facing up on top of her thighs. I wave the bottle under her nose. "Do you like that smell?" She nods so I place my fingertip on the skin just under her nose and above her lip.

"This scent is called Clarity from Young Living Essential Oils. Its formula consists of rosemary, peppermint, and a mixture of other earthy notes. I'll wave it under your nose, and you can nod if you'd like the scent applied above your lip."

Taking a couple minutes, I access each attendee before stopping at Silas. His beautiful eyes are closed, his long, ebony-colored lashes lying like a perfect fan against his cheeks. He's breathing deeply and his aura is a cool, calm, buttery yellow. Still not completely relaxed but definitely back to himself. I swirl the bottle under his nose. His eyes open, and I'm staring into pale-green pools I could swim in for days on end.

"Do you like this smell?" I whisper.

His eyes darken as he leans forward. I don't move a muscle, wanting to experience whatever move he makes next.

He inhales long and deep behind my ear against my hairline. I shiver at his nearness. He does it one more time, but this time, he adds his lips to the sensitive patch of skin, lingering there. My heart is pounding out a staccato beat, and the space between my thighs swells as my nipples tighten against the flimsy top I'm wearing.

"I like your smell. Up here." He breathes against my neck, taking his time. "Here you smell sugar sweet." I watch with rapt attention as his hand comes down on my leg and caresses his way up. When his thumb reaches the apex of my thighs, he covertly swipes my cotton-covered sex.

A soft moan slips past my lips, but he covers my mouth with his, obliterating any sound. The music weaves through the sound system, a hypnotic beat that only adds to the rhythm of my heartbeat. We both keep our eyes open as we kiss lightly. No tongue involved, just a simple press of lip to lip. A reminder of what we had, of what we could have again.

He pulls away slowly. "Here"—he circles his thumb over the exact spot I need—"you smell of coconuts and trees." He growls low in his throat. "I always did have a fondness for coconuts."

I suck in a breath and back away. If I let him touch me any longer, I'll be a goner.

Clearing my throat, I address the class once more. "Now imagine you're sitting on the edge of a cliff overlooking the ocean. The sun is high, there isn't a cloud in the sky, there's nothing but you, Mother Nature, and the ocean crashing against the cliff's edge beneath your feet. Sprays of mist tickle the soles of your feet. The wind is cool and calming against your skin. Your hair is blowing in the breeze. Now breathe it in, the sanctity. The stillness of this place. Soak your soul in

AUDREY CARLAN

its essence and breathe. Nothing but beauty and light resides here. Your beauty and light...

"Breathe..." I tell them, but really, I need to take my own advice.

The second Silas laid his cheek against mine to inhale my hairline, I lost all rational thought. All I wanted to do was drown in him like we did weeks ago. Wrap my arms around him and lose myself and the world around me.

I glance over at his form. A small smile plays on his lips, but I can tell he's meditating. Being able to read auras helps me to see when a student is having a hard time. So far, the guided meditation I started with has worked for the entire class. It doesn't always, but I'm so very thankful it is today. My own energy center is hopping all over the place, supercharged and focused on one thing and one thing alone.

Having sex with Silas McKnight on the next available surface, at the very soonest opportunity.

I'm such a slut.

CHAPTER SIX

Energy healers often believe that when an aura is out of balance or polluted by negative forces, it can affect the body in harmful ways, leading to health problems. This will present itself in the aura color surrounding the body.

SILAS

While Dara ends the class, I simply stay seated and take the opportunity to watch her. The way her body moves gracefully. How she crinkles her nose when she's focusing. The sound she makes when she laughs, accompanying it with a little snort. Unbelievably cute. Even her hair is something to behold. Long, falling down to where the ends just graze her fine bubble butt. The brown and gold tones shine like silken waves under the track lighting. Though nothing compares to the ethereal quality of her eyes. Those aquamarine orbs do something wicked to me. All she has to do is look at me, and I turn into a lustful puddle of mush.

I haven't had these types of feelings in so long it's hard to remember when I last did. Perhaps back when I first met Sarah our freshman year of high school. Only the yearnings were those of a fourteen-year-old boy wanting to get in the pants of a pretty blonde, not the carnal, possessive desires of a grown man who's tasted a woman and knows exactly what he wants.

This thing with Dara is unusual. Since I lost Sarah, I have had a few one-nighters, but nothing that did a number on me. I was able to write those occurrences off as the simple, basic need to fuck. Never once did I bring the women to my home, nor did I feel used when I woke up alone. And I did the walking those other times. No phone numbers were exchanged. Hell, I can barely remember their names. It took quite a few drinks just to go through with it the first two times. The regret I felt after having sex with another woman broke my heart and reminded me how much I missed my wife. The second woman wasn't any easier. She was white and blonde, and when I narrowed my eyes while fucking her, I pretended she was Sarah. That practically did me in, like I'd tainted what I had with Sarah.

As I watch Dara finish up, I try to assess her race. She's definitely got some African American in her, but I'm not sure if the other half is Caucasian or what. Doesn't matter to me. All I see is beauty. She's the exact opposite of everything my Sarah was, darker in every other way but lighter in essence; maybe that's what makes her special. She's the best of both worlds.

A pang of guilt pierces my heart like an icepick straight through my chest.

No one compares to Sarah.

I can't think like that. Still, I can't seem to stay away from Dara. There's something about her that calls to me. For three years, I've been wading through the days and months without Sarah. Meeting Dara three weeks ago and taking her home changed all of that. I now have more of a reason to get up. A purpose to look forward to, and it's seeing those ocean eyes staring at me from across the room like they are right now.

"Earth to Silas..."

I shake my head, coming back to myself.

"Are you ready to try some of the best desserts of your life?"

Pushing to a stand, I head over to the riser and place my hand out for her to take. I don't know why, but I need to touch her. Feel that she's real, not a figment of my imagination. "I don't know... I have a pretty healthy sweet tooth, and my sister's been known to bake cookies that are out of this world. It would be pretty hard to top her snickerdoodles." I grin.

She pouts prettily and then smirks. "I'll take that challenge on. Starting with my homemade cinnamon buns. People drive from San Francisco just to get one of my gooey homemade buns."

I lick my lips and squeeze her hand, forcing her off the riser and flat against my chest. While holding her hand, I put my arm around her back so she's flush against me. "Not sure anything is going to be sweeter than the taste of you."

I press my lips to hers. For a second, I allow her the opportunity to push away before I deepen the kiss. When she doesn't move, I cup her cheek and lick her bottom lip until she opens her mouth. Once she does, I delve in with long licks of my tongue against hers. Not even a second after our tongues touch, she's moaning into my mouth, offering eager flicks of her tongue and nibbling on my lips, her arms around my neck.

For what seems like hours but is probably only a couple minutes, we kiss, rekindling the fire inside us that brought us together three weeks ago.

Letting her arm go, I cup both of her cheeks with my palms and plunge my tongue in and out, sucking on hers until I hear a familiar little hum in the back of her throat. My cock hardens in my flimsy pants, and I grind against her. She doesn't so much as move away. No, my queen is bold and brave. Her hands wrap around my back and run a path down to my ass, where she squeezes me before pulling our bodies together.

She tastes of vanilla custard, and the more I taste, touch, smell, and kiss, the more I never want to let her go. Her lips are two soft, velvet pillows I can't help but nip repeatedly, showing her my desire for more. More of this, more of everything. Just fucking more.

A sing-song voice breaks through our make-out session. "Uh, oh, wow! Okay. Sorry."

Dara's eyes widen and she smiles, covering her mouth before she spins around. The gorgeous redhead who works at the counter is standing near the door, looking at the floor, kicking her bare feet and trying her best to avoid making eye contact. She's wearing black yoga pants. Her green tank top makes her hair look like its glowing a fiery red.

"It's okay, Luna. Um, this is Silas McKnight. He works with Atlas."

Once Dara and I move a comfortable couple feet apart, she no longer seems uncomfortable and she smiles widely.

"You own the studio he works at," she says.

I nod. "We really work together, but technically, yeah, my family owns it."

"Cool. This is my studio. Well...technically, my family owns it," she repeats, and I laugh, walking over and extending a hand.

"Good to meet you, Luna. We're just about to go next door and try out some of Dara's baked goods." I hook a thumb over my shoulder toward the wall shared with the bakery. "Would you like to join us?" My manners got the best of me, inviting her to come along when all I want is to be alone with Dara. Preferably with a bed nearby.

Please say no. Please say no.

Luna grins and shakes her head. "Aw, how nice of you. I can't. I have a class to teach. In this room, actually, which is why I interrupted your uh...hmm..."

"Kiss," Dara announces directly.

I like it. I'm finding there is a lot to like about Dara Jackson.

Luna's cheeks pinken, so adorable against her pearly white skin. "Yeah well, be that as it may, I need your room."

Dara squeezes her friend's bicep. "Course. Come over later?" Dara offers, and I frown. That means she has no intention of seeing *me* later, which was my initial intention.

"Sure thing. Looks like we've got some catching up to do." Her clear blue eyes run up and down my form.

Dara loops her hand with mine, the buzz between us picking right back up where it left off. "Come on. I've got a challenge to destroy."

I allow Dara to lead me out of the studio, into the cool Bay Area breeze, and onto the busy street. "Is it always like this over here?" I gesture to the street and the number of patrons on the sidewalks.

"Yeah. We're kind of a hidden gem in Berkeley. Similar

to Telegraph Avenue without all the street vendors, bums, and potheads offering weed surreptitiously as you walk by."

I stop in my tracks and laugh out loud, remembering a time when I walked down Telegraph with Sarah and two separate guys offered me weed. Only they did it by bumping into me and saying, "Smoke" or "Green Bud."

She smiles and tips her head, watching me laugh. "You know, Si, you're a very attractive man normally, but when you laugh...panties implode."

I lick my lip and tug at her hips, smashing her up against my body. "Are you saying that your panties have disintegrated?" I whisper in her ear, nuzzling at her hairline behind her ear where her natural sugar scent is the most intense.

Her face presses against mine, and she lifts up onto her toes and rests her lips against the shell of my ear. "If I were wearing panties they might have. But since I'm not...no." She slips back, winks at me, and turns toward the door to Sunflower.

I'm assaulted by two things at the same time: A powerful image of this woman's bare pussy, which I'd very much like to become reacquainted with, and the scent of cinnamon and powdered sugar. "Fuck," I gasp and then grab her form and bring my body up close to her backside. "Tease," I whisper in her ear as I hold the door open and place a hand to her lower back to nudge her forward.

She crooks an eyebrow and offers a saucy smirk. "Not a tease if you're perfectly willing to follow through."

Before I can question her statement, a round black woman who's obviously in charge calls out to Dara.

"My child. Looking beautiful as ever. How was your class, honey?" The woman holds her arm out, the other holding a plate of treats up high in the air.

Dara snuggles against the woman's side and kisses her cheek before glancing at me. "Really great, Mama. I brought a friend of mine to try out our desserts. He says his sister's cookies are the best thing he's ever put into his mouth..."

The black woman gives me the once-over with shrewd, knowing eyes. "A friend, you say?" She raises her eyebrows in what I can only assume is disbelief.

Not knowing what to say, I just wave. I can't exactly tell Dara's mother I'm the man she spent an evening fucking until she left in the wee hours of the morning because she thought I was married and cheating on my wife. Nor can I tell her I'm technically not married anymore because my wife died, and I'm officially seeing her daughter, because I'm not. This thing between Dara and me is casual. It can't be anything else.

"Yeah, Mama, a friend." Dara confirms flippantly.

"Mmmhmm. Well, go on child and get him something that will knock his socks off." She waves her off.

Dara lifts up a wooden, hinged section of counter and escapes behind the bar. A tall man behind the display loops an arm around her waist and places a series of kisses along the side of her cheek, which makes my girl laugh hysterically. Such a familiar touch for an employee. Too familiar, in my opinion. He rests his hands above her ass at her lower back. She presses her hands against his chest, and she looks up at him, smiling away.

What the fuck?

Is she seeing this dude?

Just five minutes ago, she was in a serious lip lock with me.

Hell, only three weeks ago I had her body in so many positions I lost count. No, I didn't. I remember every second like it was on a dirty movie reel in my mind. Nothing but flesh on flesh, lips on lips, skin on skin. All night long. Until I collapsed from exhaustion with a tight little woman in my arms, only to wake up in the morning and find a cold bed.

Scanning the bakery, I find a table off to the side and proceed to plant my shocked ass in the chair.

Maybe I'm not the only man she's seeing. Then again, it's not like we discussed our relationship status. Mostly because we drank to our hearts' content and then fucked until our bodies wore out. Now we're somewhere in between a weird dance of seduction, lust, and keeping distance from one another.

Frankly, I don't know what we are. I just know I want more of her and less of seeing another man's arms wrapped around her slight form.

I grit my teeth as the man slaps her ass like he owns it before she hustles to fill a tray full of goodies. She hollers something over her shoulder, and the man gets to work making a couple coffees. I'd prefer my coffee with a double shot of whiskey added to it right about now.

Rubbing at the tension in my neck, I pull out my cellphone and focus on it. A text message from Atlas pops up when I bring the display to life.

Did you take my advice and wait? You're not at work yet. What gives?

I smile and click the reply button.

Yes. At Sunflower Bakery. Went to meditation.

The second my message goes through, the little bubble

pops up, showing Atlas is typing. Of course, the guy is attached to his phone. He's always checking to make sure his wife or nanny haven't called about Aria, their baby. The man is freaked to the max about something happening to his family. I get it. Boy, do I get it, so I don't ever give him any shit about it. Knowing what I know now, about how short life really can be, I would have made a few different decisions myself. Like never having bought Sarah a brand-new Lexus SUV. I regret that decision every day of my fucking pathetic existence.

The text pops up with another message.

Dude! You went after her already. Awesome!

Glancing up, I see Dara is still working on something behind the counter. Her smile is wide and easy. I type my reply.

*Do you know if she has a man? She's pretty
tight with a guy behind the counter.*

Not that I know of.

Atlas's messages don't make me feel any better when Dara runs her fingers across the man's neck playfully when she passes by on her way to my table.

Her hips sway as she walks, and her long hair swishes along with her movements. But it's her eyes that hold me captive. The startling color against her caramel skin is breathtaking. I've never seen anything like it. I'm awestruck, lost in their blue depths.

"Thanks for waiting."

"Not a problem." I swallow around the dryness of my throat as she sets the tray down. It's filled to the brim with a variety of goodies and two steaming lattes, both with hearts in the foam.

Hearts.

And the guy who was groping her made them that way. Is it to remind her about his affection?

"I think you'll forgive me when you wrap your lips around this!" She lifts up an icing-covered cinnamon roll chunk she's ripped off the whole swirl. Her tantalizing fingertips are out, daring me to take the bite from them.

Leaning forward, I wrap my lips around her fingers and flick at her digits with my tongue. I grab her hand with my other, not letting her get too far from me while I chew and swallow. Once done, I pull her fingers to my mouth and swirl my tongue around the sticky remains. After I've licked off every bite, I drop her hand.

"Incredible," I whisper, my gaze hot on hers.

Her blue eyes have darkened to a smoky color I've seen before, specifically when she was underneath me, crying out her release.

"So incredible," she mimics.

"I just said that, sweetness." I lift up the cinnamon roll, tear off a piece, and pass a much smaller bite to her, getting close so she'll have to invade my personal space to get it.

"Challenging me in my own bakery?"

Taunting her, I lift the piece up and wiggle it. "You afraid someone will see me feeding you?"

She moves lightning fast, stealing the bite from my fingertips like a treat-thieving ninja.

I drop my mouth open and then close it in awe of her speed.

Dara makes that cute little snort-laugh before leaning

back and clapping wildly. "Got ya!" she boasts.

I laugh along with her. She's beautiful all the time, but when she laughs, a glow sets up around her, making it almost hard to take in her beauty. Blinding. Positively blinding beauty. That's what Dara exudes when she laughs.

"All right, crazy, tell me more about you. Now that you know a little bit more about my situation, I want to know more about you." I pick up a cookie and bite down into it. It's softer than it looks, but the instant the mixture of powdered sugar and vanilla hits my tongue, I'm closing my eyes and moaning around the heaven-sent combination blessing my mouth.

When I open my eyes, Dara is sipping her latte and smirking. "Best cookie ever?"

"Fuck yes!" I groan and take another delicious bite.

"Told you. I'll take on any challenge. Including you, Mr. McKnight," she warns, and for some reason, I think she's referring to more than making excellent cookies.

I point the cookie at her. "You. More info. Go."

She chuckles. "Not much to say. Graduated top of my class in high school. Got scholarships to Berkeley, but I didn't want to go. The bakery is my calling. Just like my parents. I've known since the day they brought me home when I was eight, I'd do anything to make them proud. Baking came naturally. The universe provided me the perfect family. I spend my days giving back that gift, only to others."

The phrase *since the day they brought me home when I was eight* sticks out in my mind like a flashing light. "You're adopted?"

Dara nods excitedly, not at all sad or uncomfortable about where the conversation is headed.

"When you were eight?" I confirm.

"Yeah. They picked me out of a lineup at a girls' home for orphans. Before that, I spent time bouncing around foster homes. Then my mother, Vanessa Jackson, looked at me, and something clicked between us. You'd never know I was adopted. They have treated me like nothing other than their very own blood my whole life. I hit the jackpot of parents. And the bakery chain and I are their legacy. I'm happy to raise that legacy up and one day share it with my own family."

I set down the cookie and plant my elbow on the table, my head in my palm. "Amazing. You seem so well-adjusted."

She grins. "Because I am, silly. And I have them to thank for it. What about you? Besides the production company, tell me about your life."

Before I can filter my words, I blurt out, "I have no life."

Her eyes narrow, and she places her warm palm on my forearm. "Everyone has someone, something to give them purpose and reason."

I let out a long sigh. "My family needs me at the helm of Knight & Day Productions since my father passed two years ago. Only a year after my wife."

Dara scoots closer and places her hand on my thigh. "My goodness, that's a lot of loss to manage. What I gather from what you're saying is you've been putting the pieces back together. Am I right?"

Instead of responding, I shrug. I can't tell this incredible woman I haven't done that. Not even close. She'd be ashamed. Hell, I'm ashamed, and more importantly, Sarah would be ashamed.

Dara squeezes my thigh, her gaze searing through mine, probably expecting me to share the way she did. I just can't. My entire body heats up as feelings I have long since forgotten rush to the surface like a bullet train, ready to roll. They clog my chest, closing around my throat, making the decadent pastries I just ate feel like lumps of coal in my gut.

Abruptly, I stand and back away from her touch, brushing her hand off my thigh. "Thank you, uh, for the coffee and treats." I swallow down the anxiety and fear threatening my every nerve ending so I can get out what I need to say, what she has to hear. "You have a gift, Dara. A beautiful gift. More than you know. I appreciate you sharing it with me."

Her hand shoots out and grabs mine, and the sizzle of magnetism hits like a jolt of electricity. I shake off her hand.

"I'm not the right man for you. I gotta go."

Without allowing her to say a word, because even one utterance from her pretty pink lips would have me begging for another taste, I bail.

Bailing is all I'm good at anymore. Dara doesn't deserve a fucked-up man like me messing with her head and screwing up her perfect life. She's got everything she needs right here in this bakery. A mother and father who love her and a doting man behind the counter who's obviously in love with her.

A handful of nights between the sheets are all I'm willing to offer, and even I know that's pathetic.

While I sat there, though, listening to her share her life, her joy at having a family who chose her over loneliness...it hit me. I will never be the man for her. I'll never be able to give that to her. I'm emotionally unavailable. The part of me that could share and give of himself to a woman died the day my wife and daughter died.

CHAPTER SEVEN

THIRD EYE
C H A K R A

The third eye is where your conscience lives. Here, an individual not only can sense and see what's going on but evaluate its true meaning. Ethics and a sense of justice originate from this chakra.

D A R A

I'm not the right man for you.

His last words clang around my mind as I sit in utter shock, my gaze still locked on the bakery's glass doors. He walked out on me. We were having a nice time; there was even some sexual tension buzzing around our bodies, as though we both wanted more. Much more.

I think about the intensity of his kisses in the studio and on the street. The sensual way he swirled his tongue around my fingers as I fed him. He was into me. All in. And then...nothing.

Worse, I watched it happen in living color. Literally. His aura changed so fast it was like watching a mood ring change color when different people put it on, one after the other.

Red...sexual desire.

Orange...excitement.

Shades of green...insecurity.

Shades of blue...fear of speaking the truth.

Indigo...deep feeling.

Black...grief.

All of it speaking to a man who's confused. He seems down-to-earth, pleasant, easygoing, and then when something stirs his feelings, he doesn't know how to handle it. He shuts down. Closes off to me and those around him. I don't get it.

I'm dumfounded, trying to figure out what I did wrong.

While I sit there staring, Ricardo comes over, making a big show of resting his ass in the chair Silas vacated.

"Two thousand five hundred sixty-one dollars and some change." He grins wickedly.

I frown, trying to understand what he's talking about but mostly just stare at him blankly.

"The amount of money in my bank account." His chest puffs up with pride. "Told you that boy would be back. Now give me all the deets. He ran off so quick I didn't even have a chance to make up a reason to come over to your table and introduce myself personally." Ricardo's hopeful tone and smile make my heart sink.

"He's gone, Ricky. I think this time for good." I don't even recognize the sorrow and sadness in my own voice. It's unlike anything I've ever felt before. Worse because I know what it means for our child.

Silas isn't going to be capable of being a part of the baby's life if he is unable to be near me. I can't imagine what it feels like to go through the tumultuous myriad of emotions the way he did when he sat with me. It was like one of those kaleidoscopes. Peer through the looking glass, spin the base, and see all of the colors change, weaving into one another. Only his colors didn't provide beautiful new images to gawk at. His were like watching a man being shot in slow motion. One second he's alive and full of life, the next, he hears the shot—shock, fear, and surprise on his face—and then the bullet strikes. That's when his face shows recognition of his fate, of the lifeforce bleeding out of him, and then resolution and, finally, death.

I could never willingly put him through that again. Heck, I don't want to put *myself* through it.

He cringes. "No way. Nuh-uh. No man can look at a woman all enamored and hanging on his every word like that and not be interested. How'd you mess up with him? Tell me, and I'll tell you how to make it better."

I shake my head and grab his hand. "No, I'm serious. I think he's *gone* gone. He said something about being the wrong man for me. Like he wasn't good enough."

He purses his lips and rubs at his chin. "Well, that I believe. No man is good enough for my baby girl."

I slump into my chair and run my fingers through my hair, pulling the long mane over to one side. In a moment of clarity, I make the most important decision of my life: I'm not going to let this go. He needs to at least be given a chance to conquer his demons. There's something far more important on the line than whatever is plaguing him, and that's the little love growing inside me. Our child.

"I need to get through to him," I say, absolutely committed to my mission.

Ricardo frowns and squints. "Why is it so important? If he's just another guy you hooked up with, it shouldn't matter that much. It's not like you have a vested interest in him."

I open and close my mouth, not sure how to tell him I do have a vested interest, a *huge* one. A life-altering one. Except the buzzer in the back kitchen goes off.

"We gonna get any help back here?" Mama yells from the back of the bakery.

Both Ricky and I stand, jumping to action. "Tonight, Luna's coming over. We'll order pizza, and I'll tell you everything."

He narrows his eyes. "Meaning you haven't already." The sass in his voice cannot be missed.

"Ugh. Let's just talk about it later, okay?" I lift my hands, clasped in prayer, to my chest.

He puckers his lips and clucks his tongue. "Fine. I'll bring the wine."

I'm about to tell him not to bother and then think better of it. He'll definitely need it when he hears my news. "Great."

★ ★ ★

Two separate knocks sound on my door at the same time. I hustle to the door, already knowing who it is. Both Ricardo and Luna have the security codes to get into the building, but Ricardo has a key.

I open it to find both Ricky and Luna all smiles and welcoming energy. One is holding up two bottles of wine, the other a box of pizza.

My mouth starts watering instantly at the smell of cheesy

goodness. I'm not sure if it's mental, but since I found out I'm pregnant, I want to eat all the time. As though my mind and body had a discussion and agreed now was the time to have the largest appetite in the world. This does not bode well for my physical appearance. If this keeps up, by the time the baby comes, I'll be the size of a house. Mentally, I remind myself to add an extra yoga class into my normal weekly schedule. Maybe that will make up for the overabundance of extra calories.

"Hey, guys!" I swing open my door, letting them both in.

Ricky goes straight for the wineglasses while Luna sets down the pie. She's wearing a pair of tattered jeans, a skintight tank, and a gazillion bangles that clink and chime like little bells as she moves. Two separate crystals hang from her neck. One on a long chain that runs down past her breasts, the other on a choker right at her neck. I finger the quartz.

"Feeling the need to ward off some negativity today?" I question, noting her aura is a pensive silver at the tips of her normal gold tones. Luna takes after her mother and is a natural healer and divine spiritual leader for all the yogis in the area. It's not typical to see something hinging on concern in her aura.

She flattens her lips into a thin line, her facial expression one of uncertainty. "Yeah, I got a weird call from the building owner. He warned me he was thinking of selling. Did you receive a similar call?"

I shake my head. "No, but my father would have been the one to receive it. I imagine apartment sales are like this. If our landowner sells, it usually just means we are getting a new landlord essentially. Right?"

The silver in her aura flickers and pops around her. "I

guess. I just have a funny feeling about it. I'll know more in the coming weeks, I guess. Besides, we're not here to talk about me. We're here to talk about you and that yummy cocoa bit of sexy I saw you sucking face with earlier." Her blue eyes sparkle with mirth.

"You were sucking face! You did not share that information with me!" Ricardo walks around the kitchen counter and sets down two glasses. Luna grabs hers and instantly takes a sip. I stare at mine like it's got a virus attached to it. Even the smell of it is strangely turning my stomach a little.

I grab the glass and move our little party over to the couch before groaning and flopping down onto it. Luna sits gracefully next to me. Always the one with poise and tact. Ricky sits across from us in the single chair. My studio apartment isn't big and has an open floor plan, so my bedroom is completely visible to the rest of the space. It means I always have to keep my bed made and clothes off the floor in case I have visitors.

"It was so hot, Ricardo," Luna gushes, making me squirm in my seat. "They were totally going at it. I swear if I hadn't interrupted, they would have been on the floor doing the naked pretzel." She laughs and smacks her thigh.

"Not true!" I pick up a throw pillow and nail her with it.

She nods repeatedly. "It is!"

I sigh and flop back into the couch. "Not that it matters now. He came over to the bakery to talk. We chatted a bit, talked about his wife, who passed away. That was part of my original issue..."

Ricardo sips his wine and shakes his head. "Wait a minute. You never told me he had a wife."

I glance down at my lap and away. "I didn't know at first. We had the best night of sex, all over his house, and then when

I woke up, I saw pictures of him and his happy wife all over the place. I freaked out. Thought he betrayed his wife and daughter. So, I bailed."

"His daughter! He has a kid?" Ricky asks, shock in his tone.

"That was the other thing that freaked me out. I opened a door and found a pink nursery. Except... I didn't see even one baby picture with his wife. Only pictures of them together. Weird, right?" I cringe and rub at my suddenly throbbing forehead.

Ricky nods. "Yeah, it is."

"My mother still has baby pictures of me in the hallway, and I'm twenty-six years old," Luna adds.

I inhale fully and let it out slowly. "It is strange. Anyway, long story short, I jumped to conclusions, thinking he had a wife and I'd accidently jumped into bed with a scumbag cheater."

Ricky's and Luna's faces contort into expressions of disgust, but neither interrupts.

"When he came to class on Saturday, I yelled at him for making me his mistress. He said I had the wrong idea, but I didn't believe him and left thinking that was it. This morning, he shows up outside Lotus House again, waiting to talk to me."

"And how did it get from a one-night stand, to a yelling match at Lotus House, to you and him making out, to him coming to the bakery and walking out?" Ricky queries, summing up my drama rather nicely.

"He walked out?" Luna gasps. "No!" Her voice crumbles with misery as if it happened to her.

Man, I have good friends. Worried about me to the point they're sad for me.

"Yes!" Ricky answers for me, his indignation obvious.

I groan and cover my eyes. "When he came today, he was flirty, which reminded me why I was attracted to him in the first place." I frown, forcing those thoughts out of my head. "Anyway, he made me listen to him. He cornered me up against the hallway wall, which was so hot, you guys, you have no idea." I fan my face, my temperature rising with the retelling. "Then he told me he'd been married, but he's now widowed."

"Oh no." Luna's voice lowers, filled with emotion for a person she doesn't even know. Kindhearted, my girl. "Do you know how long ago?"

"He didn't say, but his aura was showing he's still grieving, yet I get the feeling it wasn't that recent. Also, he never brought up his daughter." Which is weird. Period.

"Do you think something happened to his kid and wife at the same time?" Ricardo's eyes seem to get bigger by the millisecond, a sheen of sadness passing through them.

Holy shit! That could be it.

"Oh, my goodness. What if he lost his kid too?" I gasp and place my hand over my mouth and belly, gut-wrenching acid swirling in my stomach. "Losing both at the same time could easily break a man like him."

Both Luna and Ricky nod and take swallows of their wine.

Not thinking straight, with this possible new information swirling around in my head like a tornado, I add, "Makes the secret I'm keeping from him even harder to tell."

I shake my head, the misery coating my tongue, clogging up my throat and making tears prick at my eyes.

"What secret, baby girl?" Ricky asks softly.

Luna places her hand on my knee. "Yeah, what are you not sharing?"

I close my eyes and sigh heavily. "You know the one-night stand we started talking about?"

"Yeah. Go on..." Luna nudges.

"Well, I got a little more out of it than a half dozen orgasms and a lifetime of memories to relive."

Ricardo shakes his head. "No, baby girl. Don't even say it..." he warns, his face paling, expression guarded.

Luna's brow furrows, and she looks at Ricky and then at me and back again. "Say what?"

I swallow down the fear and doubt I'm doing the right thing by telling my best friends, but I can't go through this alone. Not anymore. Especially after Silas left the way he did this evening.

Mustering up all my strength, I whisper the two words I've been afraid to say: "I'm pregnant."

Ricky hisses, and Luna gasps.

"Fucking hell, baby girl!" Ricardo stands up and starts pacing. "And with a fucked-up creeper who may look exactly like Jesse Williams, which means your baby is going to be fine as fuck, but damn it all to hell. The man has a screw loose!" He keeps pacing, to the kitchen and back to the couch, all of ten feet, before turning around again. "Obviously, if he got up and walked away from you after a night of carnal delights. Sweet baby Jesus. Now I'm going to have to be a father figure. Shit!" He runs his hands through his slick black hair, messing it up, layers falling to the sides of his head.

I can't help it... Watching him rant sets me off into a flurry of much-needed giggles. The situation is dire, yes, but it's not like I don't have a job, a family, and amazing friends, all who will love this baby to the moon and beyond. I've got money in the bank. I can be a single mom if I have to and still be completely fulfilled.

Ricky stops pacing, sets his fists on his hips, and glares at me. "This is not funny. You're pregnant, and the baby daddy's jacked in the head! At least tell me he has a good job. Please!" He looks up at the ceiling and repeats himself. "Please, for the love of God, make this man rich!"

Prayers granted.

"He's the owner of Knight & Day Productions," I admit.

"No way! He's Atlas's boss." Luna taps at her wineglass.

I nod. "Yeah."

"Have you talked to Atlas about him?"

"Honestly, the thought never occurred to me. Besides, I kind of need to see a doctor, make sure the baby is healthy and everything is all right before I tell him. And I definitely want to tell him before I start telling the people he works with." I'd be pissed if the situation were reversed.

She bites down on her lip. "Yeah, that would probably be wise. What are you going to do right now, though?" Her hand comes back to my leg, and she rubs a soothing path along my thigh. Her energy switches, green tones mixing with her usual gold.

"Nothing I can do besides eat right, take prenatal vitamins, which Mama already stocked my cabinet with, and wait. Maybe he'll come around." I shrug, trying to play nonchalant, but every fiber of my being is telling me to hunt him down and make him see I'm worthy of his attention. And he's worthy of mine.

I'm just not confident what the end result will be. Will he even care I'm pregnant with his child? What if he did lose his daughter and wife at the same time? He never told me what happened to her. Maybe this is the universe's way of giving

Silas a second chance at having a family.

Ricky pulls me out of my thoughts by putting two slices of pizza in front of me. "Eat. The baby needs food."

"The baby isn't even a real baby yet." I roll my eyes but pick up the plate because *I am* hungry. I glance at his lap, and there's no plate of pizza on it. "Where's yours?"

He grabs my untouched wine glass and pours it into his almost empty one. "Liquid dinner."

I snort-laugh once more, the situation so ridiculous, and yet, I'm glad I told them. Having a couple of friends and my mother to lean on right now is exactly what I need.

"Thank you both for being here. For not judging me." I pick at the crust on the edge of my slice.

Luna clutches at her chest and almost chokes on her wine. "Heavens no! Dara, we're your friends. We're here to support you in whatever life throws your way. And a baby is something to rejoice in." She beams daggers at Ricky, her voice rising in accusation.

He holds up his hands. "What! Speak for yourself. I'm allowed to be nervous. I'm about to be a dad!" he fires off as though my problem is his problem.

"No, you're not. Relax, Ricky," I implore tiredly. God, all I want to do is go to bed early and forget this day ever happened.

"Oh yes, I am. If this baby needs a male father figure, I'm going to be it." He points a thumb at his chest with pride.

I shake my head. "You'll be Uncle Ricky and an important part of his or her life, yes. The baby already has a dad, and something in me believes...no, *knows* Silas will step up. I just have to get up the nerve to tell him. Eventually. When I know for sure the baby is fine. I have a doctor's appointment in a month. After that, I'll know more. The baby should be around seven weeks by then. The books say it will have a heartbeat and the doctor will be able to make sure everything is moving along as it should."

Ricky comes over to my side of the couch and squeezes his lean body in next to me, placing a hand on my flat belly. "Have you thought about names? Ricardo is a really nice one."

I tip my head and look up at him. "Really?"

"It is! Strong. Hispanic."

"My baby's father is African American...and maybe some Caucasian. I'm not exactly sure, but I know he's a brotha. Definitely not Hispanic."

"What about your biological family? You could be Hispanic! You don't know! You look like you've got some Latina in you. Swear it!" He makes a show of crossing his finger over his heart. "Sassy and spicy like one for sure!" He holds out his forearm against mine. "See, our skin tone is almost the same hue! Definitely Latina! So Ricardo fits."

I chuckle and shrug. "My birth certificate only has my mother listed. No father. And she's listed as African American, but my guess is I'm half and half. My father thinks I'm half white, but it's really anyone's guess."

Luna sits up straight. "Is it true what they say about...you know..."

"Yes," I answer swiftly, already knowing what she wants to know. It's a female thing. We have radar on this type of question.

She tips her head. "I mean about his..."

"Yes," I answer directly.

"I'm talking about his..." She gestures to the general vicinity of her lap.

"Luna, honey, I get you, *girl*. Totally *get* you. And yes. He's hung like a freakin' horse."

Which reminds me: I'm not going to be getting any more sexy time, so I flop back and sigh dramatically.

"What?" She rubs at my arm.

"Now who's going to want me? I can't drink. I'm going to get huge, and I'll be having another man's child. I'm going to be a statistic with a baby daddy but no man. Ugh!" I groan and cover my eyes. It never really hit me until right now: I'm going to be alone raising my baby. Sure, I'll have help from my parents, but it's not the same. A child deserves two loving parents like I had when the Jacksons adopted me. I went from nothing to something amazing. I want that for my baby. I'd always hoped to have a huge family. Every dream I've ever had consists of me being a mother, wife, and baker. The perfect life.

Ricky puts his arm around my shoulders and forces me to cuddle against his side. "You have no idea how you turn heads everywhere you go, sweetheart. Hell, half the time I see you in one of your short dresses, I get a semi."

I cringe and push at his chest, but he doesn't let me go. "Gross! You're like my brother."

"Don't I know it," he says solemnly, as if he really is hurt that I don't see him in a romantic light.

"You're joking. Please tell me you're kidding. You don't want me like that. Do you?" I choke on the question. It tastes so weird on my tongue I can hardly breathe.

He shakes his head. "God no! But your body is banging, baby girl. Tits and ass don't lie, and I am a man. I may tend to go for the pretty boys, but I've been known to get down with a woman when the moon and the stars align."

Luna gasps. "You mean you're not totally gay? Whoa! Now that is news to me!"

Ricky shuffles his shoulders. "It ain't no *thang.* It's not like it needs to be spread around. It's like when you hate coconut the fruit but love the water or the rum! If the ingredients are just right, you can be swayed to sample the dish."

Luna laughs. "So, you're mostly gay, but you reserve the right to be swayed to the opposite sex."

He perks up, smiling widely. "Exactly."

She takes a deep breath. "Ooookay. Remind me never to try to hook you up."

His eyes bulge. "Hook me up a million times over. If you've got a hunky ginger brother, I'm *all in,* honey-pie!" Ricky shifts his chin from left to right in a "Mmmhmm" gesture.

I slap my hand over Ricky's mouth. "Just stop talking. Your I'm-gay-not-gay-sometimes is cray-cray."

"I'm into people and sex, not labels," he asserts emphatically.

"Now that I can live with." I wink, and he kisses my temple.

The three of us look at one another and then all sigh, loudly and heavily.

"So, what now, preggo?" Ricky asks.

"Don't you dare start calling me that!" I dig a finger into his ribs. "We're keeping this secret, which means on the *down-low*. Definitely until I know the baby is okay and I've figured out how to tell Silas. Got it?"

Luna nods, and Ricky follows.

"I can't believe I'm going to say this, but..." I hold up my hand. "Solemn pinky swear on this shit right now."

Luna has zero problems hooking her finger with mine. Ricky purses his lips, ruffles his hair, and tries to ignore the request.

"Ricky, I need you quiet on this one. Pinky promise, or I'm

never talking to you again!" I threaten.

His eyes narrow. "You wouldn't last a week without talking to me, baby girl." He links our fingers dramatically and swings them.

He's not wrong. I wouldn't last a week without begging him to talk to me. We've been best friends since junior high. I'm the first woman he ever kissed. He's the first boy I ever kissed. That kiss freshman year sealed the deal on us forever being friends and never more than that. Then, four years later, he confided he was into boys as well as girls, which started a whole new era, but I was there for him as he's always been there for me.

As crazy as my BFF is, he's one of the most important people in my life, and not being able to talk to him for a week makes my heart ache just thinking about it.

"You're right. I love you too much," I admit.

He grins. "I knew it! You've always been in love with me. Since our first kiss freshman year."

Luna has heard this story a million times, so she just plays along and laughs.

"Time to get some music going. We are not at a funeral. We are going to celebrate this new life and my pending awesome uncle status." Ricky jumps up and heads for the stereo, a jitterbug in his step.

"Hear, hear!" Luna lifts her wineglass.

I pick up a slice of warm pizza and raise it up. "Hear, hear." Then I take a massive bite, chew, and thank God for good friends.

For the next eight months...I'm going to need them more than ever.

CHAPTER EIGHT

Yellow and Green Aura Colors and Meanings: Starting with a bright sunshine yellow, this connotes that the individual is creative, playful, self-aware, feeling powerful, and is knowledgeable and curious. When the yellow starts to mix with green on the color spectrum, it shows the person as more passionate, communicative. As the aura moves into a full, brilliant green, the individual is dealing with growth, balance, love. If the green darkens dramatically, the person may be jealous or have low self-esteem and resentment.

SILAS

Week one since I walked out on Dara has been a study in my own personal self-restraint. I've convinced myself she doesn't need me, regardless of how much I want to run back to her, fall at her feet, and apologize for the way I left. Except I know leaving was the right move. Dara is young, beautiful, and knows what she wants out of life. She doesn't need a broken man who can't love her. A woman like her should be worshipped the way I did Sarah.

I've been making a few strides with setting Sarah free. I'm not capable of removing every piece of her from the house all at once. Her disappearing from my life forever all in one night was enough of a shock. Removing all evidence of her existence...not a chance. With my mother's urging and continuous chastising, however, I've made progress.

I told myself this week I'd tackle the hallway. I've removed all but two pictures of us in the living room. That took the entire week. A couple per day is my goal. With each image, I allow myself the time to mourn her loss. It may not be healthy, but remembering those times with the woman I loved and lost is the only way I'm going to be able to get through this. Sarah deserves that much.

"Christ! Sarah deserved so much more than dying at twenty-fucking-seven!" I holler at the image of the two of us on the beach together. One of our quick weekend getaways to Santa Cruz. She loved the beach. The sound, smell, the sand. All of it. Much to my dismay. But I loved her, so I went. I'm so glad now that I did.

I grit my teeth and pull the next picture off the wall. One of her with her parents. I'm such a schmuck. Their only daughter dies, takes the only grandchild they will ever have with her, and I haven't really been there much since it happened. I couldn't then. It was too fresh.

Who am I kidding?

I still can't. Between the three of us, the people who loved

Sarah more than their own lives, together, our grief would drown us whole. Except the guilt and shame has its own way of drowning me. Sarah would despise the fact that I haven't visited her parents in two years.

I glance down at the picture of her, tears filling my eyes. "Then come back and do something about it!" I growl and throw the picture across the room. The glass shatters into a million tiny pieces. "Fuck!"

My heart pounds. I'm hot as hell, and sweat is trickling down my neck, running in a perfect line down my spine. There's no sound but the cadence of my labored breaths. I squeeze my hands into fists as a hurricane of loneliness spins a vortex around me. I lean against the wall and slide down to my ass. With my knees up and my head in my hands, I let the tears fall.

★ ★ ★

Week two has come and gone since I last saw my meditation teacher. Hell, I could use an hour session with Dara, even just to find that sense of peace she brings to her students.

My heart, my mind, and my soul have been ravaged the last two weeks with thoughts of my life with Sarah. Every picture in this godforsaken hallway has brought up a different phase in our lives I'm never going to have back. I'm down to the last two pictures.

The ones taken shortly before she died.

Chills run up and down my spine as fear and anxiety rip into my heart like a monster with razor-sharp claws.

The first image was taken by the sonogram technician. The happy couple holding up a sonogram of our baby girl. We were ecstatic. After two miscarriages, we finally had the proof our baby was healthy, and it was a girl. We could not wait to call our families and tell them the good news. One of the happiest days of my life, knowing I would soon be the father of a baby girl.

The next image is of our daughter's face at the seven-month 3D scan. Sarah didn't want to do the scan at first. Thought it was bad juju to see what God had given us before we were supposed to. I couldn't help it. I was too excited. Then when the technician showed us our baby girl on the screen, Sarah sobbed happy tears and thanked me with a million kisses all over my face.

I caress the cheek of the infant in the picture. She looked just like her mother, and I suspected her skin would be dark like mine. I thought she was the most beautiful thing I'd ever seen.

I lost the beauty of her before I ever even had the chance to touch her. Kiss her face. Tell her I loved her and would protect her forever.

All of it gone.

My entire world destroyed.

Taken from me by a junkie needing a fix.

I hold the two frames close to my heart.

"Why, God? Why did you take them? Sarah never hurt anyone."

My head falls forward as if it's working independent of my brain. I rest my forehead against the cold wall.

"How am I ever going to get over her?"

Out of nowhere, flashes of Dara's ocean-blue eyes pierce my vision. The scent of sugar filters through my nose, and I breathe it in, taking huge gulps of air, wanting the peacefulness she brings to push away some of the darkness invading my every thought.

Dara.

She'd know how to fix me.

I shake my head and pound at the wall with my fist. "No!" I can't use her, chew up all her goodness, and spit it out like a wad of tasteless gum. Like Sarah, she deserves the best.

I'm so far from the best man for her it's almost comical.

A dry laugh leaves my lungs, and I push off the hallway wall and check my handiwork. My heart squeezes as I see the empty walls.

That's what I am now. A bunch of blank walls once filled with a beautiful life. It's fitting because that's how my heart feels.

Empty.

★ ★ ★

Three weeks since I've tasted powdered sugar and cinnamon on my tongue. I haven't even been able to walk past a bakery for fear I'd get in my car and drive over to that quaint Berkeley street and beg Dara to share one of her homemade masterpieces with me.

I've fought the pull of her for a full six weeks. I would have thought by now the desire to go to her would dissipate. It hasn't. There's nothing I want more than to hunt Dara down and lose myself in her essence.

Kiss her soft lips.

Taste her succulent mouth.

Make love to her luscious body.

Over and over until all the holes in my empty life have

been filled with her light. I fear I'm losing my mind. Either I'm crying over Sarah and the loss of our daughter, or I'm bemoaning the loss of Dara who's alive and well and only twenty minutes away.

Except I can't move on yet. I'm not ready. There's still more to do. More I have to let go of.

Set your loss free. Dara's words haunt my sleepless nights. I want to call her, tell her I'm trying, but I don't know how. She wouldn't want me anyway.

I stare at the closet. One half is completely filled with every single piece of Sarah's clothing, exactly as she left it. Like my mother with my father, every day I look at her clothes and expect her to come in wearing a pair of panties and a bra to pick out her outfit. Every day, for close to a decade, that's how Sarah entered the closet, ready to pick out the day's outfit. How do I look at this closet and not remember that?

I stare at one of her evening dresses. She wore it to one of our anniversary dinners.

Which one?

The question surprises me, but on top of it comes a sense of uneasiness because, for the life of me, I can't remember where she wore that dress. Suddenly, it's the most important thing in the world. As if the thought of not being able to remember means I'm forgetting her. Forgetting Sarah.

Why can't I remember?

A tightness squeezes my chest, and my heart thumps wildly. I press my fingers against both of my temples. "Which anniversary?" I cringe, racking my brain, trying to remember.

My breath comes fast. Too fast. I tug at the tie around my neck.

I can't breathe!

Remember, Silas! Fucking remember! I mentally scold myself.

Which anniversary?

I swallow around what feels like a golf-ball-size piece of cotton in my throat. I rush to the bathroom, panting, sweat breaking out on my forehead, at the back of my neck. My pupils are tiny pinpricks of black when I catch my reflection in the mirror. Shrugging off my jacket, I let it fall to the ground in a heap. I twist the cold water on, cup water in my hands, and splash my face several times. The cold doesn't even register against the heat engulfing me.

For a long time, I breathe in and out the way Dara taught us in her meditation class. In for five, hold at the top, out for five, release entirely.

It takes a long time, but eventually my heartbeat slows and I can breathe more evenly.

What the fuck was that?

"Hello!" a sing-song voice I recognize instantly calls out.

My sister Whitney comes into my room.

"Bro! It's me, Whit!" she calls out. "You in the can?"

I close my eyes and smile before grabbing a hand towel and patting my face dry before exiting the bathroom.

I'm not alone.

"Just washing my face. What's up? Why are you here?"

She tosses her purse and keys onto my big, lonely bed. "Mom said you were going through Sarah's clothes today. As her best friend and your favorite sister, I thought I'd help you go through it. Pick out a few things we can give her mom, our sister, and of course *moi*, before donating the rest."

"Give them away?" I choke out, knowing it makes sense, a lot of sense, but still hating every fucking second of the words leaving my mouth.

My baby sis nods. "Yeah. Sarah was really into helping the women's shelter, remember? She used to volunteer all the time. And I know for a fact, that's where she took all the fancy clothes you bought her when she was done wearing them. Those clothes help women get back on their feet, get jobs, et cetera."

Sarah did love helping the women's shelter. She couldn't stand knowing what they went through. "Yeah. She'd like that." I nod. And my Sarah would. Selfless and giving all the way. "Whit, it's the perfect plan."

Whitney smirks, puts her hands on her hips, and cocks her head left and right, giving serious attitude. "Don't I know it. I've always been the smart one out of the sibs."

I chuckle, put my hand to her shoulder, and squeeze. "You keep right on thinking that."

"Oh, I will. Because it's fact...yo! Boom!" She makes a motion of her hand exploding. "I'll start in the closet. Why don't you work on boxing everything in the bathroom?"

The bathroom.

So much safer than the closet.

Then I remember what's in the closet, and my heart starts up that erratic rhythm again. I take a few steps and find my sister already putting some things on my side in a hanging pile and leaving others. The black evening gown is hanging on the right near my stuff.

She stops with a sweater in her hand.

I finger the gown. "I can't remember what anniversary she wore this to." My voice cracks at the admission, but I won't be able to rest until I know.

My sister looks at me, her brown eyes revealing she

knows this is important. She stares at the dress for a minute, appreciating the crystals at the top of the shoulder before she snaps her fingers. "Bro, it's because it wasn't an anniversary dress! She wore it to the huge album release party for the boy band Daddy signed like six years ago."

I think back to that party. Sarah all in black, walking down the red-carpeted staircase, holding my father's elbow, looking like a princess. That was the night we decided to start trying to get pregnant. Must be the same reason she kept the dress.

The flush of anxiety creeping up the back of my neck eases. I reach out and grab my sister's hand and squeeze. "Thank you."

"Course. But I'm keeping the dress. Sarah said I could wear it anytime I wanted, and I plan on blowing Mack's mind at the next launch party."

I snicker, thinking about my sister's poor boyfriend. "That boy needs to put a ring on it." I frown and lean against the doorjamb.

"Mmmhmm. Don't I know it."

"Want me to have a talk with him?" I offer, knowing I've shirked my big brother duties the last couple years. Now that Dad's gone, I need to step it up.

She nods. "Could you without scaring the bejeezus out of him?"

I scowl. "Uh, no. What's the point of having a talk unless he's scared shitless? Trust me, Whit. I got you, girl." I promise.

She sighs. "At this point, I'll take any help I can get. We've been dating for two years."

"True. Except the last time we spoke, he was working really hard to set himself up. Pay off his school loans and get himself a nice pad. Has he done that?"

Whitney folds up another item and sets it on a shelf where she's accumulating a stack. My guess, the stack is the donation pile. I refrain from looking at it because I don't want to know what's being donated or kept. If it were up to me, it would stay right where it is forever, but then I'll never let her rest.

"Yeah, but get this. You know what that *baller* says he's saving up his money for?" She sneers and makes an ugly face. "I'm gonna give you one guess...and it's not a ring!" Her tone is scathing.

I gesture up with my chin, not even wanting to attempt a guess.

"Dubs. Fuckin' rims for his ride. And why?" Her voice lowers for the rest of her tirade. "'Oh, because I can't be taking my shawty in a POS,' he says. Like I care about his car!" She grumbles under her breath.

Unfortunately, I can't help but chuckle behind my hand. Whitney sends a blast of daggers from her gaze. "Don't you be takin' his side! You're Team Whit. Period. Feel me?"

"Girl, I can feel your heat a mile away. I'll talk with him."

"Great." She smiles for a second before it turns into a frown, and her dark eyes assess me. "What d'you think you're doing? Sitting on your ass watching me slave away while you do nothing? I ain't yo mama. Get to steppin'. That bathroom's not going to pack itself. Jeez-us." She pushes her long braids over one shoulder and fans herself with one hand. "And turn on the air. I'm hot as hell up in here."

"I love you too, Whit." I laugh.

"Air conditioning, fool!" she hollers.

"Got it!" I leave her be.

I turn up the air, see a stack of boxes she must have brought with her, and grab those too, setting them on the bed.

"Oh good. You're not blind." She winks, grabs a box, and heads back into the closet. I take a box and head to the bathroom with a smile. First time in three weeks I've cracked one.

"And I love you too, Si-low!" she randomly yells across the room.

I smile into the mirror and set the box on top of the vanity. I open the first drawer and inspect the contents. All makeup. I'm not even going to look at it, instead, pulling the entire thing out and dumping it all in the box. Sarah never cared much for the stuff anyway, so why should I?

Keeping up my momentum, I take on the rest of the drawers. I'm doing fine until I chance a look at the vanity. Her perfume, brush, and daily products are sitting in an untouched basket in the corner. The only reason it doesn't have years of dirt is because I have a cleaning lady come every two weeks. I grab the basket and assess that most of it can go in with the rest.

The hairbrush, though, is harder to let go of. It still has strands of long blonde hair tucked in the tines. Seeing it brings the crippling feeling crawling back up my neck. I lean over the vanity and breathe the way I did before my sister arrived.

"You done?" Whit comes into the bathroom and notices me breathing in and out. She grabs the brush. "I was coming in for that. May I have it?" she asks softly.

"You're not going to throw it away?" My voice sounds rough, emotion spilling out with each utterance.

Whitney shakes her head. "Nope. I'm going to use it when I have my hair out of braids and think of Sarah every morning."

I nod and swallow down the sadness. "Good." The only word I can croak out.

Whitney grabs for my wife's perfume and opens her mouth to speak. I stay her hand and bring it to my heart. "I'm keeping that for me. My wife's scent stays with me."

This time, she nods, but her dark-chocolate eyes fill with tears. "You're not the only one who misses her, Si-low. Except we're not allowed to talk to you about her because you won't allow it."

I suck in a harsh breath and let it out just as harshly. "Fuck. Why does it still hurt so much?"

Whit lays a hand on my back and rubs in a calming circle. I try to focus on the soothing gesture, much like how our mother comforts us when we're sick or hurting.

"Si, I know this is going to sound harsh, but I think you need to see someone. These steps you're taking toward letting her go are great. Really good. I mean that."

I narrow my eyes and clench my jaw tightly.

"It's just, three years is a long time to hurt. Maybe you need to share some of that hurt with an impartial outlet. Give yourself some time to accept what happened and move on with your life."

I grind my teeth hard enough to feel pain. "I don't want to move on without them."

"Si, I know you don't, but you have no choice. None of us do, but we're trying. You're not trying as hard as you could be."

Not being able to run or escape is making me feel cornered in the bathroom. I push back away from my sister and lean against the wall, crossing my arms over my chest. "What are you talking about? Therapy? Like a shrink?"

She nods. "Yeah. Exactly. When I was at the studio earlier today, I saw Atlas. He gave me a card to give to you."

"Why didn't he give it to me himself?" I huff.

Whit purses her lips and rolls her eyes. "Maybe because you'd act all affronted, like the big man on campus who doesn't need help from anyone. He may be your friend, but Atlas is also your employee. Don't forget who has the ultimate say around Knight & Day Productions."

I sigh and rub my head, allowing the tiny prickles to tickle my palms. "You think he was afraid to approach me? He hasn't been afraid on anything else. More than that, we're friends. Bros."

She shrugs. "Maybe he thought the suggestion would come better from me. Whatever the reason, I think it's a good one."

I turn to say something and get her back, following her into the bedroom. She digs through her purse, which could easily double as a suitcase it's so huge. "Here. Monet Hart. He claims she's the best there is. Apparently helped a girl you know. Someone named Honor?"

"Honor Carmichael. I met her a few weeks ago. Songbird. White as a ghost but looks like an angel. She's hooked up with Atlas's friend Nick Salerno."

"The guy who owns the boxing gym and fitness center, Sal's or something?"

"Yeah. They're all connected through Atlas, I think. Though the name Hart sounds really familiar."

"All I know is that Atlas suggested her. What do you say?"

I flip the card over a few times before flicking it with my middle finger. "You really think it will help?" I ask, my heart laid out for her to see.

Whit holds both of my hands in hers and brings them up between us. "I do. It's time to make changes. It's time for you to live again and for Sarah and the baby to be free from this world. No matter how much we all wish they were still here, they're not. But we are, big bro. What do you say? You'll call?"

I pull my sister into a tight hug. "I'm so thankful you're my baby sis."

She rubs her head against my chest. "I love you, Si-low."

"I love you too, Whitney. And I'll make the appointment."

CHAPTER NINE

THIRD EYE
C H A K R A

The third eye chakra is the center of our divine wisdom. From here, we seek to know the truth in all things. To delve into our own spiritual and inner demons and expel them so we can live a harmonious life.

DARA

"Baby girl, I'm so excited I can hardly stand it!" Ricardo squeezes my hand with exuberance. "We're going to see our baby today!"

Mama leans forward and tilts her head toward Ricky, sitting to my right. She's on my left. "Calm down, boy. You're going to frighten the girl. She's already nervous. Chill out before I make you take a long walk off a short pier."

I giggle, the fluttering in my stomach relaxing a little while the two of them bicker. Mama holds my other hand and brings it up to her mouth, where she places it against her lips. "Look at me, child."

When Mama speaks, I listen. I turn my body toward hers and focus on her loving face.

"Everything's going to be okay. No matter what happens in there today. I'm here, Ricky's here, and we're going to take this step together. You hear?"

I nod and snuggle against her soft curves, not caring about the armrest digging into my ribcage. The need to be near her love is more important right now. I can tell from her aura she's frightened but putting on a big front. This can't be easy for her. My mom and dad had a hard time getting pregnant and suffered a series of miscarriages and painful fertility treatments before they chose the adoption route.

"I'm scared," I admit. Since the moment I found out I was pregnant, I've wanted this baby. More than anything else in the world. Even with Silas not in the picture, I still want to have his child. My child.

My mom pulls both of my hands up to her mouth and kisses each one of my fingers. "Me too. Jacksons can brave anything as long as we're together, right?"

"Right!" I grin at my mom.

Every day I thank the good Lord for Vanessa and Darren Jackson. They've given me the perfect life. I couldn't have asked for more loving parents.

"Dara Jackson?" a nurse calls, holding a clipboard and flipping through the pages.

All three of us stand up and head that way.

"Dara?"

I nod, unable to speak through the fear coating my throat.

"Follow me," she says cheerily.

The nurse leads us through what feels like a maze of hallways and doors before stopping at one that has a number flag on the top labeling it room number three.

"Lucky number three." Mom smiles happily. It's her favorite number. She says because when she got me, her family of three was complete.

I smile and enter with my peeps behind me. Ricky is about to jump out of his skin, all smiles and positive energy. His aura is beaming a healthy orange. At least one of us is putting out the positivity. My mother and I are too worried about whether or not the baby is okay, is alive, and has a heartbeat.

"Grandma and Dad, you want to step out of the room so Dara can get undressed?"

Ricky grins wildly at the dad comment. He's still convinced he's going to be the baby's male influence. I have hope Silas will eventually come around and do the right thing. Once I get around to telling him he's going to be a father. Well, a father *again*, since he likely has a little girl.

Still, there is that niggling fear because he never mentioned his daughter, and I didn't see even one picture around his house among those of him and his wife...

I shake my head. I can't think about that right now. This is about me and the little life I'm carrying inside of my womb.

Mom and Ricardo leave the room while I change into a dressing gown with the extra-long paper blanket to place over my lap. A machine with a penis-shaped wand sits beside the bed, a TV monitor on the wall.

The doctor comes in, followed by my mother, who instantly takes up her position at my side, holding my hand. Ricardo stands to the back where my head is. Far away from where my unmentionables will be showing at the other end.

The doctor introduces herself as Dr. Hathaway.

"All right, let's see what we've got. The urine test you took tested positive for pregnancy. And you said your last period was supposed to arrive how many weeks ago?"

I clear my throat and squeeze my mama's hand. "Uh, around seven weeks ago."

"Then we should be able to get a good visual. Lie back, put your feet in the stirrups, and bring your bottom to the end of the table."

I follow along with her directions and push down the insecurity of being in such a vulnerable position. This is about seeing my baby and making sure it's healthy. I can survive any amount of embarrassment for that outcome.

The doctor gels up the wand with what I can only assume is lube before inserting it inside me. It feels like a huge dildo but really hard. As she maneuvers the wand a little inside me, she taps at a keyboard and stares at the monitor.

"Yes. Right there." She holds the placement and points to the monitor. "See the black circle and that white blob?"

All three of us stare at the screen. "Yeah," I answer.

"That's your baby."

Tears fill my eyes. I hold my breath as a cold sensation runs down my arm. I glance at my mother, and she's crying outright, tears running down her face and falling onto my arm.

The doctor continues. "And see that flicker right there." She does all of this one-handed, which is beyond impressive, but I imagine she's had a lot of practice. "That's your baby's heartbeat."

I focus on that flicker and let out the breath I'd been holding. It blinks on and off so fast. "His heartbeat?" I choke out.

"Mmmhmm. Healthy too. Although we don't know what the sex is. We won't be able to tell that until around your twenty-week ultrasound. I'm going to measure the length and determine how far along you are."

My mama kisses my cheek, keeping her face near mine. "Look at that heartbeat. Fluttering away like a butterfly. Just perfect, child."

I lift my hand and hold her face to mine. "Mama..." I barely whisper, the awe and emotion too much.

She kisses my cheek again and then my temple, whispering only to me, "We're gonna have a baby."

"Everything looks great, Dara. Based on the size, you're measuring seven weeks and three days. Your due date will be slated for..." She smiles widely and laughs.

"What? When am I due?"

"February fourteenth, Valentine's Day. Dad, that should make you happy!" She gestures to Ricky.

"Oh, it does!" He gushes, his hands clasped together at his chest, his face beaming.

I chuckle. "Fitting," I say, thinking that my baby is due on the national holiday dedicated to lovers, and I got pregnant from a one-night stand with a man who can't bear to be around me. "And he's not the father."

His excitement dwindles, and he narrows his eyes. "I'm better than nothing!" he counters.

"Best friend, best uncle status, remember?" I remind him softly, not wanting to hurt his feelings.

Ricardo shrugs. "Whatever. This is awesome!" he practically squeals.

"All right, Dara, here's a set of pictures of your baby." She hands me a set of four photos.

They all look like a bean-shaped blob, but it's still the prettiest blob I've ever seen. I clutch the photos to my chest and sigh. Physical proof of my baby bean.

"I'll leave you to your privacy. Schedule an appointment for five weeks from now. We need to do another ultrasound at the twelve-week mark. Once you've hit that, the chances of any problems occurring are significantly reduced. For now, you can follow the dos and don'ts on this sheet." She hands me a piece of paper detailing harmful things to my baby. Smoking. Drinking. Shellfish and a host of others I'll review later.

"Take your prenatal vitamin every day, drink lots of water, and get as much rest as possible. Otherwise, you can do everything you normally do. Have you experienced any sickness?" She marks something on my chart.

I shake my head. "No. Though I'm pretty tired."

She nods. "That happens in the first trimester. You'll get back that spring in your step in your second trimester but then lose it again in the third." She grins. "It's different for everyone, though."

"Thank you, Dr. Hathaway."

Ricardo follows her out and leaves me with my mother. I pull off the blanket and rip the paper gown off before throwing it all in the trash. My mother hands me my undies, which I put on, and then my bra. I toss on the flowy maxi dress I wore and slip into a beaded pair of multi-colored flip-flops. When I'm dressed, my mother holds out her arms. Without missing a beat, I fly into them, resting my face on her chest. Her warmth and love feed my soul, and we stand there, hugging and sharing in this moment.

"My baby is gonna be a mama." There's a beautiful sense

of awe floating around her form, and I revel in it.

I nod against her chest. "I'm still scared," I admit. I can tell this woman anything, and she'll always be there for me, never judging, just accepting.

She runs her hands through my hair. "I know you are. One day at a time, remember. Have you told Silas about the baby yet?"

I cringe and push away. "I didn't tell you his name."

"No, baby, but the second you brought that boy into our bakery a month ago and looked at him as though he walked on water, I knew he was the man who had my daughter's heart. I am not blind."

I push away and frown. "He doesn't have my heart. I barely know him."

"Child, you think I was born yesterday?"

"No," I mutter petulantly.

"Baby, when you brought Silas into the bakery, you glowed like the sun cresting over the horizon on a new day. No man has ever made you glow like that except your daddy the day we brought you home. I hadn't seen the shiny new glimmer with anyone else until he walked in. And let me tell you something." She turns me around and cups both of my cheeks. "That boy looked at you the same way. 'Cept he has shadows in his eyes. Something he's battling."

I nod. "He was married. She died."

"That would do it," she says before pulling me back into her arms and leading me out the door.

We schedule my next appointment, and my mother leads me out. I'm dumfounded, staring at my ultrasound pictures and tracing the edge of my baby bean.

"I'm going to love you so much," I promise the bean.

The sun hits my face when we exit, and I stop to let it soak into my being before I start walking and bump right into a hard form. Strong arms hold both of my biceps.

A deep voice I recognize grabs my heart and squeezes. "Dara?"

I open my eyes and come face-to-face with the most handsome man I've ever seen. The face that appears in all of my recent dreams. My baby daddy.

"Silas?" I shake my head and back away from his hold.

He squints, confusion marring his features. "What are you doing here?"

"What am I doing here?" I repeat his question, fear rushing through my limbs and causing the hair on my arms to stand.

My mother comes up. "Oh, hello again, friend. Silas, is it?"

He nods. "Mrs. Jackson, hello. What brings you to this side of the Bay?" He's referring to downtown Oakland.

I glance around and look for a sign, a reason, anything I can say to avoid answering the real question. My mother, on the other hand, has different ideas. And where the hell is Ricky? It just dawned on me he isn't with us.

"Doctor's appointment." She points behind her at the large building we just exited.

"Oh. I hope everything's okay." He frowns.

"Right as rain," she says, not giving anything away or leading on to the fact that it was *my* doctor's appointment and not hers.

I couldn't love the woman any more than I do right now. Keeping my secret, knowing I need to tell Silas in my own time.

"What are you doing here?" I ask, trying to keep the conversation light.

He nods to the building next door. "Knight & Day Productions." He smirks, and that small twist of his lips sends thrills straight through my body, down to my lady business.

I grit my teeth and nod. "Cool. Well, we gotta go..."

"Hey, I've been meaning to come to class again. I wanted to apologize for the way I left things, and I..." He stops and takes a deep breath, but before he can continue saying what I'm dying to hear him say...

That he misses me.

He wants to see me.

He thinks we have left something unfinished between us.

None of those things can leave his lips because at that exact moment, Ricky comes barreling out of the doctor's office holding two streams of black and white ultrasound photos.

"Look, baby girl...I got copies of the baby's first photos for me and your mom! Totally schmoozed the nurse who brought us into the exam room...and...oh fuck!" His gaze has reached the tall man standing before me.

My heart drops, and I cover my belly protectively. Silas's gaze clocks the photos and then goes to me and down to where I placed my hand. His voice sounds like a box of shaken rocks when he speaks. "You're...p-pregnant."

"Um..." I'm unable to get anything else out for a full thirty seconds as we have a stare-off. "Yeah, about that...I gotta go." I turn around on a heel and get maybe four feet forward before an arm is hooked around my upper body and my back is flattened against a hard, muscular chest.

His breath is at my ear, sending tingles all through me. "How far along are you..." he grates into my ear, and I lock my body, preparing for anything. Fight. Flight. I'm not sure.

"Look, it's none of your business," I start, feeling the need to protect myself and my baby from whatever may happen. Not that I think he'd hurt me.

"I asked you a question, Dara." His voice is shaking, emotion pouring out of every word.

Closing my eyes, I take a slow breath.

"Just over seven weeks."

"My God." He lets me go as if he's been shot and the force of the hit has knocked him back.

I turn around to find him stumbling a few paces backward, his hands coming up to his face.

"Silas...I, meant to tell you. I just, the way you left. And, what you told me. I needed to know..." I'm fumbling for the right words and failing miserably.

He stands still, his hands forming fists at his sides.

My mother sidles up to me and hooks me around the waist. Ricky takes up my other side, a united front. Two people I love, protecting me from what they think might be the big bad wolf. I know different. He would never hurt me. But he, on the other hand, is hurting. A lot. His aura is screaming pain and confusion. Sadness and fear.

"It's...it's...mine." He runs a hand over his head and closes his eyes.

"I'm sorry." I don't know what else to say. Digging in my purse, I find a business card for Sunflower Bakery. It has my cell phone number on it. I walk over to him and hold out the card. "When you're ready to talk..."

He snatches the card out of my hand and surprises me by pulling me into his arms, hugging me, tightly. "I don't know..." He burrows his face into my neck. "I don't know what to say. What to feel." His body trembles against mine. "I'm dead inside, Dara."

His words ripple through me like a physical blow, an ache he holds inside of him I need to assuage. "You're not dead inside. You're sad. You need help."

He nods into my neck. One of his hands holds the back of my head; the other locks around my waist. "You're not going to keep my baby from me, are you?" His voice is filled with dread and loss.

Grabbing his head with both of my hands, I pull his face away from my neck so I can see his beautiful pale-green eyes. Everything around us is gone, disappeared the moment he brought me into his arms. The busy street. My mother. Ricardo. All a whisper in the wind as I make a deep connection with the man who is plagued with loss.

"Silas, I'd never keep your child from you. You can have as much or as little participation in his or her life as you want."

His expression contorts into one of agony, his body bucking as though he's received a physical blow. I hold him through it.

"The man who took my wife's life took my unborn daughter's with it. You can't take away my second chance..." He gulps, tears filling his eyes and falling down his face, wetting my fingers where I'm holding him.

I hear my mother's voice from not far behind me. "Sweet Jesus."

I don't address her. All my attention is on this one tortured, beautiful man.

My worst nightmare was true. He lost his wife and daughter on the same day. Going on instinct, I tilt Silas's head forward and lay my lips on his forehead. "You beautiful, beautiful prince."

"Don't take my chance away," he repeats, agony coating

every syllable.

With my heart in my throat, my forehead to his, I grab the hand he has curled around my hip and ease it to my belly. "He or she is seven weeks and three days. The heartbeat was perfect. I have another appointment in five weeks. At that point, we'll have passed the twelve-week mark," I tell him, trying to reach the place in him that needs this information to break out of his past misery. Give him something beautiful to focus on.

His hand cups my belly warmly and then—shocking me, my mother, and my best friend, based on the triple gasps—Silas drops to his knees. He plants his face to my belly and holds my hips. I wrap my hands around his head, rubbing his scalp while he nuzzles my abdomen.

My mother is a mess of tears when I glance over. She's got a handkerchief held to her face. Ricky is the opposite. He's been taking photos. I don't care. It's a moment in my child's life, and I'll be thankful for his efforts later.

"Hey, you gotta get up." I try to lift his head, but he shakes it.

"Need to connect with my child." His voice is muffled by my dress where he's kissing my belly over and over, speaking in a hushed tone, saying words that aren't for me but for our baby.

I gesture to Ricky. "Give me a set of those pics."

He frowns. "But..."

"Ricky!" I warn and snap my fingers.

He grumbles but hands me one of the strips of four images. "I've got a better idea, Silas. Stand up."

Silas does what I say as if on autopilot. His aura is a jumble of happiness, sadness, excitement, grief, and every possible feeling in between. It's changing so manically it reminds me of a strobe light.

"This is our baby bean. Take these photos and give yourself some time to let it soak in. When you have, call me. I'll be waiting." I run my hand down the side of his face, lean up on my tiptoes, and kiss him softly on the lips.

As I'm backing away, he locks his hand around my head and smashes our lips together once more. Only this isn't the goodbye, sweet, sentimental kiss I planned to give him.

No, his kiss is filled with desperation, desire, and longing. He holds my face, turns it from side to side, delving deeper with each plunge of his tongue.

I can't breathe.

I can't stop.

I can't pull away.

It's too good. My mind spins with need while emotions battle for attention reminding me that, a month ago this man left me. He's lost so much in his life he doesn't know what he's doing. He's clinging on to the one thing that's real. Me. And our baby.

Finally, the need for air wins out, and I pull back. He chases my lips, starved for more. I am too, but I have to be smart. He needs time to process what he's learned today. What's about to change in his life, forever. I turn my cheek, so he kisses me there and runs his lips down my neck to my hairline.

A million prickles run rampant through my nerve endings. I'm enjoying every press of his lips, every nip of his teeth, but I can't lose myself in him, in this. It's everything I want, but it's not real. He's a desperate man holding on to anything he can right now. He doesn't know what he's doing, what he's implying with each brush of his lips.

Finding strength deep down, I nudge his head away from my neck and step back from his grasp. On instinct, he comes after me, as though I'm a life preserver and he's floundering in open water.

I put a hand up in front of him. "Stop."

He does, his eyes wild, *hungry*. For me. For our baby. For a new life. I know better than anyone it's not that easy. I'm not a substitute for his loss.

"You need to work through your pain, Silas. I can help. Our baby can help. But you have to take the steps toward healing. Dealing with your grief."

He firms his jaw and nods.

"Okay. You've got my number," I remind him softly, as though I'm speaking to a child.

He pulls the card out of his pocket, shows it to me, and then puts it back.

"Take some time. Think about this. And we'll talk." I hold out the strip of photos once more.

Silas claims them like he would a priceless, porcelain Fabergé egg. I smile, loving that he's being so tender with something so important. Shows how much he cares already.

I walk over to my mother and grab her hand but keep my gaze on his. "Call me."

Ricky jets over to his car at the curb and opens the door. My mother enters the front seat. I move to enter the back.

"Dara!" Silas calls out, still standing in the same place I left him moments ago.

I turn back to look at him before getting in the car.

"I want this baby," he says, tossing his heart and emotions out in the open for me to catch them.

"I'm glad. I want this baby too." I smile and get into the car.

Ricky speeds off toward home.

He wants our baby.

CHAPTER TEN

Red and Orange Aura Colors and Meanings: When an aura is a deep red, the individual is likely grounded, strong, and survival-oriented. A darkening color could be anger, but if the hue turns into a bright cherry red, that suggests energetic, competitive, sexual, and passionate feelings. Going to the next color in the rainbow, orange hues connect with vitality, creativity, stamina, courage, and excitement.

SILAS

When the door to Dr. Monet Hart's office opens and she calls my name, I'm stunned stupid in my seat in her comfortable waiting room. Greeting me is an attractive Asian woman with long ebony waves that fall down around her shoulders. She's wearing a pink, silk blouse and tan dress slacks. A pair of matching Louis Vuitton stilettos grace her feet. I know this because my sister Whitney owns a pair of the exact same shoes, which I know because I bought them for her birthday six months ago.

All of that is not why I'm sitting stock-still in the middle of her waiting room. That's because not only is the woman attractive and well dressed, she's also very heavily pregnant. She looks like the goddess of fertility with a serene smile and warm, knowing black eyes.

"Mr. McKnight?" She gestures to her office with a sweep of her hand.

I get up on shaky legs, as though I'm a newborn deer just learning to walk, and enter her inner sanctum. The room is aesthetically pleasing, with a comfortable-looking couch in the center divided by a table opposite a single arm chair. I'm guessing the chair is where the doctor sits.

She walks to her desk, picks up a yellow pad and pen, and then gracefully takes her place in the single chair, which leaves the couch for me.

I make my way over to it, open my suit jacket, and sit down, crossing one ankle over my knee.

"Now, Mr. McKnight, you told my receptionist when you made your appointment that you are a friend of Atlas Powers?"

"Uh, yeah, we're buds and we work together."

"At Knight & Day Production? Am I assuming correctly you are his employer?"

"Yeah. We're friends, though." Probably one of the only real friends I have left after I disappeared from all the relationships Sarah and I had together.

I bounce my knee up and down in a nervous cadence, not sure how this works and what I'm supposed to do.

"Mr. McKnight..."

"Silas is fine."

"Okay, Silas. I need to have full disclosure before I start seeing you as a client. Your friend Atlas is my best friend's husband."

"Mila?"

She nods with a small smile. "I believe we know many of the same people, and yet we haven't run into one another."

"No, I'd remember you." I smirk, not being able to help it. She's beautiful. A blind man would remember this woman.

She purses her lips. "If there comes a time when our worlds do collide, I may have to suggest alternate therapy. For now, I can and am willing to work with you if you are."

I swallow the lump in my throat. "Yeah, I gotta do something or I'm going to lose them." The words roll off my tongue without thought.

"Well, that's as good a place as any to start. Who are you afraid to lose?"

"Dara and my unborn child I just found out she's carrying four days ago."

"And what makes you think you're going to lose them?" She sets her elbow on top of the arm of her chair and rests her chin on her knuckle and thumb.

A river of feelings ram up against my subconscious, and I blurt it out. "Because I already lost my wife and unborn child three years ago."

Dr. Hart sits up in her chair. "Let's back up a bit so I'm up to speed. You were once married. What's her name and from when to when, so I can keep track of the details as we discuss."

I suck in a fast breath and push out everything I can think of just as quickly. If I say it fast enough, maybe I won't have to

AUDREY CARLAN

hear it myself. "Sarah. We were high school sweethearts. Met freshman year. Dated until we were out of school. Moved in together at eighteen. I went to college, and she worked until she was twenty when we married. We tried to have a baby right away. Suffered a couple miscarriages, and then...I lost them both. Three years ago."

Dr. Hart doesn't say anything for a long time while my chest rises up and falls back down, a weight so heavy on my ribcage I can barely breathe. Its arrival always coincides with discussions of Sarah and the baby.

"Okay, that's an awful lot of hardship you experienced. To have suffered even one miscarriage can be tough." Her tone is soft and soothing, thoughtful, bordering on considerate. I can see why people like telling her their secrets. She doesn't seem to take the hurt and make it her own, yet she's still offering up a little of herself in her body language, her words, and the small crinkle at the corner of her eyes that tells she's taking it all in and also finds it sad.

I nod. "Sarah got depressed. Then when we lost the second one, I could barely get her out of bed. Until we found out we were pregnant with our daughter."

"And what happened then?" Dr. Hart asks.

"She got better, started to live again. For her. The baby. And the day we got to the twelve-week sonogram and the baby survived, was healthy, that was the day she broke out of her deep depression. It came and went so quickly. I didn't question it. At the time, I only cared that I had my wife back."

Dr. Hart scribbles something in her notepad, and I wait until she sets her dark gaze upon me once more. "Now tell me about three years ago."

I swallow the bile that crawls up my throat. The

monster that owns my heart when I talk about Sarah makes its appearance, putting a vise grip around the small mass of muscle and squeezing hard. I rub at my chest, above my heart, trying to quell the pain remembering brings. Not being able to contain it, I burst out of my seated position and pace behind the couch, stopping in front of the window. It's going to rain. The clouds are dark, bloated with moisture, filled to the brim and ready to offload a torrential amount of cold wetness from the sky. I welcome the bad weather. Suits my current mood.

"Silas...what happened three years ago?" she asks again.

I close my eyes and go back to that very day before my wife headed off to work.

"You look like a juicy red apple in that dress, sweetie," I tell my wife as she fluffs her hair, looking in our bedroom mirror.

I wrap my arms around her waist and place my hands over her huge belly, feeling our daughter kicking away.

"She giving you trouble already?" I chuckle and kiss her neck.

Her blonde hair falls to one side as she holds my hands against her baby bump. "Never. She's perfect." My wife turns around, pressing her belly against mine while she reaches up on her toes to kiss me. I take her mouth willingly.

"Just. Like. You." She pecks me three times in a row. "I've got to go, though. Training my replacement at the law office."

"Good." I'm happy she agreed to quit her job, be an at-home mom, and take care of our daughter. Then the red color of her dress reminds me of the secret I have for her. "But, before you go, I have a present for you." I waggle my eyes and grin.

Her eyes sparkle, and her smile fills my heart full of joy.

"Come on." I grab her hand and lead her to the garage.

"What in the world have you done, husband of mine?" She

waddles along with me.

I chuckle. "You'll have to close your eyes and wait and see, wife of mine."

She dutifully closes her eyes, and I lead her into the garage, standing her in front of the present I bought her.

"Okay, open them." I let her hands go, and she opens her eyes.

Her pink pout opens on a gasp. Those blue eyes I adore so much cloud with fresh tears. "It's...so...so...my goodness!" she finishes.

"Red! Beautiful. Expensive!" I offer up, excited to hear what she thinks of the brand-new, off-the-lot, red Lexus RX 350 I bought her.

She hovers her pale, white hands over the hood. "It's so shiny. I can't believe it, honey."

"Believe it, sweetie. You're about to be a mother. You need an SUV with class and style. The car spoke to me when I saw her, and I knew she was perfect for you and our girl."

My wife spins and flings herself into my arms, tears running down her face. "I love you so much. Thank you, honey. Thank you!"

Still locked in the memory, I shake my head from left to right, bringing the room back into focus, trying to forget again.

"Keep going," Dr. Hart urges.

Pain lances through my chest, and I grit my teeth, taking several deep breaths. "And that very day, when she stopped her car at a stop sign close to her work in downtown Oakland, a drugged-up junkie saw my wife's shiny, new red car as his meal ticket to more drugs. He pulled a gun on her, yanked her out of the car, and shot her in the face. Killing her and our baby. He didn't care that she was pregnant. Only twenty-seven years old, with an entire life ahead of her. A home and a husband waiting for her. He looked into her beautiful face and saw nothing but a woman who was getting in the way of getting his next fix."

I can feel my shoulders drop as I lean my forehead against the cool glass of the window, allowing the sound of the rain pelting against its surface to keep me standing, the cadence soothing.

"So you think because you bought the car for her it's your fault they are dead?"

With zero time to think about it, I turn my head and match my gaze to Dr. Hart's. "Yeah. It's obvious. Had she been in the piece-of-junk Honda she'd been driving around since she was sixteen, which was a hand-me-down even then, I would still have my wife. My daughter would be three years old. Yeah, it's absolutely my fault."

Dr. Hart shakes her head. "Silas, it's not that simple."

"Isn't it? No car, no death." Seems pretty fucking simple to me, but I leave off the last part. It's her job to ask me the tough questions.

She gestures to the couch. "Please sit down."

I do what she says and ease back across from her.

"Do you believe in fate and destiny?" Dr. Hart asks randomly.

"Yes." I was raised believing our lives are already laid out for us. Free will allows us to take one step or another, certain paths, but for the most part, God is in control.

"Then if you accept that fate exists, you accept the knowledge that events happen and occur beyond any one person's control. And by the same token, if you believe in destiny, you accept that events are meant to happen. It's already decided before we are born."

I close my eyes, the guilt hammering a beat in my heart so loud I can hear its *thump thump* resonating through my body as I sit. "I'm not sure it's so cut and dried, Dr. Hart."

"I'm afraid that if you believe in fate and destiny, it is that cut and dry, Silas. You just want to accept it's your fault they're gone. That had you reacted differently, say, not bought the car or given it to her, the outcome would be different. This is simply untrue based on the logic that fate and destiny mean everything is predetermined and a supernatural power holds all the cards."

"You mean God?"

"Do you believe in God?" she counters.

Damn, this woman is good. "Yes."

"Have you ever experienced what you believe is a miracle?"

"Every day I see God's miracles. Through the love of my family, my friends, the success of my business. He's everywhere."

"Then why can't you believe it was God's decision to take your wife and daughter that day?"

"Because God wouldn't be so cruel. He'd have known they were my everything."

"Unless he was preparing you for this moment. Right now. When you were to be the man in the life of this woman Dara and your child with her?"

Her suggestion blasts me like a fireball to the gut. "Fuck!" I gasp, allowing it to resonate internally.

Could Dara and this baby be my fate? My destiny?

I stand up, not knowing what else to do with myself.

"I gotta go." Too many images and thoughts are swirling around my head for me to sit in this room and focus any longer.

I need to think. Figure this out.

Dr. Hart smiles, sets the legal pad on the table, and stands, holding out her hand for me to shake. "You have a lot to think about, I gather."

"Yeah." I shake her hand.

"Don't be too hard on yourself. You've suffered a great deal, Silas. These kinds of tragedies mark us. They lay a hurt on our souls, which can take a long time to heal. Sometimes they never do. It's up to us to try to manage that hurt. You've made the first step." Her words dig deep, coating my nerves with a soothing balm. "I'd like to see you again."

I nod, already recognizing this woman is capable of putting things into a different perspective. One I could never see through my own self-pity and sorrow.

"When should I come back?"

"When do you want to come back?" She cocks an eyebrow and lays a hand over her swollen abdomen.

"Tomorrow?" I clear my throat.

She chuckles. "I think next week, around the same time, would be good. Don't you?"

"I need to solve this as soon as possible." I force as much sincerity into my voice as I can so she understands how important healing is to me. "My life with Dara and our baby depends on it."

She shakes her head. "You can't force the mind or the heart to heal. It happens naturally, organically. What you can do is offer Dara your progress. Discuss some of what we talked about with her. Perhaps the two of you can help one another through this until you find a happy plane of existence where your past life and future can coexist together."

"Thank you." I walk over to the door and grab the handle.

"You really helped. And uh, congratulations on your baby too. When are you due?" As I ask the question, it dawns on me I don't know when my baby is due. Suddenly I need to know that more than I need to take my next breath. Only I'm not sure I'm ready to see Dara just yet. This new logic the doctor presented needs to be fleshed out in my mind, mulled over, given some breathing room.

I'll text her instead.

"Two more months."

"Exciting," I mumble, thinking about how exciting a new life would be. A baby. *My baby.*

"It is. See you next week, Silas."

"I'm looking forward to it," I offer and push through the door.

Once I've made my appointment for next week, I escape outside. The rain pelts my jacket, face, and chest, soaking right through my clothing and chilling my bones. I need the cold. It reminds me I'm still here.

★ ★ ★

I'm seeing a therapist. She's great. I think she's going to help me work through my past.

I read the text over and over again to make sure it conveys what I want to tell Dara. I'm seeking help. I'm working on my issues. She's still on my mind.

While I wait for the text to be seen and responded to, I pull from the fridge one of the readymade dinners Ma made for me. A Post-it is stuck to the top. *Cook on 350 degrees for forty minutes.*

I lift open the lid and sniff the contents. Looks like some

type of chicken bake. Anything will do. I'm a shit cook, and my mother knows it. When Sarah died, I lost thirty pounds in six months. Eating wasn't a priority, and I didn't know how to cook. Plus, I didn't care about me. My mind was wasting away; why not my body too?

My mother had other ideas. She and my two sisters started up this plan. Each of them would cook two dinners big enough to put some aside for me. Mom would pick them all up and deliver them each week. She picks up the clean casserole dishes I leave sitting on the counters and fills them up with the new meals. It's pretty pathetic. A thirty-year-old man whose mom and sisters make his meals and take care of him.

I'm going to have to put a stop to that too. Maybe I could take a cooking class or something. Learn a few things.

I'll bet Dara could teach me.

The thought runs a race through my mind. She loves to bake, and I'll just bet a million bucks she knows how to cook a fine meal too.

My phone pings, and I practically jump out of my skin to get to it. A text from Dara.

That's fantastic. I'm happy for you.

My heart starts pounding, and I lick my lips, trying to think of what to say.

Instead of typing her a message, I take a deep breath and hit the call button. It rings twice before she picks up.

"Hi," she says almost shyly. I like hearing her low, sexy timbre. It reminds me of her whispering in my ear when we couldn't get enough of one another.

"How are you doing?"

"Fine," she offers, and I rub at the back of my neck, not sure how to best respond.

"And the baby. Everything going okay? You're not spotting or anything?"

"Nope. Everything's great. I've been really tired, so Ricky's been taking the mornings alone on my behalf."

The mention of another man rankles against my nerves. I twist my hand into a fist and set it up on top of the counter, willing myself not to punch anything. If she needs something, I should be the one there to help.

"What needs to be done in the morning?" I ask, not even knowing what she was talking about but still frustrated someone else is doing it. Someone who's not me. Another man.

She yawns and sighs as if she's snuggled up in bed. I am enjoying imagining her in her bed. Which reminds me, I don't even know where she lives. God, there's so much I don't know about the woman who's got my heart in a vise and is carrying my future in her womb.

"The bakery start-up. A night crew comes in, remember, and then Ricardo and I take over baking the fresh daily pastries and get set up. He's handling it, though. I think he likes to know he's helping me. He's got this plan to be the best uncle in the world. And since children need all the love they can get, I'm allowing it."

"Makes sense. So, today marks eight weeks."

She chuckles. "You're right. I didn't even realize it. I need to read my weekly pregnancy announcement."

"What's that?" I ask, eager for any information about our baby.

"I have this book, and it goes week by week and tells you what your body is doing and what's happening with your baby in this week."

"Read it to me?" I ask, wondering if the request is too

stupid but not caring if it is. I'm in desperate need of anything she'll share with me.

"Okay, hold on."

I can hear the sound of paper rustling. "Okay, I'm back. Oh, cute. Our baby bean has a little head." Her voice softens, sounding very girly. "Baby has webbed fingers and toes, the lungs and throat are forming. Oh..." She starts laughing.

"What?" I find myself smiling into the phone.

"It says here our baby's tail is almost gone. Did you know they have a tail?"

I chuckle and respond with a low, "Yeah." I did know because I've been through this phase before. Still, I never read through these things with Sarah. And right now, hearing Dara read about our child's growth is making it more real. Making a lightness enter my chest. "What else?"

"Says our baby's genitals are not completely formed so we won't know if it's a boy or a girl. Do you care either way?"

"No. Healthy," I choke out, when I really want to just say, "Alive."

"Ah, our baby is the size of a kidney bean. See, baby bean, you really are a bean!" She laughs, and it's music to my ears. Like a fresh rain shower in a dry desert.

"Baby bean sounds like it's going through a lot of changes," I say, wanting to add something to the conversation.

"Yeah. And my body too. Yowza."

"Like what?" She's the mother of my child. I want to know everything.

"My uh... Well, it says my boobs are going to start getting bigger. Great." She says the last word as if it's the opposite of greatness.

"What's the matter with that? You've got an amazing rack!

The more the merrier." My voice lowers to a sultry timbre, remembering just how great her rack is.

"It's not like I needed any more, though."

I'm laughing into the phone. "You're right about that. Just more of you to love." I laugh again and then realize what I said when the line goes completely silent. "Dara..."

"No, it's okay. I'm just, a little hormonal right now and tired. I should go to bed."

Not wanting to stop hearing her voice, I scramble to get out anything I can that will make her keep talking to me. "When can I see you and the bean?"

"I don't know if that's a good idea right now."

"Dara. I need to see you healthy and alive." I close my eyes and grit my teeth.

"Oh. Yeah. Okay. I'm sorry. How about you come to meditation on Saturday?"

"That's five days away." I regret it instantly.

"It's better than nothing."

"You're right. Meditation on Saturday morning. Take care of yourself. And feel free to call and talk to me about anything," I offer, wanting her to take me up on it.

"I will," she says rather stiffly, meaning she definitely won't. Still, I have to take what I can get right now. Earn my place in her life. Heal the hurt I've caused with my actions.

"Good night, Dara. Sleep well."

"You too, Si. Sweet dreams."

If I dream of her, they will be sweet.

CHAPTER ELEVEN

THIRD EYE
CHAKRA

Couples driven by the third eye chakra tend to be very self-aware. They know their own problems and don't deny they exist. They simply are. A couple will use self-realization to work together toward self-perfection. This allows each person to give freely of themselves to the other. Since they often have a spiritual and psychic harmony, they are one another's best resource for problem solving.

DARA

Please come at 7:00 a.m. before the 8:00 class. I want to work with you privately.

I send the message to Silas Friday evening. Today, I spent

the day hunting down the perfect item to help him find peace amongst all of the distractions his mind is dealing with.

Namely...

His wife.

His daughter.

Me.

Our baby.

Not to mention I'm sure he has a whole host of other things to worry about as the CEO and primary shareholder of Knight & Day Productions. I hold up the mala prayer beads I bought. A hundred and eight in total. Each bead is about the size of a large pea and slightly different in color. The strand I own is primarily made of wood and turquoise, a teal silk tassel hanging at the end. I've had it blessed by a Buddhist monk, and today, I bought a set of beads to assist with Silas's meditation too.

The black beads interspersed with a smoky quartz bead called to me the second I arrived in the small store. The Buddhist that runs the shop offers a variety of meditation tools, and when I came in today, he already knew what I was looking for. Strangely enough. He led me right over to the mala beads and left me alone to finger them individually and feel their energy. When I got to the black one I hold in my hand now, an image of Silas sitting in my room at Lotus House came to me so clearly, I knew they were the ones.

Together the shop owner and I put our combined energy into them, blessing them the only way I know how, by giving love and extending loving energy into them while I held the strand. Silas will have to set his own intention through his meditation practice, but this is another step in the right direction.

I just hope he won't think the gift silly or strange.

Something inside me encouraged the purchase. It was all I could think about when I woke this morning. With that type of energy spilling from every pore, I couldn't deny the compulsion.

Now I sit in my room on my bed, holding my own meditation beads as I breathe deeply, set my intention, which is to help Silas heal, and let everything else go.

★ ★ ★

Silas is waiting by his car when I exit the bakery the next morning. "Hey, how are you?" His eyes scan me from head to toe and then stop at my belly. I haven't gotten any bigger yet, so I'm not sure what he's looking at.

"Good. Baby's fine."

He takes a full breath when I mention our child growing inside me. He hangs his head and then glances at me when I start to walk.

"Why are you at the bakery so early? I thought you gave over the mornings to Ricardo?"

I smile shyly, appreciating that he paid close attention to our conversation a few days ago. "I live in the apartment above the bakery."

He smiles widely. "Yeah?"

"Yeah."

"It's cool. You live where you love to work. And then, of course, you're right next door to your other passion."

"Perfect setup. Though I'll have to figure out what I'm going to do when the baby comes."

He frowns but continues to follow me in. I unlock the door and, since I'm the first one in, head over to the alarm panel and press the buttons, turning off the alarm. I keep the door locked because it's safer, and I don't want anyone intruding on our meditation session. Besides, Luna will be in within the hour anyway.

"Why? What's wrong with your apartment?"

"Nothing. It's just small. Eventually, the baby and I will outgrow it. There's not a lot of room to put a crib, but I'll probably get a bassinet for the first few months."

He grabs on to my arm. "Um, don't do that."

I stop and turn toward him. "Do what?"

"Get a bassinet." His voice changes, lowers. "I, uh, have one."

My shoulders fall. "Silas, we're not using something you bought for your daughter."

He shakes his head, takes a deep breath, and lets it out. "The bassinet I have is the one my grandmother made for my mother. She brought me and all of my siblings home from the hospital to it. I'd like for our child to have that sense of home when he or she lies down at night. It's a family heirloom. My sisters and brothers will want to use it when they have a child too."

A surprising sensation comes over me. Peace. He's thinking about our child individually but, more importantly, as part of a bigger family. "I'd like to hear more about your family."

"After meditation?" he asks hopefully. "I can come to Sunflower."

I chuckle. "Well, I teach my normal class after, but if you want to wait around, we could."

"Absolutely." His matter-of-fact response sends me smiling.

"Okay. Please take a seat wherever you feel most

comfortable."

"Where are you going to be?"

"Why?"

"Because wherever you are is where I'm most comfortable."

His eyes are a brilliant green, his aura filled with honesty and light. The man is pouring his emotions out, and he doesn't even know it. I'll have to let him in on my little, somewhat rather well-known secret. At least in this community, I'm known for being the resident aura reader.

"Place two mats side by side on the riser there." I point to my regular location and then head for the candles and music. I set the mood and then dig through my bag for my gift.

Silas is sitting cross-legged, all in white, a V-neck T-shirt and white sweats. His brown-sugar-colored skin looks positively edible in this light. Finding what I need, I pull out the silk-wrapped item and take my place in lotus position in front of him.

"I've got something for you." I hand him the parcel.

He unfolds the indigo silk until the prayer bead necklace is showing, gleaming in its ebony glory. Silas holds it up to the light, and the smoky quartz catches a ray of light and sparkles against his shirt.

"What is it?"

"These are mala prayer beads. They are traditionally used in the Buddhist faith but more often to assist with meditation."

He fingers a bead. "How do they work?"

I take the ones I have around my neck and place them in my hands, letting the strands spill through my fingers.

"We're going to start with you closing your eyes and breathing the way I taught you before. In for five, hold at the top of the breath, out for five, release all the air and repeat."

Silas closes his eyes dutifully, and it gives me such pride. His energy seems positive, his aura glowing a brilliant yellow like it usually does when he's happy and his body language relaxed. He's not at all taken aback by this unique gift. Seeing him open to new things is refreshing.

"Now that you're relaxed, allow the beads to slip through your fingers as though you are connecting them to you and your energy. Imagine your energy filling up each bead with light. While you are doing this, I want you to state your intention to the beads..." Before I can say "silently," he blurts his intention out loud.

"Forgiveness."

The single word smashes into my heart along with a wave of guilt. This poor man has suffered so much loss, and here he sits before me, wanting to be a part of his unborn child's life. Still trying to find forgiveness for losing his family.

Needing to be close to him, to share in this moment, I shimmy my booty closer, making sure our knees touch. He opens his eyes the second our knees make contact.

"Close your eyes." I smile but lay my hands over his thighs, grounding him in this moment.

"Visualize each bead you turn with your thumb and middle finger as if you are receiving forgiveness and letting go of negative thoughts."

I watch as he spins each bead and then moves on to the next.

While he's doing this, I lean over and flick on the music. "We're going to chant together. But first, I'm going to explain what each word means so that you have a deeper connection to it. We're going to do the *Om Nahma Shivaya* chant we did the last time. You seemed to enjoy that one."

He smiles and nods but doesn't speak or open his eyes. Good, he's getting into the zone he needs to be in.

"Om is the sound of our transcendent eternal God, the universe, all things. You say the word long enough to feel it resonate in your throat and into your heart."

Na is the earth.

Ma is water.

Shi is fire.

Va is air.

And Ya, is the ether or absolute conscience.

"When you say them together, *Om Nahma Shivaya*, you are essentially offering up a prayer of sorts, stating you want to be one with the universe and all things, until eventually, you find the place in your mediation where you are enlightened. Now let's chant together. After each utterance of the chant, send your energy into the beads along with your intention. On the next chant, turn the next bead."

Together we sit, chanting, sending energy out into the universe and our beads and letting our intentions shine, until the music runs out. The CD runs for forty-five minutes. At the end of our session, Silas is rocking along with his chant, continuing to whisper the phrase even without the music. He's in the sweet spot, and I'd love to keep him there, but I have to start the next class.

Shifting my hand from his thighs, I cup his cheeks and press our foreheads together. The second our foreheads touch, a shimmer of rainbow light sparks around the both of us, our auras and energy merging into one.

His eyes flash open, and he cups my neck, keeping me close. "Thank you. For this gift. For everything."

I'm so overrun with emotion all I can offer is a nod. Our gazes hold one another's for what seems like eternity, neither moving nor speaking, just being with one another in this safe space.

Until the door opens and the first of my clients enters.

The spell is broken.

★ ★ ★

I expected Silas to leave when the class filled up. He didn't. Instead, he sat off to the side of the riser, his back against a mirrored wall, two bolsters under each knee, and closed his eyes. He used his beads and meditated for the entire next hour, following along and going back into his safe space. I wanted to clap and cheer. Meditation is not easy for the most spiritual of individuals. Turning off the monkey mind and getting into the right headspace, letting go, is hard to do. For someone like Silas, who has so much tragedy to wade through, I'm happily surprised he was able to go so deep unassisted.

When the class is over, he stands and holds up my bag for me while I put my things in, put on my hoodie, and reach out for it.

He shakes his head. "I'll hold it. What do you have in there?" He lifts the bag up and down, gauging its weight.

I chuckle. "Books."

"Seriously?"

"Yeah. I carry around my pregnancy guide, a journal in case I want to write something I'm thinking or feeling, my Kindle in case I get bored, and my daily meditation. Plus, of course, all the other stuff women carry around."

He frowns. "Women carry around too much baggage."

I snort-laugh. "Says the man who did two hours of meditation class today."

"*Touché.*"

Seeing his beautiful grin lights up my day. I smile and look down.

Silas reaches for my hand and twines our fingers. "I need to touch you."

"'K," I say without further comment. He squeezes my fingers in what I can only assume is thanks as he leads me down the hall, out the doors, and to the bakery.

"Is your, uh, mom here today?" He bites down on his lip and focuses on the road.

"No. She doesn't usually come on Saturdays, preferring to spend the time with my dad. It was a fluke she was here last week."

He nods. "Ricardo?"

"Yep. He comes most days. He has as much vested in this bakery as I do."

Silas clenches his jaw, and a muscle ticks at the side. His aura starts to glimmer with a little red anger.

I stop him before we enter. "Hey, just so you know. There's nothing but deep friendship between Ricardo and me. He's my best friend. When we met, we tried to be more..."

Silas pulls me against his chest, wrapping his arms around me. When he said he wanted to be close, I guess that meant full frontal touch. "Continue," he growls, as if it's physically hurting him to hear me talk about my past with Ricky.

I loop my arms around his body, resting my hands above his ass and looking up into his piercing green eyes. "We kissed, freshman year of high school. It was gross. We both knew from that day on we'd be nothing but best friends. Besides, he's mostly gay."

"Mostly?" He cocks an eyebrow.

Giving him a cheesy smile and a shrug within his embrace, I add, "His words, not mine. I don't think he's been with a woman in years, but he says he's still attracted to them. He's just *more* attracted to men. He's got a thing about labels."

Silas nods, brings his head down, and presses his lips to mine. "As long as he's clear that your kisses are mine now, we'll be cool."

"Is that right? You're claiming my mouth?" I smile, loving this but not wanting to push.

He grins wickedly. "And everything connected to it." His words are like Fourth of July and Christmas rolled into one. They're everything I want to hear. Still, I'm not sure he's fully capable of giving me all of himself.

"Is this your way of saying we're together *together*?" I mutter around the question I've wanted to know but was too afraid to ask.

"Dara, you're carrying my baby." His words are said with a tone that might as well have said, "Duh."

I narrow my eyes. "Lots of women have baby daddies as well as have babies on their own..." I start.

He presses a finger to my lips, cutting off my next phrase.

"Not my baby mama. My son or daughter is getting a family. It may take time, and I know I've got some demons to work through, but it doesn't change that I'm connected to you. Shit, Dara. Every time I see you, I'm destroyed all over again by your beauty, by your *soul*. You're everything I could ever want... I just need to set the part of my heart Sarah owned free. I'm working on that. It doesn't mean there isn't room for you and our baby."

"Si..." My voice catches.

"We went about this backward, sweetheart, but it's happening sooner rather than later. Let's just feel it out, okay? Prepare for our baby and figure out the nuances as we go."

"One step at a time?" I blink up at his firm jaw, perfect wideset pale-green eyes, and excellent bone structure.

"Exactly."

"I can do that. Starting with feeding you another treat, which will be the best thing you've ever put in your mouth."

He shakes his head. "Girl, I already told you, nothing tastes better than you. That cinnamon roll, though, was a close second."

I laugh out loud as he holds the door open for me.

"After you, my sweet," he says.

"Now I'm your *sweet*?"

"Babe, you smell and taste like powdered sugar and honey." He rubs up close to my back. "I won't even get into what you smell and taste like in other places. But I can attest to your sweetness being *all over*."

I fan my face. "Lordy. You need to shut that mouth, or I'll be taking you to my apartment, not a table in the corner."

"Woman, don't threaten me with a good time." His eyes spark with mirth and a lot more with desire. I'm sure my own are no better.

"Sit down and behave." I point to a seat.

"Yes, my queen." He uses the endearment he's called me a couple times before. If I'm honest, it's my favorite one, but I'd never admit it to him.

Once he's settled, I hit the display case and shoot a smile to Ricky. He gestures to Silas and gives me a thumbs-up only I can see behind the counter. I give him one back but motion to keep it on the down-low. He nods and grins, going back to assisting the next customer.

Pulling out the trays, I select another cinnamon bun because I know Silas loves that and I appreciate the memory of him swirling his tongue around my fingers. Then I add in an éclair, a chocolate-dipped cookie, a couple Danish, and a pumpkin cupcake. I've had my eye on that cupcake since I made the batch last night.

I practically drool as I maneuver around the display. Before I get far, Ricky calls me. "Latte for your man, large decaf latte for you, sugar pie!"

"You're the best."

"Don't I know it!" he cracks.

Silas is waiting when I come back and sit down with my tray loaded to the gills.

"Tell me about your family."

"Eager?"

"I'm adopted, Silas. I don't have any biological relatives. I'm excited that my baby will have both, people who chose her in their life as well as blood relations. Lay it on me!" I smile and grab the cupcake before he can even consider it an option.

Silas picks up the cookie. Interesting choice. Why go for the cookie when you can have the warm cinnamon roll? But whatever. To each his own.

"To start, my mother's name is Darlene, my father, Devon 'Daddy' McKnight, as he was known in the music world."

"I can't believe it. I actually have records of your father playing his soul music. My mother is a fan. She couldn't believe you are Silas McKnight, son to Daddy McKnight. My father might want your autograph."

"What? Why?"

"Because he thinks you're famous by osmosis. And just so you know, he now thinks our baby is famous too."

He chuckles, and the low rumble makes my stomach dip pleasurably.

"I have four siblings. I'm the eldest of five. Two sisters, two brothers."

I stop mid-chew, a chunk of cupcake catching in my throat before I cough and swallow it down with a sip of coffee.

Silas's expression is worried when he speaks. "You okay?"

Nodding, I sip more of my drink. "Yeah, it's just, my goodness, that's a lot of family members."

"That's not all. My father has four siblings, my mother seven. Our baby has a very large family. Including your mother and father, this child is never going to feel unwanted."

My face snaps up at the use of the word that clouded eight years of my life in sadness. Being an orphan, I always felt unwanted. Until the Jacksons chose me. Then my life changed.

And my baby will never go unwanted. Ever. He or she already has a huge family to count on.

"Silas, you can't possibly understand how happy your large family makes me." My voice is thick, coated with an emotion I can't hide.

He grins huge. "That's good, Dara, because you're now an important part of it. You, me, and our baby."

CHAPTER TWELVE

Blue and Purple Aura Colors and Meanings: If an individual's aura is blue, the person is cool, calm, and often sensitive. When the blue darkens, they may currently be experiencing a fear of self-expression and doubt. Indigo, which incidentally is the color of the third eye chakra, proves the person is intuitive, visionary, and clear-minded. If the aura shifts into violet it means the individual has a divinity, a sage wisdom, and enlightenment surrounding them.

SILAS

A pang of guilt and sadness wiggles down my spine as I watch the Realtor hammer in the For Sale sign on my lawn.

Sarah's house.

In my heart, I know this is for the best. I can't continue to live in this house, attempt to have another woman in my life, and bring a child who is not the baby Sarah and I dreamed of having into the nursery. It's not right.

Besides, as Dr. Hart continues to remind me, living in the past is not healthy. Dr. Hart has spent the last couple weeks working with me on making advances and changes, which are based on me and my needs *now* and not the life I lived with Sarah.

Seeing Dara every day is helping, even when it's only for thirty minutes in the morning while she works and I drink her coffee and eat her mouthwatering confections. Plus, I've gone to meditation two more weekends in a row since she gave me the prayer beads, and I've even been working on my own personal practice at home. Still, it's been hard to do with the reminder of my old life pushing all around my senses.

The Realtor makes his way back up the walk. "Good asking price, great condition... It's going to go fast," he surmises, looking at the lawn and the white sign announcing the property's availability to the world.

I nod and sigh. "It's time for a change. Any tips on a home in Berkeley?"

He frowns. "Sorry, not yet. It's a very old area you want to be in. There aren't a lot of people willing to sell, but it does happen. I've given a heads-up to all of my associates, as well as friends of mine in other companies, so we can be the first notified if something pops up."

"It's all you can do, right?" I shrug.

"Yeah."

"Let me know what bites you get on this place. Yeah?"

The man looks at my white one-story with a perfectly manicured lawn. "Shame you want to leave. You know, this isn't that far from the area you're looking at in Berkeley. Twenty minutes, tops. Thirty, if traffic is bad."

"I'm starting a new family, and my woman works in that area. I don't want her driving thirty minutes a day." Which sounds ridiculous since thirty minutes in Bay Area traffic is nothing. For others, that would be a dream. Some people drive three hours from the Valley to work in a city they can't afford to live in.

I'm really thinking I don't want Dara driving *ever*. Especially in her condition and even after. I make a mental note to discuss this fear with Dr. Hart. She'll have a field day with it, but it's not something I can bend on, not anytime soon.

The Realtor puts on his sunglasses and holds out his hand. "Well, I've got all I need. Please make sure you leave the key in the lock box on the front door, and let me know if there are certain times you don't want visitors. We make sure properties are seen before seven p.m. so we don't disturb your life too much."

I take his extended hand. "Thanks. Have a good night."

"Will do. You too, Silas."

The Realtor leaves my house, zooming away in his Mercedes.

I walk back into the house and look around. Whitney has been helping me box up things and sort for donation. As much as I would have liked to keep everything of my life with Sarah, it's not fair to Dara to have her sitting on a couch I picked out with my wife or sleeping on a bed we shared.

Besides, one day, I fully intend on having Dara and my child in my home every night. I know it's early, and Dara and I are getting to know one another, but there's something about her I can't stay away from.

She's beautiful, that much is a given. Wild in the sack, from what I remember of our drunken night of debauchery. I chuckle every time I hear her cute snort-laugh. None of this compares to her scent, though. Coming home to a woman who smells like a bakery every day...not a hardship for sure. And then there's her smile... It's so pretty, it could light up a room. Nothing gets to me the way her voice does as it wavers and lowers when she's teaching meditation; the sound weaves into the fabric of my being and calms the chaotic place inside me. The one that tells me I'm not enough.

Not good enough for my company, my family, Dara, or our new baby.

Dara makes that anxiety go away.

As I look around my empty house, my heart starts to throb. A painful reminder I'm alone, except now, I don't have to be.

Grabbing my coat, I'm through the kitchen and then jumping into my BMW within a minute flat. I glance to the right and notice my wife's old Honda still sitting there collecting dust. I'm going to donate it to the women's shelter we took her clothes to. One more thing Sarah would love to have shared with someone who needed it. I put it on my list of to-dos for tomorrow. Tonight, I need to see Dara, feed her a meal, and make regular plans to see her more than for my morning cup of coffee and a pastry. She hasn't been open to dating me yet, thinking I needed more time to sort myself out, but what I really need is to be around her. Spend time getting to know the woman who's going to have my child in the next thirty weeks.

Speeding down the road, I make it to the bakery in just over twenty-five minutes. The Realtor was right. It really doesn't take that long from my current neighborhood, but it would mean Dara would need to drive to work quite a distance every day. I can't have that hanging over my head. Not right now.

When I jump out of the car, I can see Dara at the window just turning the sign over from Open to Closed.

I grin and run up to the window. She sees me and smiles one of her own.

God, she's pretty.

"Got time for one more customer?" I yell loud enough so she can hear me through the glass.

She unlocks the door and opens it.

"Hey, didn't I see you at breakfast?" She smirks, and the tightness I felt in my heart back at my empty house dissipates.

Not fearing her response, I loop an arm around her waist, plaster her to my chest, and kiss her without warning.

She gasps, probably surprised at this sudden development in our relationship, and then melts into the kiss quickly, pressing her lips to mine just as eagerly. I slip my tongue along the seam of her lips, and she opens, allowing me entrance. She tastes of lemon and frosting. I lick her up, humming and moaning my appreciation of her tastiness as our tongues duel. She digs her fingers into the muscles of my back, rubbing her breasts against my chest. I run one hand down and palm her plump ass.

God, she feels good grinding up against my length, so I do it again until she moans her delight.

The kiss quickly gets out of control, both of us warring for dominance. Dara slants her head, holds me around the neck, and dives in. I give her everything she wants and more, grabbing both of her butt cheeks and yanking her up, pushing her against the nearest wall so I can grind my cock against her.

"Oh my God, Silas, it's *so* good," she murmurs around my lips.

"Is that right?" I press my dick harder between her legs, and she mewls like a baby kitten.

"I'm so...so...*hot* for you." She digs her nails into my back.

Taking my time, I run my nose down her neck and nip, lick, and kiss along the golden column, working her into a nice little frenzy.

"How do we get to your apartment?" I whisper in her ear and then bite down on the outside of her earlobe.

She moans. "Through the kitchen, up the stairs."

I work her neck for another few seconds, licking up and down, enjoying her sigh as I do.

"Um, Si...just let me down. I'll take you there. Need to make sure the bakery is locked up."

I let her unlock her legs and slide down my body. Except before she can go, I need her lips again. She returns my kiss with fervor, making my jeans tight as fuck with how hard my dick is. Letting her free, I adjust my package, trying to find a little more space and failing miserably.

Dara smiles and locks the door I just came through. Her hair is a wild mess of curls, more so now that I've messed them up. I don't care. She's still unbelievably beautiful.

Like a lost puppy, I follow my girl around the bakery as she closes up shop. I pay close attention in the hope she'll let me help her one day soon.

"The night team will be here in an hour, so don't worry when we're upstairs and you hear the alarm beeping. They'll unarm it and rearm it while they're here and again when they leave. It's a safety precaution and works well, especially so I know it's them coming in when I'm alone upstairs. My dad made sure the apartment was well insulated, so it's not like we can hear one another, hence the reason for the alarm."

"Makes good sense." I keep track of her movements. "What's the code?" I ask, not even thinking she may not want to tell me just yet.

"Three two seven two," she says automatically. "It's Dara when you type it on a phone keypad." She winks.

"Clever."

She shrugs, letting the compliment roll off as she presses the buttons. "Okay, we can go upstairs." Her eyes light up to a stunning daylight blue, the hint of excitement still floating in them as she licks her lips, looking me up and down.

Even though the bulge in my pants has not gone down even a little, I still feel as though I should make a valiant effort to woo her instead of tossing her on the nearest bed. "As much as I'd like to take you into your apartment and make love to you all night long..." I try.

"Yes, please," she says automatically, and I laugh.

"You and the baby need to eat. You've made it to ten weeks now without any problems, and I want to ensure you and our lil' one are getting all the nutrition you need. Meaning, can I take you to dinner?"

She scrunches up her nose and shakes her head. "No, but I can make you something to eat if you don't mind? I'm honestly far too tired to go out. I made homemade spaghetti and meatballs last night, if you're interested?"

"If I'm interested? Woman. Are you crazy? What man wouldn't be interested in a home-cooked meal?"

Dara smiles widely. "Then come on. Let's get you and this baby fed."

I follow her up the stairs, watching her ass jiggle the entire way. For someone who works out at the yoga studio next door, she's still got some seriously lush junk in the trunk, and I'm a man who loves a woman with a juicy ass. I can't wait to sink my teeth right into it, leave my mark.

My dick hardens more painfully, and I groan while looking away.

Focus on the stairs and the food, not your woman's ass.

Like a homing beacon, my gaze goes right back to it. Thank Christ she made it to the top and was opening her door, because I was two seconds away from taking a bite right out of crime, and I'm not sure how she'd have reacted. Maybe pleasantly, maybe not.

Dara tosses her keys into a ceramic bowl next to the door and keeps walking through to her small kitchen.

She was right. As I look around and see her homey apartment, comfy-looking couch and chair, neatly made bed with a ton of throw pillows on it, I try to find a place where she plans to put our child and can't find one. All I see is all there is. One big room that's maybe eight hundred square feet total. There's absolutely no room for me or our child.

Grinding my teeth, I head to the small kitchen and plant my ass on one of the two stools available. My closet is bigger than her kitchen. And there is one thing I know about Dara: My girl likes to cook. She's a fuckin' baker. Woman needs a top-of-the-line kitchen and appliances.

Breathing slowly, I attempt to get a handle on my nerves. It wouldn't be good for me to launch an all-out attack on the life Dara has created for herself. She lives simply. Runs a bakery she loves by day downstairs, works at the yoga studio next door, and spends time with her friends and family, all on this one street. And she doesn't seem put out at all by having less.

"How long have you lived here?" I ask, making polite conversation and wanting to learn as much about her as possible.

"Five years." She's chopping up some cucumber and dumping it on top of a bag of salad she'd already put in the bowl while I was taking in her place.

"What do you do for fun?" I ask the lame question every guy asks when you're first dating a woman.

She grins and waggles her brows. "You mean besides making you crazy with wanting to bang me?"

I cough and cock an eyebrow high. Damn girl has my number, that's for sure. "I'm pretty sure I'm the one who said let's eat first."

She flicks her hair over one shoulder, giving me a lovely view of her cleavage as she mixes up the salad, dropping in cherry tomatoes and black olives. "Yes, but I also know that every day for the past two weeks your eyes have followed my ass, my tits, and my legs around while I've served people in the bakery or taught class. I'm willing to bet you can't wait to get inside again." She licks her lips and runs a finger down her neck and between her breasts. Boldly, she cups her large tits in both hands and gives them a healthy jiggle.

"Christ, woman, you're driving me crazy," I grit through clenched teeth.

She winks. "I know. And I love every second of it." With a grin, she spins around and bends over, giving me a front-row seat to her bootylicious ass while she puts a pan of garlic bread in the oven.

Moving on pure instinct, I'm off the stool and around the small island just as she lifts the oven door up and in place. I've got an arm around her chest, my front plastered to her back, and my other hand around her waist, lips at her neck.

Dara stills for only a moment before pushing her ass against my renewed erection. "See something you like, my prince?" The little vixen is taunting me into action.

"Yeah, and I'm gonna take it." I bite down on the space where her neck and shoulder meet.

"Is that right?" Her words are a breathy, turned-on whisper, but her hips and ass are devious as she grinds back against me.

"Hands to the fucking counter," I grate. "Now, woman."

I can feel her heartbeat pick up against my arm where I've got her locked to me. She shifts her body away from the hot oven and to the counter two feet from it. As she does this, I slide my hand up her shirt and pull it up and over her head. She's in a hot-pink bra.

"Fuck me," I growl against her skin before rubbing my dick against her ass. With nimble fingers, I pull down both of the lace cups, letting her big breasts spill over the tops. "Christ, your tits are meant to be worshipped, lil' mama."

Dara moans as I thumb both of her nipples and then pluck and pinch at them until she's a squirming mess.

"Silas..." The word is a breathy gasp when I bite down on her neck and suck at her sugar-coated skin.

"Fuck, baby. You smell like apples today."

She hums. "Fresh apple pies."

Using one hand, I push down her ever-present yoga pants, taking her matching pink lace underwear with them. Her perfect mocha-colored ass comes into view, and I fall to my knees and put my mouth on one fleshy cheek. I bite down while gripping both globes. Fascinated, I squeeze and mold her flesh while shivers and gooseflesh rack her body and skin.

"Baby...need more," she murmurs, her head falling forward, all that mass of hair covering her face from view.

I stand up and pull off my shirt, because I need skin-on-skin action, but I only undo my jeans and push them far enough to get my dick free.

With my right hand, I rub at her ass cheek, and she mewls. Something inside me snaps, and I pull my hand back and smack that ass with a resounding whack. Her body arches, presenting her booty in offering for more.

"Yes!" she cries out as I smack that ass again.

"Jesus fuck, my queen loves her ass spanked. Which is good, Dara baby. *Real good*, because there is a lot I'm going to be doing to this ass." I press my dick in between her cheeks and crowd her body so she can feel me from ass to neck.

I run my hand up her chest until I have her slender, delicate neck in my hand. I wrap my fingers around her throat and tip her chin up, turning her face toward mine so I can take her mouth. Her lips press to mine willingly, greedily, and she's generous with her tongue. Makes me want that mouth on my cock and soon.

"What more do you want to do to my ass, Si?" she gasps.

"Oh...my girl is a little dirty. She wants me to tell her about all the filthy things I'm going to do to it." I pull my hand back and smack the same cheek hard, working my cock between her globes, thrusting until a bead of pre-cum spills out the top. I take that drop, back up, and rub my thumb around her pink little hole. Her body jerks but not away.

I spin my thumb around that tiny rosette in little circles. "You into ass play, lil' mama?" I bite down on her shoulder and kiss it better.

"Don't know." She gasps as I press a little bit of my thumb into the tight heaven of her ass.

"Fuck me. You tellin' me I'm going to be the first man to have this ass. All 'dis sweet ass." I push my thumb all the way in, and she cries out.

"Yes, yes...oh, God. Baby...please," she begs as I work her hole in and out, until she's pushing back into my thrusts.

Putting my other arm around her form and down, I find her slippery and ready. "You like my thumb in your ass, baby?" I tweak her clit and her body jerks, her ass tightening around my finger so much it could cut off the circulation. Shit, I can't wait to get my dick in that tight heaven.

"Yes! Si, plea—"

She starts to beg, but before she can get out the final please, I'm slamming my cock home. Her body lifts up off the floor, hands gripping white-knuckled on the counter.

"God, yes!" she cries out.

I have her hung up on my cock and thumb and, better yet, loving every second. Out of nowhere a timer buzzes, but it adds to the heated action going on before me. Neither of us pay any attention to it because I'm buried deep in tight, wet pussy, and she's enjoying being ridden.

"Si, baby, I'm gonna go off." Her voice is raw, filled with lust and sex.

"Then get there. I'm riding you until I get mine and you get it so good you'll *never* forget who rides this cunt."

"Jesus." Her inner walls lock down on my cock at every dirty word I say. Hell yeah, my baby likes it dirty.

Dara cries out her release, and I go at her harder, working her pussy and her hole. I wrap an arm around her body and pinch her clit so she's got no choice but to go off again. This time, though, she cries out so loud she loses her voice.

I release her clit and ass, grip her hips, and go to town. "Hold on, baby. Hold the fuck on!" I growl as my body goes blazing hot. A sizzle hits the base of my spine, my balls draw up, and my heart explodes with a fierce beat at the same time I feel my release ricochet up my cock and into my woman.

"Fuck."

Thrust.

"Me."

Thrust.

"Tightest."

Thrust.

"Cunt."

Thrust.

"Ever."

Thrust.

"Goddamn!" I grit my teeth and plant my dick to the root, my body losing strength and falling on its own accord over smooth skin.

Shivers rack my frame, and I kiss every bit of skin I can reach as I come back down. Her back, shoulders, spine, and up to her neck.

Her breath is coming in labored pants. I wrap an arm around her chest, one hand gripping her massive tit. "You good, lil' mama?"

I lift her up to a stand, my dick sliding out still semihard. That's what this woman does to me. I fucked her hard, came hard, and my dick is ready for more of her.

"Oh yeah, so good, but baby...the bread."

Hearing the word bread, I come to, noticing the timer still blaring and the stench of burned toast hitting the air.

"I think it's burned." She moves out of my hold, turns off the timer, and then, wobbly like a newborn calf walking for the first time, grabs the oven mitt and opens the door.

A billow of smoke pours out and the smoke detectors go off.

"Fucking hell! Get out of the kitchen. I got this. Open a window and turn on the fan."

I grab the mitt, get the burned bread out, and set it on the top of the stove. I wave the mitt around the smoke-filled kitchen, hitting the exhaust fan, putting that sucker on high.

After a couple minutes, the sound goes away and my gaze finds Dara. She's standing under the smoke detector, naked from the waist down, her boobs still out of the cups, tits bouncing wildly as she spins a dish towel in the air where the smoke alarm is.

Then I look down at myself, dick getting hard at the sight, pushed out past the top of my boxers with my jeans falling down around my ass, an oven mitt on my filthy hand.

I lock gazes with Dara. "We're crazy." I laugh.

She licks her lips, stops spinning the towel, and places her hands on her naked hips. "Crazy hot. I don't know about you, but it was worth a loaf of burned bread."

Simple and sweet, she says it like it is. I could so easily fall in love with this woman.

A rumble of laughter bubbles up my chest and out my lungs. "Yeah, lil' mama, it was, but next time I do you..." I shuffle over to the sink, let the mitt fall to the ground so it can be washed, and clean my hands at the sink before putting my dick back in place and zipping up my pants. "I take my time and we do it on a flat surface." I point to her pretty bed. "That spot will do."

She grins, fixes the cups on her bra, and saunters her sweet body toward me. "Bet I could make you fuck me again right now."

I shake my head. "You could, but you're not." I cup her stomach, thinking maybe I can send some love and energy to our baby. "Baby needs to eat, and Mama needs to rest and clean up."

"You worried about our baby, Si?" She frowns and presses her body against mine in a bear hug.

"Always, Dara, but I'm trying not to worry so much."

"'K. And I am really hungry."

I smack her bare ass. "Then get that fine ass cleaned up and back in the kitchen and tell me what to do so we can get you fed."

She smiles as she moves around me to snatch up her undies. She puts them on, and also her yoga pants and shirt, and then rushes to the small bathroom and does her business. She comes back into the kitchen, grabs a pot, and holds it out. "Boil water for the noodles."

"As you wish, my queen."

CHAPTER THIRTEEN

THIRD EYE
C H A K R A

The sixth chakra is unique in that, when this chakra is fully activated, both sides of the brain function in synchronicity. The left brain's analytical and logical thinking is balanced with the right brain's creativity.

D A R A

"Read it out loud to me." Silas snuggles his warm chest against my side. He's holding a cup of coffee on his sheet-covered hip.

One thing I learned about Silas after a night of what seemed like endless rounds of delicious sex was that he sleeps naked. Secondly, he runs hot. His entire body was a cauldron of heat throughout the night. This worked well for me because I run cold. All the time. Plus, I am a cover hog. I like to sleep bundled up in gobs of covers surrounding me. Though I will say, having a heater pressed directly to my back all night? Bliss.

"I swear it says I can have minimal amounts of coffee. My doctor confirmed a cup of caffeine a day was fine for me and the baby. Stop fretting." I smack at his hand when he tries to read over my shoulder.

He chuckles and kisses my bicep. "No, read me week eleven since we'll be in that week in a few more days."

I smile around my cup and flip the page of my pregnancy book farther ahead a week. "Usually I don't skip ahead. I enjoy reading the new week on the day, but I guess I'll forgo that rule just this once."

Silas gives me one of his megawatt smiles, his teeth looking extra bright white against his darker skin this morning. "Much obliged, baby."

God, I love when he calls me baby. And lil' mama. And his queen. Each and every time, a small, pleasurable tingle runs up my spine.

Turning the pages, I get to the right spot and settle in. He leans on his side, head in his hand, waiting patiently for me to read "Week 11" of our pregnancy journey.

"Says here our baby is the size of a lime!"

"Sweet and sour. I like it."

I chuckle and read on. "Baby is fully formed and just over an inch and a half long."

Silas lifts up his fingers measuring to the amount stated. "Tiny but significant. What else?" His tone is eager, which gives me a little thrill. Silas wants this baby. Probably as much as I do, which makes having a baby out of wedlock a lot easier to swallow.

When I'd thought of my future, there were always children

in it. As many as God would grace me with. Only that future included a doting and loving husband and father. A home. A true family. Besides being a baker, it's all I've ever wanted. At least I can feel and sense Silas's happiness in our little lime.

"Baby has about a one to one head to body ratio, meaning the head and body are about the same size."

"Say what?" His head jerks back, and he frowns.

I run my fingers down his forearm. "Says it will even out, no worries."

His expression distorts into one of mistrust. He fingers the book, trying to raise the cover. "You sure you're reading the book on human babies and not animals?"

I nudge his shoulder. "Stop it. Our baby is fine."

"Okay, now what does it say is going to happen to my baby mama?"

Scanning the page, I read through so I can summarize. "Fatigue, nausea, mood swings, leg cramps. Oh, and I might get a dark line running down the center of my belly."

He furrows his brows and tugs the sheet, uncovering my naked body. "Lemme see." Silas runs a finger down my belly to the top of my pubis and then runs it back up before circling around my nipple until it furls and hardens.

One of his eyebrows cocks up as he leans forward, making his intention known. He sucks a hardened tip into his mouth, swirling his tongue around the tightening nub until it tingles and throbs.

Swiftly, he knifes to the side and puts his coffee on the bedside table and then flops back around, crawling between my thighs and resting his upper body on my lower half. He makes a detour to my belly, where he places a series of kisses in a circle around my belly button, and then he whispers something so low I'm not sure I catch it all—it sounds like "Love you."

I melt on the spot as he kisses his way up my body until he's back at my breasts. His hands form around each globe as though they are balls of dough and he's kneading them. Shivers of excitement race from my chest to center hotly between my thighs.

"Do you have any idea how magnificent your tits are?" He swoops down and locks his lips around one, laving me with his tongue before flicking just the tip until it gets so hot it burns.

I moan and squirm but can't move much since half of his body is on me. "I'm guessing as good as my ass?"

He stops midlick, runs one of his hands down my side, and tags a healthy handful of cheek, squeezing it hard. "Nothing is as fine as your ass, baby. *Nothing.*"

Total ass man.

A giggle leaves me as I toss the book to the side. Silas gets to work on my tits, and I enjoy the attention while he gets me ready for some day-starting, mind-melting sexy time.

A girl could seriously get used to this.

He bites down on a nipple, and I cry out, arousal forcing my hips to buck against him.

"Hey, hey, easy." He kisses his way down my chest again, keeping his thumb and index finger on my nipples, tugging and rolling, ribbons of pleasure zipping along every nerve ending. "I'm getting there. Gonna eat you, and then I'm going to feed you."

After he takes me there with his mouth, my mind is mush because he was *hungry*. Fucking *starved*. And when he said he was going to *feed me*, it didn't mean food. No, after he ate me, he got up on his knees, lifted me up so my back was at the headboard, and then my man fed me his massive cock. I took this willingly, eagerly, swallowing down every beautiful inch until he shot off like a rocket in my mouth. Again, I took all he gave me.

Sated, he eased me down and rolled me on top of him. And that's where I was lying, naked on top of Silas, when it happened.

The door to my apartment opened.

"Child, you are late as the day is long for your shift. Ricky is getting nervous and overwhelmed with the patrons and the..." She turns the small corner and stops, eyes on my naked body slung over Silas. "Lord in Heaven! Praise sweet, sweet Jesus! My grandbaby is gonna have a daddy!" she cries out and raises her face to the sky.

Silas, unable to move because, if he did, my mom would get a crotch shot to end all crotch shots, groans. Me, I act quickly, lean over, and grab the sheet. I fling myself to the side, pulling it over both of us.

"Mama, seriously, whatever happened to knocking?"

"Overrated. My baby lives alone and was, before now, *single*. How was I supposed to know you'd be busy with your baby daddy? It's not like you've been keeping your mama updated on your relationship status. Forced me to get my information from an alternate source, finding out that my grandchild's daddy has been sniffing around regular at the bakery. Word is he's taking your meditation classes too. So when I come up here to find out why my child is so late for work, thinking maybe she's sick and needs her mama, I find her naked as the day she was born on top of her hunky baby daddy. What am I supposed to think?"

Silas's body starts to shake, and as my anger rises, his emotions go in the opposite direction, and he busts up in heaving bouts of laughter. "This is too goddamned much. And I thought my family was nutty. Your family takes the cake, baby."

"No, we *make* the cake," Mama clarifies, much to Silas's delight.

"Lordy be. Mama, get out of my house! I'm naked. Silas is naked. And neither one of us is too comfortable having my mother find us in this particular situation."

Vanessa Jackson is not about to take lip from her daughter, and I know this the second she puts her fists to her rounded hips.

"Child, you will take whatever I'm giving because I'm yo' mama. And like I said, if you had been keepin' me informed, I wouldn't have had to come up here and check in on my lonely girl, who is the furthest thing from lonely, since she's got a six-foot-plus hunk of brother lying bare-ass naked in her bed, looking mighty pleased with himself. Speaking of..." She turns her gaze to Silas.

Oh, shit. Here it comes. This is not good. Vanessa Jackson in a snit is all bad.

"You going to be making an honest woman out of my girl and bring up this baby in a family?"

Silas's laughter cuts out instantly. He sits up, sheet falling to his waist, giving my mother a beautiful expanse of his sexy-as-hell male chest before he swallows and firms his jaw. "Ma'am." His voice is raw and not from laughter. "My child will have me as a father. Full fucking time. Period."

"'S'wat I wanna hear. However that comes about, I trust you to see to it and do right by my only child."

"Yes, ma'am. Working on it. As you can see, things are progressing in the positive."

She glares. "I don't see a ring on her finger. I see a naked man happy to be in her bed. You want to stay in that bed next to my beautiful girl, you'll do something 'bout it now, won't you?"

"Mom!" I screech, jump out of bed, not caring about my nudity because, well, she's my mom. She's seen it all before. I nab Silas's shirt and tug it over my head, the cotton soft, comforting, and smelling of apples, fresh-cut wood, and leather, the length falling down around me at midthigh. "We're not ready for that kind of commitment."

"And yet you're having a baby with him. You just rolled out of bed naked, a bed you were sharing with him. I'm not exactly seeing a commitment issue here," she continues, not knowing the full details behind what happened in Silas's past.

"Trust me, Mama. Silas is committed to our baby. We're working on us. Okay? Now, if you could please go downstairs and tell Ricky I'll be down soon, I'd appreciate it."

My mother sucks in a huge breath, lets it out in a sigh, and then turns around toward the door. "No more secrets from me, young lady."

"Yes, Mama. We'll talk more later."

"I'll be waiting." She huffs and closes the door.

I wait a few seconds before walking over and locking it. "I'm sorry about that, Silas. I had no idea..."

Silas gets out of bed buck-ass naked. He pulls me into his arms and holds me. "It's okay. Am I embarrassed your mother caught us naked in the sack? Yes. Am I cutting and running?" He curls a hand around my nape on one side and uses his thumb to lift my chin so I'm forced to look him in the eyes. "No way. What we got is good. Really good. I'm working on me and setting some demons from my past free and looking toward my future with you and our baby. One day at a time. And for me, last night and this morning were nothing if not phenomenal."

"For me too," I whisper, meaning every word with my entire soul.

He rubs his nose against mine and then kisses me softly, biting down on my bottom lip before pulling back. I love feeling the sting of the bite. "That's all that matters. We know what we're doing and we're moving forward, yeah?"

"Yeah." I nod.

"Okay, I'm going to take a shower. Can I take my girl out for dinner later?"

Him saying it doesn't make it real. Not until he confirms what it means.

"Your girl?"

He dips his chin.

"Am I your girl? Your only girl. For good?" My voice cracks as I force out those words.

"You carrying my baby?"

"Yes," I mumble.

"You just take my cock down your throat?"

"Yes." This time it comes out with more conviction.

"Sleep next to me all night long, giving me the best sleep I've had in years?"

"Uh, yeah." I'm not sure where he's going with this.

"Then I think you should get that you are my girl and I am your man. We are having a baby together and starting a family. You, me, our baby. We on the same page?"

I swallow and nod my head.

Silas dips his head down only a couple inches from mine. "We on the same page? You, me, our baby?"

"Yeah, Silas."

"Okay. Dinner tonight?"

"Sounds great."

"I'm gonna hit the shower now and get to work. As your mother confirmed, we're both late in starting our day." He kisses me slowly and sweetly before pulling away and eating up the distance with his masterful thighs and masculine physique. When he gets to the door of the bathroom, the only room in the house with walls, he stops, fingers gripping the doorjamb. "Worth it. You. This. Us. I'm all in, baby. All. Fucking. In."

I love you, I whisper in my mind when he winks and enters the bathroom. As much progress as we've made, I do not think my man is ready to hear that. If he ever will be.

My man.

Silas McKnight is my man, and I am his woman.

Inside, I girly scream...

Yippee!

* * *

After Silas left and I came down to the bakery, I received a cold shoulder from my mother and a ball of grins from Ricky.

"So, someone's baby daddy spent the night?" Ricky shimmies across the floor, a bag of frosting in his hand.

"Shut it! Why didn't you come up and knock instead of sending my mother up?" I growl, not even a little bit of humor in my question.

He snorts. "Because I saw baby daddy's car in front of the bakery when I arrived at the crack of freakin' dawn, and the hood was cold. Meaning he stayed the night."

I couldn't stop my mouth from falling open in shock. "You knew he was upstairs with me, and yet you didn't think to call my cell, come up, and knock? Instead, you sent my mother? What in the hell were you thinking? Do you have any idea how embarrassing it was to be lying naked on top of your man when your mother comes barreling in, thinking you're sick or something!"

Ricky's mouth drops open this time, and then he falls all over himself laughing. He laughs so hard he starts to wheeze and has to lean against the bakery table to hold himself up. "Even better!" he screeches like a hyena.

"You planned that scene up there?" I point to the stairs leading to my apartment.

"Not at all, but I did think it would be awesomely funny for Mama Jackson to find your baby daddy with you. I thought she'd be excited." He nudges my shoulder. "Which she is. Came down those stairs smiling like a loon, happy as a clam, ready to serve customers. I'd have sworn you told her you were naming your baby Vanessa if it was a girl."

The name hit my heart. Vanessa for a girl. Secretly, I wanted a boy, and there was only one reason for that. I didn't want Silas thinking about the daughter he lost when we were having our child. Though being able to give my mama a namesake gift like that bulldozes me like a ton of emotional bricks. I'd love to give my child the name Vanessa like she and my dad gave me the last name of Jackson.

I shake my head, dispelling the thoughts and focus back on my soon-to-be *ex*-best friend. "You have no idea how much that sucked up there."

Ricardo comes over to me and wraps his arms around my chest. "I'm sorry, baby girl. I honestly didn't mean anything by it. I got so excited when I saw the car outside, I lost my mind a little. I should have been protecting you and the budding relationship, but I figured since he spent the night, things had definitely progressed. So...did they?" He doesn't beat around the bush at all, wanting to know the details, even though I'm mad at him.

He also knows I can never stay mad at him. It isn't in my genetic makeup to hold a grudge. I have very little family. When someone lets me in, loves me, that love needs to be treated with care. I know with my whole heart Ricky'd just as soon cut off his own arm than intentionally hurt me.

I blow out a long, frustrated breath. "Yeah, they did. We agreed he's my man and I'm his woman. Which I think in macho manspeak means we're boyfriend and girlfriend."

Ricky whoops and hollers. "Right on! That calls for a celebratory cupcake!" He dances his way out to the display case. On his heels is my mama.

She doesn't say a word; her silence says it all.

Concern.

Frustration.

Betrayal.

Apology.

Compassion.

Love.

She opens her arms without speaking, and I run into them, plastering my face against her ample bosom. "Mama," I whisper.

"Child."

"I'm sorry," I croak into her chest.

"Me too. Shouldn't have walked in like that and caught you unawares. I'll take more care in the future."

Tears prick the back of my eyes and clog my throat. "I didn't mean to keep anything from you. We were taking things really slow, and I...I'm scared."

"Why you scared, baby? He seems like a good man."

I sniffle and let a tear fall down my cheek. She wipes it away without even needing to see it. She just knows it's there because she knows me.

"He is. The best. But, there are things you don't know about Silas, Mama."

"Like the fact that you're in love with him?" She hits the nail right on the head, first try.

I nod into her embrace.

"Love can be scary, child. Especially when you do things a little backward, but you'll turn it around. Ain't no man in the world gonna turn down love from my beautiful girl. Just not gonna happen. Get that outta your head right now," she demands as if it's her right to do so.

I swallow down the lump in my throat and pull back. "As you may have heard a little on the street, he was married before to a woman he loved for a long time. She was pregnant, and both of them died three years ago."

My mother closes her big brown eyes and whispers what I know is a prayer. A prayer for Silas's dead wife and daughter and maybe even one for me too. Then she grabs me around the waist and holds me close once more.

"Sometimes the things we love most in this world come with loss. Like you, baby. I love you more than anything in this world, but I had to lose a lot and let go of a lot to find you and make you mine." She pets my hair and kisses my temple. "Maybe that's what God brought you here on this earth to do. For me, your dad, and now Silas."

"Which is what, Mama?"

"Be the love he earns when he lets go of all the loss."

CHAPTER FOURTEEN

Pink, Gold, Silver and White Aura Colors and Meanings: Pink auras are connected to artistic, sensitive, affectionate types. However, if the pink darkens, it shows the individual's immaturity and dishonest side. Those who are graced with the gold tones tend to be intuitive, wise, and enlightened, but not as much as a person who has silver and white. Those shimmery colors signify the individual is a nurturer, pure and transcendent, ethereal. A true innocent and often spiritual leader.

SILAS

Today is the day. It's been two weeks since Dara and I rekindled the physical side of our relationship. Since then, I've wined and dined her, sans the wine of course due to her pregnancy. I've been seeing Dr. Hart regularly and working on letting things go. My house has already received several offers, making it easier to move on from my past life.

Do I still miss Sarah?

Yes. Absolutely. She'll always be a part of me, one I plan to keep forever. There will always be a piece of my heart that beats for Sarah and our lost child, but the rest has to stay open for Dara and our unborn baby.

Every day I'm shocked at how easy it is to be around Dara. Spend time with her, laugh, take her out, share a meal. But nothing beats the quiet time where we hold hands and talk about our child, the hopes we have for the baby's future. All the things I had started to do with Sarah but never got to live out. And every day I can wake up and drive over to the bakery and see my girl with my baby alive and growing inside her is another day toward healing the past.

Dr. Hart has yet to convince me I'm not partly to blame for what happened to Sarah. I still feel guilt over buying her the new car, not doing something, *anything* to have made her safe. The shit deal is I bought her that car to keep her safe. It had great safety ratings for accidents and the like. Though none of those things can ward off junkies looking for a fix. I still can't get past it.

I shake my head to force out the negative memories and guilty feelings crawling up my spine ready to latch on to my heart. Today is supposed to be the day where I get to see my baby on the screen and hear the heartbeat for the first time.

This is the appointment Sarah and I only made it to once in three pregnancies. The twelve-week checkup and the beginning of the second trimester.

The minute I've showered and dressed, I pull out my

phone and find Dara's name in my contacts.

I press "Lil' Mama" and wait while it rings.

She answers, her breath labored as if she's just run a mile. "Hello."

"Dara, what's going on? Why are you out of breath? Are you okay? Is it the baby?" I ask, concern coating every word, my heart instantly pumping a mile a minute.

"What?" she says distractedly. "No. I just ran to the phone from the shower. Slow your roll." She laughs and lets out a long breath as if she just slumped down into a chair. "God, I'm tired."

"Baby, it's eleven in the morning. I tucked you into bed at eight last night because you were tired, and then I met Atlas for a beer."

"You did?" She yawns.

I chuckle. My girl is nothing but sweet in the mornings. "Yeah, it's why I didn't stay."

"Hmm, wondered about that when my alarm went off. You set that too?"

I grin into the phone, hold it with my ear against my shoulder, and put on my shoes. "Yeah, baby. I didn't want you to miss our appointment. I'm looking forward to this."

"Mmm, me too. Too bad we won't get to find out what we're having for another eight weeks. Pregnancy stuff takes forever!" she complains, and I can imagine her pretty pout, having seen it before.

"Good things come to those who wait. I'm sure your mama taught you that."

"Seeing as I had to wait eight years for a mama, yeah, I get it, but I want our baby now, not twenty-eight more weeks from now."

I chuckle into the phone. "I'm going to leave, and I'll come over and get you."

"No worries. I can meet you there. It's close to your work. That way you can do what you need to do at work before our appointment."

My throat dries, heat engulfs my form, and sweat beads at my hairline and behind my neck. I try to take a breath, but my chest is tightening.

Fuck. It's that same sensation I had when Whitney was here helping me clean out Sarah's stuff. I tighten my fists and hold the phone as close to my ear as possible. "What do you drive, baby?" I form the words slow and steady.

"Like a car?"

I close my eyes, images of Sarah getting into the red, shiny Lexus and driving off for the first and last time enter my mind.

"Yeah," I mutter, locking down the panic that's beating double-time in my chest.

She laughs. Hard.

What the fuck?

"You're funny, baby. I don't drive, and I sure as heck don't have a car."

Within a second flat, my heart rate slows, and I can finally take a breath. "Then how do you get around?" I grab the towel I used from my shower earlier and wipe at my face and the back of my neck.

"I've got two legs, and I use them. When I absolutely need a ride, I call a taxi or Uber it. Then of course there's the subway if I need to get into the city." She laughs again, and the sound is so beautiful I want to say something funny so I can hear more of it. "Not sure if you noticed this, Si, but I work in a bakery that I live above. My hobby is teaching meditation right next door. Everything I need is on this street. Except you, of course, and you have your own car. Why would I need to drive?"

A lightness fills my chest, and I rub at the back of my neck. "That's smart, baby, and very good. So very fucking good."

"'K, so I'll meet you there. I'll take an Uber. Our appointment is not for another two hours, and I know you need to get to work because I heard you on the phone with your sister Whitney yesterday. Whom, by the way, I have yet to meet." She huffs into the line playfully.

As much as I don't like the idea of someone else driving my girl, I do need to get to work, and Dr. Hart would lose her mind if I told Dara she had to wait for me.

I can hear her words already. "Silas, you can't keep living in the past. Taking chances and calculated risks are necessary. You cannot prevent something from happening. You just need to accept that life comes with the good and the bad."

"Okay, lil' mama, you win. Just be careful. Make sure the car is big and safe. Text me the driver's license plate before getting in."

"Aye, aye, Captain! Will do." She makes the cute snort-laugh sound I love. "Get to work. And hey..."

"Yeah?" I ask, not exactly wanting to let her go.

"Think of me," she whispers before hanging up.

I smile at the phone and then put it in my pocket. "Always, Dara. Seems I can't stop thinking about you since the day we met."

Which is true. The woman has been on my mind from the minute I tasted her lips. That drunken night changed my life in so many ways and all for the better.

Glancing at the clock, I realize I need to get to steppin'. I grab my blazer and head for my silver baby, a lightness in my movements and a smile on my face.

I don't drive, and I sure as heck don't have a car.

Those words spin on repeat, leaving me smiling like a crazy man all the way to work.

Safe. My woman and my baby are going to be just fine.

★ ★ ★

"How was that, baby?" Mallory coos into the mic through the sound booth.

I sigh and press the talk button. "Great. Let's give the second verse another go, with the backup vocals live this time."

The two women standing to Mallory's side nod.

"You're the expert, big boy." Mallory smiles and presses her chest out, smashing the mic stand between her overly enhanced breasts.

I cringe and think back to a couple nights ago when I had my hands pushing a pair of perfect tits together, my dick sliding between them, Dara's little pink tongue poking out to flick at the tip of my dick as I titty-fucked her. God that woman melts my mind and makes my dick hard as stone. Even now, just thinking about fucking her, I'm getting a semi.

Shit. Not what I want at work, especially when, in thirty minutes, I'll be meeting her next door at the doctor's office. Thinking of that, I grab my phone, which has been on silent while I focus on the music, and check the display. Seven minutes ago, I got two texts: One was a picture of a license plate. The other was a picture of Dara, offering me a beautiful smile, her blue ocean eyes gleaming with excitement. Under the picture, there was a single line of text which said the following:

Heartbeat day, Daddy! Woot woot!

I grin and chuckle behind my hand. My girl is such a nut.

Though thinking back, this experience is far more hopeful than the ones I had with Sarah. The two times we got pregnant before our daughter, Sarah lost the baby before we could hear the heartbeat. In the second pregnancy, we went in for the twelve-week check to find out there was no heartbeat. The baby had passed somewhere around the eight-week mark, not long after the first sonogram. She had to have a D & C, otherwise known as a dilation and curettage, to remove the fetus. The third pregnancy we made it to the twelve-week mark, but there was no happiness, no smiles. We were prepared for bad news and ended up getting great news.

For me, the twelve-week mark is a mixed bag. This is the fourth time I've thought I was going to be a father. Two miscarriages and one death. No baby to hold in my arms or a child to give my name. To say I am excited is an understatement. I am scared out of my fucking mind, but I'll never squash Dara's exuberance. The way she lives her life in the light, bringing joy and happiness everywhere she goes, gives me hope that her energy will carry on to our unborn child.

Mallory's voice cuts through my thoughts, the rise and fall of the harmonies working perfectly. Magical. When they're done, I press the talk button.

"Fucking magical, ladies! We're going to have another hit on our hands. Go ahead and stop; we're breaking for lunch. I have an appointment to get to."

Mallory jumps up, her boobs practically smacking her chin in the face.

Leaving them to get their things, I turn off the equipment, set the tracks to the right spot for when we come back, and turn around to grab my blazer. I want to look perfect for Dara today. Be there for her, no matter what happens.

Behind me, the door to the room opens and Mallory comes skipping in. "That was so great, Silas baby. You are a master!" She flings her arms around me, pressing her hard breasts into my chest. "We should celebrate. Right now. How's about I lift my skirt and you fuck me right here?"

"Mal, what the fu—" I try to get out before I feel a tight grip on my soft cock and her lips slam onto mine, her tongue invading. The taste of candlewax hits my tongue from her lip gloss.

Just as I'm trying to push her off, the door behind her opens.

"And this is where Silas makes all the magic happen." I hear Atlas speaking to someone. "What the hell? Goddamn..."

Before I can push Mallory off, her body is flung from mine, her grip on my dick painful when she lets go. I cower over myself, gripping my cock and wiping my soaked mouth at the same time. "Christ!" I growl, disgusted.

"Bitch, what in the world are you doin' putting your skanky-ass hands and filthy mouth on my man!" Dara screeches, one hand on her hip, the other pointing a finger.

Mallory is gasping for breath, her body slanted across the leather couch in the back of the booth where visitors sit to watch the acts record. "Your man!" she says with a raised voice and tries to stand.

The second Mallory stands, Dara smacks her face and shoves her back down. "Bitch, did I say yo' skanky ass could get up? No, I did not! Sit the fuck down before I hurt you." Her voice is nothing like the sweet meditation teacher I am most often graced with. This Dara is a sista from downtown Oakland ready to open up a can of whoop ass and scratch a bitch's eyes out.

"Dara," I try, but she swings around, her face twisted with anger and a hint of hurt in her pretty blues.

"Did you willingly kiss her? Put your mouth on her, let her put her hand on your dick?" she roars.

"Baby, no, but please—" I shake my head.

She lifts a hand between us. "And did you lead this skank on?"

I shake my head instantly because *holy shit*. My girl is pissed. As in *pissed*. And I do not want to be the recipient of her wrath.

She continues undaunted. "Last I recall, it was *my* mouth you were kissing. *Me* you were fucking. *My* body that is having your baby!"

"Shit yeah. No way, dude!" Atlas gasps, his mouth opens, which he immediately covers with both hands when Dara flings her gorgeous locks around and glares at him.

"Silas was meant for me!" Mallory stupidly bites out.

Dara tips her head back and laughs. "Girl, you are wacked in the head if you think he'd want fake when he can have all of this." She runs her hands down the sides of what I gotta admit is a spectacular body. My wife Sarah was beautiful. She looked good. Dara is a straight knockout. No man on this earth would deny that. Petite height but the body of a *Sports Illustrated* swimsuit model. Normally, she's sweet as pie. Just apparently not when a woman is stomping on what she considers her turf. And though I hate to think it, I'm pretty fucking pleased and a tad turned on that she's putting on such a show. I just wish it wasn't with my cash cow.

"Baby..." I approach Dara with my hands up in surrender. "We have an appointment with our baby doctor to check on our little one," I say, reminding her what's really important.

Her shoulders drop, and I slide my hand around her waist, covering our baby protectively. "Mallory, I'm sorry this went down the way it did, but Dara's my woman. She's having my baby. We're building a life together..."

"Righteous!" Atlas says, clearly in awe of the entire thing.

"Silas, baby, I don't care. I can have babies for you," Mallory keeps on.

"Bitch! Please!" Dara's body tightens in my arms, and I swear she's a second away from getting in another scuffle, this one to knock Mallory out.

Gripping Dara, I turn her away from Mallory and hand her off to Atlas. She snarls and scowls.

I put my arms out and grab Mallory's hands. "You are sweet, talented, and there are so many men out there who would want to be with you. I'm not that man. I have a woman. Dara. She's my future, and we're having a family. Please hear me. This, between you and me, is never happening. I'm sorry. And for this reason, I'm putting Atlas on as your producer. We need to keep a professional distance from one another."

Mallory's brown eyes tear up. "But..." Her lip trembles. "I know you could love me."

I shake my head. "Not when my heart has been taken by another woman. I'm sorry. Atlas, please..." I gesture to Mallory, and he steps up.

Atlas places a hand to my shoulder. "Dude...you have some serious explaining to do." Regardless, he smiles widely, showing his happiness in the news he's just heard.

"We gotta go."

I clasp hands with Dara and intertwine our fingers.

Before we leave, she calls out, "Better stay away from my man, blondie, or you deal with me!"

Tugging Dara out the door, down the hallways, and out the front door into the open air, I spin her around and press her into the wall.

"Si, I know what you're going to say, but seeing her hand on your package, her mouth on your lips, I lost it. I went a little crazy, but I'm not sorry. She had no right to put her hands and mouth on my man. Those are *my* lips. That's *my* dick!" Her voice is petulant and immature.

I love every fucking word, but the woman needs to shut up in order for me to tell her what I want to say. So instead of hollerin', I place my lips on hers and kiss the daylights out of her. It takes a nanosecond for her to catch on and participate. Her rigid, angry stance melts into me, her tongue dancing with mine, giving me all of her when she wraps both arms around me and moans her pleasure into my mouth.

After I've kissed her long and hard and her eyes are half open and lustful, I lay it out for her.

"Baby, I'm not mad. I should be, but I'm not. You stood up for me against Mallory when you could have blamed me. It didn't even cross your mind I was cheatin', and that says a ton about the trust you have in what we've got. I fuckin' love that. Thank you. Thank you for having my back."

Instead of saying anything in reply, she hauls up on her toes, wraps her arms back around me, and kisses me long and hard at the same time. Her tongue delves deep, and she moves her head to the side and drinks from my lips hungrily, only stopping when she needs air.

I take a few deep breaths, pressing my forehead against hers. "We okay?" I ask, my breath coming in harsh pants.

"Yeah. You ready to see how our baby is?"

"Thank God you didn't get into a full-on fist fight. Doesn't take much but your mouth and your quick hands to put an admirer in her place." I crack the joke, putting an arm around her shoulders.

"You'd do well to remember that. I don't share, and I don't like women all up on what's mine." Her sass is magnificent and surprising since she's been mostly Zen this entire time. I mean, I know the girl has some attitude, but it had never reached this proportion until another woman was threatening her claim.

"I agree. If the situation was reversed, no telling what would have happened."

"Good thing we won't ever have to worry," she says, a bit of humor in her tone.

I, however, am not amused. She garners attention wherever she goes. I've never been with a woman who gets so many eye-fucks from the men she passes on a regular basis. Restaurants, shopping centers, movies. The yoga studio. Hell, half the people coming to the bakery are men dressed to the nines just wanting a piece of my woman. Her time. Her pretty smile. Her tasty baked treats. I can't wait until the day she is showing. Bet business goes down fifty percent when those men can physically see they have no chance in hell with the shit-hot baker.

Dara leads me into the waiting room, where we don't even sit before our name is called. Since we got here right to the minute of our scheduled appointment, I was relieved. Spending thirty minutes thinking nothing but negative thoughts was not high on my list of things I wanted to do. Still, I couldn't help it. I've been in this position before. Nerves were tight at this point.

We are brought into a room, where Dara is told to change out of her clothes. I stay for everything, enjoying her groan when she has to put on a paper gown and place the equally scratchy paper blanket over her lap. Instead of focusing on my anxiety at what the doctor may find, I put my attention on Dara. Rubbing her shoulders and neck, kissing her cheeks, her forehead, nose, and lips until the doctor finally enters.

When Dara lies down, the doctor lubes up the probe for the transvaginal ultrasound. Dara spreads her legs, and both of us look anxiously at the screen. The doctor is silent, clicking buttons and moving the wand until finally...she smiles.

That single tip of the lips from the doctor says it all. Our baby is in there and more importantly...alive.

"There. There's your baby." She stops the screen and holds it in place, lifts her hand, and points at the white curved bean-shaped form.

The image increases as the doctor zooms in, and what I'm gifted is absolutely perfect. A baby. Rounded head, profile of a face with a little nose and lips, legs, arms, and back. Then, right before our eyes, the baby kicks its legs and moves its hands.

Tears fill my eyes and fall down my cheeks. My child. Kicking. Moving. Alive.

"Wanna hear the heartbeat?" the doctor asks.

I can't respond. I just stare at my child moving around inside its momma.

"Yes, please," Dara says.

The doctor pulls out another contraption I don't really remember the last time with Sarah and places it over Dara's belly.

A *swish swish* sound enters the room. "And that's the heartbeat, Mom and Dad."

Dara's hand squeezes mine, and I force myself to look down at her. "Silas..." she whispers, her own tears sliding down her cheeks. "Our baby is beautiful." Her words crack, emotion bleeding through them.

I glance at the screen, living for every movement, every *swish swish* I can hear.

"Yes. Beautiful," I murmur and then kiss her lips. I give her everything I can in that kiss.

My time. My commitment. My heart.

I pull back and look into her ocean eyes, my own leaking nonstop. "Thank you. Thank you for giving me something to live for."

CHAPTER FIFTEEN

THIRD EYE
C H A K R A

The third eye chakra is associated with intuition and devotion.
Individuals driven by this particular chakra can be counted
on to know what their partner needs, instinctively. They also
tend to be people who mate for life.

DARA

Silas has not left my side for a solid week. Okay, I'm exaggerating. He's gone to work each day, but before work, he's with me. After work, he's back at the bakery, waiting for me to finish my day, shooting the breeze with the regulars, and breaking the hearts of hopeful yogis everywhere with his fine-ass manliness. Except, of course, on the night when he goes to see his therapist. Still, right after that appointment, he's knocking on my door. After I gave him the code, he also requested his own key. Since we're making this relationship official, I gave him one. However, I did not think this meant he'd take this gesture so seriously he wouldn't leave.

Meaning, Silas hasn't gone to his own home since our twelve-week appointment. Now we're well into thirteen, scraping on the edge of fourteen, and he's still hovering. Which is weird, but I haven't been able to tell him this because I enjoy having him around all the time. He's extremely helpful and goes out of his way to be so. He lifts heavy things, helps out around the bakery, and is generous in bed. When I say generous, I'm talking two big Os a night. A woman would be stupid to complain about that, especially when it's attached to such a big, attractive, fine-as-fuck brother who's doting on my every word.

It's still strange because I have yet to meet his family. He knows every single person in my world. This is easy to do. My world is surrounded by the bakery, my small family, and the studio. My mother is now head over heels in love with him. My father thinks he's famous and tells everyone he knows that my baby daddy is a "McKnight," which he thinks bodes well for his daughter's future of becoming a McKnight as well. That particular thinking, I ignore. Silas has even made a truce with Ricky. Everyone at Lotus House knows him now, but I still can't shake the feeling something's not right. Most of my concern goes back to the fact that I have not met his family. A family, he's made a point to tell me, is usually really close.

The door to the bakery opens as I'm sweeping the floor. I closed up ten minutes ago but must have left it unlocked. Silas smiles huge as he enters, another duffel bag of what I assume is *more* clothing in his hands. He's been adding to his stockpile each day. There are so many of his suits, dress shirts, and slacks my closet is now beyond tight. And he didn't even ask if he could hang them. And when I asked about it, he just said he didn't want wrinkled shit to wear to work. As if that answered that. I once more did not dig further because I like having him around every day, and yet it's concerning.

"Hey, baby." I smile and set the broom aside.

He comes to me, lifts me up, and spins me around, his pale-green eyes sparkling with happiness. "I have great news!" He kisses me hard and quick before pulling back and setting me back on my feet.

"Great. What?" I lean against the table and place my hand over my belly. It's gotten a little harder, and Silas is convinced I have a miniscule bump protruding out. He'd know, since he spends a lot of time rubbing, kissing, and touching that space.

"Sold my house." He shrugs off his blazer and hangs it over one of the empty chairs.

I purse my lips. "Say what?"

"Got more than asking price too. A lot more. Now we just gotta keep our eyes peeled for a house close to here, and we're golden, lil' mama. Life is turning around!" He spins in a circle, as smooth as if he were Michael Jackson himself, and snaps his fingers.

Trying and failing to comprehend all that he said, I shake my head. "Back the truck up, buddy. Put that in reverse. You sold your house?" I frown, trying to catch up. He never mentioned he put his house on the market. Why in the world would he sell it?

"Yep."

"That amazing one-story closer to your work by thirty minutes?" I dig, figuring I must have it wrong. Maybe he had more than one house.

"And scored a wad of cash for it too." He smiles widely, obviously proud of himself.

"Thought you loved that house. It's where you and Sarah started up, where you wanted to bring your baby home." My tone is filled to the brim with emotion, cracking as my throat constricts and my heart starts to pound.

Silas clocks the tone and comes to me, wrapping me up in his big arms. "What's this I hear in your voice. Sadness?"

For a long time I stare into his eyes, seeing nothing but concern. The house he bought with his wife is sold. She's gone, and now the home they were going to bring their baby to is gone. He's got me and our baby. "You were not kidding about moving forward," I whisper.

He shakes his head. "Dara, baby, what did you think we were doing here?"

"I don't know. Getting to know one another," I respond rather lamely.

"Baby, I knew you the second I tasted you."

His words are nice, *so nice*, but I didn't expect him to give everything up for me. "You're going to miss that house."

He presses his forehead to mine. "Being in that house alone with a ghost of my past was not helping me move on with my life. You and this baby are my life now, and I love what I've got. No more living in the past for me, baby. I'm right here." He places his hand over my belly where our baby is growing. "Where I'm supposed to be, with you and our child. Not leaving that."

"So that's why you've been bringing clothes over every night? Because you sold your house?"

He chuckles and kisses my forehead before dipping his gaze to mine. "No, my queen. I've been at your house every night because I can't stay away anymore. Don't want to. Shouldn't have to. If you're not kicking me out, I'm not leaving. Told you weeks ago, wherever you are is where I want to be. That hasn't changed today, and it won't change tomorrow. What will have to change is a bigger pad for you, me, and our baby."

"A bigger pad?"

He laughs. "Yeah. A home. For the three of us."

I'm in love with you.

Again, I think it but don't say it. Something inside me is scared to say it, blurt it out and ruin this moment. What if he doesn't love me back?

He couldn't. Not when he's been dealing with loss. I know he cares and loves to be with me, but only time will tell if that turns into love. He loved Sarah. Married her, spent ten years loving her. He's only known me three months, and I'm carrying his child. We need more time.

My mama was right. She's always warned me, "Watch out, baby girl. You fall hard, and you fall fast. Just don't fall for stupid." Unfortunately, I've been down that road a couple times already, yet Silas is so much more than any man I've ever been in a relationship with. He's everything I could ever want or dream of in a man. I just need to know he's mine and no longer Sarah's. I can appreciate he'll always have a place in his heart for his wife who passed, but I want the rest. My baby and I deserve that.

"I'm happy for you," I whisper, controlling the words I want to set free.

"Be happy for us!" He puts his hands on my biceps. "We get to house shop!" He grins like this is something to celebrate, and maybe it is.

"Baby, you haven't even asked me to move in with you, or

vice versa, and you want us to house shop?" I shake my head and cringe.

Silas jerks his head and steps back a couple paces. "I'm sorry, baby. Did I hear you right?"

I glance around. "There's no one else here but me and you. I'm sure you did."

He shifts the right hand holding my arm and runs his fingers down to my hand. He interlaces our fingers, and immediately, our hand chakras start buzzing. "Dara, I told you. This is me and you and our baby. We're doing this. Lil' mama, I thought you were with me?"

I lick my lips and drop my head, focusing on the glitter in my painted toes. "Yes, I'm with you. It's just that you make moves and don't tell me you're making them. How am I supposed to keep up?"

He frowns. "Been bringing my stuff to your house every day. What did you think I was doing?"

I shrug. "Wanting to be with me?"

"Fuck yeah. For good, not for a night. Is this not something you want?" His facial expression guts me; I can see it in his eyes, that fear of being unwanted. His aura color changing is not helping either. He's nervous, bordering on scared. "Am I wrong to think more is happenin' between us than what really is?"

Letting it all go, I pull his form against my chest and wrap my arms around him, putting my face into his neck. "No, God no. I want you. I want this. It's just I don't want you to regret making this leap when you weren't totally over what happened with Sarah."

He holds me tightly. "Baby, I'm never going to be over what happened to Sarah. It's always going to live in the back of my mind, but that doesn't mean I can't be happy. Have a family with a beautiful woman who's kind, sweet, talented, a great fuckin' cook, an even better baker, but more importantly, a woman of substance. I want that in my life. After being alone, I've finally realized I deserve my own slice of happiness, and that's what you do for me."

"I make you happy?" My words sound raw and rough, and tears threaten at the back of my eyes.

"Dara, I haven't seen the sun in more than three years. Then you came along. And baby, you shine so bright I'm blinded with its glory. I never want that warmth to leave me. Ever. So, I'm gonna hold on to it. Hold on to you. Let you keep me in the light."

"I'm falling for you." I admit my half truth because the real truth is I already have, but this is a good first step.

One of his arms locks around my waist, the other shifts up my back, his hand curling into my hair, thumb pressing my chin up. All I see are pools of green. Love and happiness beaming down at me.

"That's good, *real good*, because I'm falling for you too."

* * *

Two weeks later...

"Yo', there a Dara up in this house?" a woman's voice calls from the front of the bakery.

Ricky pops his head into the back where I'm frosting more buttercream and raspberry cupcakes and hooks a finger over his shoulder before disappearing. I finish the last two. My man's favorite. Silas loves him some raspberry, and I love putting a smile on his face, so I've added a new raspberry item to my regular list of treats each week. He's shown his appreciation in multiple ways, most of them with his tongue or his cock. Therefore, treats are brought upstairs on the *regular*, and with this second trimester libido, I am a happy woman.

I wipe my hands on my apron and head out to the front. The bakery is packed as usual. A bunch of patrons I recognize. My mama picking up tables and chatting up the customers. Same as she does in every store we own. She likes to be in this one, not only because I'm here but because it's where they started. So twice a week, Mama helps out, mostly hanging out, shooting the breeze with the customers, sharing her sage wisdom along the way. This system works for me. I love having my mama close.

She smiles at me and tends to the table of yogis we all know. Crystal Nightingale and Jewel Marigold have been co-owners of Lotus House but are getting to the place in their lives where they want to retire, explore the world even more than they already have, and dote on the younger generation. Part of their regular routine is to hit the bakery in the afternoons. I make special vegan treats for them, which keeps them not only coming back but buying me out of those treats because they love to bring the remainder home to their husbands. Win-win.

I wave over to them and then nudge Ricky. "Who called for me? I know a lot of people here." I snort-laugh, giving him a wry smile.

He points over to two well-dressed black women standing off to the side, behind the line of people. I make eye contact with the younger one and smile. Her eyes widen, and she smacks the arm of the older woman with her. The other woman is relatively tall, thin, and wearing a purple tunic-style silk blouse and matching pants. Her hair is cut in a sleek black bob that sways as she turns around. I immediately see the resemblance. Pale-green eyes set against dark, mocha-colored skin in a face that looks exactly like the man I love.

Holy shit! This must be Silas's mother.

I swallow, wipe my suddenly clammy hands along my apron, and exit at the counter bar, lifting it up and letting it fall back down.

The two women push through the crowd and stand before me.

"You can't be Dara. You're a sista'," the young woman says with a hint of awe and distrust. Her aura is screaming leery, which I can't fathom because she doesn't even know me.

"Half, yes. Not sure what else," I admit freely because I've got nothing to hide about my ethnicity. Mostly because a person's color does not matter one iota; it's the breadth of their character that speaks to who they are.

The young woman stares, mouth gaping, before her eyes scan my body head to toe and land squarely on my bump. At sixteen weeks, I'm definitely showing, much to Silas's great delight. Even if I wasn't, the new apron Mama bought me that reads "Baby Baker" with a picture of a cartoon baby holding a cupcake right over my small bump definitely gives it away.

"You're Dara?" the older woman asks, as though I didn't make that clear by coming over to them.

"Yes, ma'am. And you're Silas's mom." I hold out my hand and smile. "I'm so excited to meet you. I wish Silas had told me you were coming in. I would have planned something special, more coverage for the store, but as you can see..." She ignores my hand, so I use it to gesture toward the line. "We're pretty busy."

"You most certainly have been busy...*skank*." The woman

standing next to Silas's mother says that last part under her breath, but I still catch it.

"Excuse me? I didn't quite hear you." My voice shakes, but I otherwise hold it together, though not by much. My heart is squeezing tight, my breath coming in shallow starts, and my palms are starting to sweat again.

"Oh, you heard me. Gold-digging whore that you are." Her dark-brown eyes, nothing like Silas's, scan me, and she scowls. "Figured it would be a white girl." She sneers. "Silas prefers milk-white blondes, or didn't you know that?"

I take a step back, instinctively holding my hand over my baby.

"Whitney! Have some class," Silas's mother scolds, though she doesn't exactly apologize for her daughter's behavior.

"Mama, he knocks up some sista, basically bails from his family for three months, up and sells his house, disappears with a woman named 'Dara' who works in a bakery. A fuckin' bakery, Mama! When my brother is the head of a multi-million-dollar record label, and we show up, and she's actin' all timid and sweet. Pa-leeze. Look at her." She holds a hand out toward me.

And that's when the room turns ice-cold. The chill coming from behind me. "What did you say about my child?" My mama puts her hand around my waist, cinching me to her side.

I swallow the tears crawling up my throat and raise my hands. "It's okay, Mama. This is Silas's mother and obviously very protective sister, Whitney. I'm sorry. I didn't catch your name, Mrs. McKnight?" My mother squeezes my shoulder, giving me her strength, knowing what his sister said cut me to my core.

"Darlene McKnight." She offers her name but nothing else.

"And what's this I heard about you thinking my baby is a gold digger? 'Fraid to tell you ladies, but my baby owns this bakery and is the legacy of our franchise. 'Sides, when it comes to the baby making, it takes two to tango. Your boy was all over my girl. Still is. Happily, I might add."

"Mama, please. Don't wade in," I plead quietly.

Whitney places her hands on her hips and puffs up her chest. "Admit it. You trapped him."

"Trapped who?" The deep voice I love so much comes barreling through the bakery door and the patrons at the back. He sidles up to me, tugging me into his side from my mother's. She lets go willingly, a wicked smirk on her face.

"Dara, baby." His beautiful eyes meet mine, and I look away. Then he turns to his mother and sister. "Mom, Whit? Care to explain what's going on here?"

Whitney, full of hubris and a lot of attitude, adjusts her chest like a snake about to strike, her neck whipping back and forth with sass. "Met your girl Dara you been hidin'. Seems you knocked her up and never cared to mention that to the family. Why? Because you're scraping the gold digger off? God willing."

"Whitney!" Silas growls and gets right in her face. "What the fuck you say? I've spent sixteen weeks getting Dara to commit to *me*, not the other way around! Yeah, she's carrying my baby. Yes, we didn't plan it, but obviously the Big Guy above did." His voice is filled with righteous indignation.

"And what about, Sarah!" she screeches, eyes filling with tears. "What about your dead wife and baby?"

Silas's body goes ramrod straight, and his aura turns a smoky gray bordering on black. He's about to unleash a wrath unlike anything I've ever seen before.

"How dare you bring up Sarah and our baby. I loved her." He points his finger directly into her chest. "I loved our baby." He pokes at her chest again, and she takes a step back. "But that was three years ago. Three freakin' years!" His voice is barely lower than a lion's roar and filled to the brim with pain and anger. "Dara came into my life, and I'm finally living!" He points to her again. "After three years. Finally, I have something to look forward to."

"She's taking advantage of you!" she hollers directly in his face.

Jesus, this family can be volatile.

Silas locks his hands to his sister's shoulders. "Don't you see, Whit? I'm taking advantage of *her*!" He swings an arm out toward where I'm standing, and he may as well have shot an arrow into my heart. "She's giving me *everything,* and I've given her nothing! But I'm changing that. We're getting a house together, having a baby, and one day when I convince her that I'm worthy of her love...I'm going to make that woman my wife!"

Another arrow to the heart, this one filled with hope.

"Now get the fuck outta her bakery and don't come back until you've got a lengthy apology on that spiteful tongue."

Tears slip down Whitney's cheeks. "But Sarah..."

"Is. My. Past," he grates through his teeth. "Dara. Is. My. Future." He shakes his head. "I thought when you helped me clean out her stuff, told me to move on, that you'd be happy for me."

"Not by knockin' up the first ho who spreads her legs!"

I cringe and tuck into my mama, who reclaimed me the second Silas went on his tirade.

"It's okay, baby. She doesn't know you. She thinks she's

protecting her brother. Sad to say, she's making a grievous mistake. One she's going to regret."

"Maybe I should..."

Mama shakes her head. "No. You are Silas's woman. You stand by your man no matter what. Good and bad. Even if the words hurt. You let him take care of those hurts. Trust me, baby?" she whispers as Silas talks quietly to his sister.

"I trust you, Mama."

Darlene McKnight's eyes are on me, head tipped to the side. She takes a step forward. "My daughter has a vile temper and a foul mouth, though she means well."

"Looks like something her mama should be settin' straight," my mother says sternly.

Darlene purses her lips and then taps the bottom one with a red-tipped nail. "I do believe you are right. I'm sorry we had to meet this way, but you can understand how we'd get off on the wrong foot with our boy keeping things under wraps, picking up and moving in with a woman we hadn't even met yet. Now I see that you're carrying his baby, which I'm sure has its own story."

"It does. One I'll let Silas share, if he chooses." I firm my chin but hold tight to my mother, needing her support.

"Respect that. My apologies for the harsh words my Whitney has spoken. I, on the other hand, would very much like to get to know you and my very first grandbaby."

I nod, not sure what else to do.

"Go!" he says low and threatening to his sister, who stands tall and strong, her pride controlling every movement. Silas spins around facing his mother. "Ma, this is not okay. This is not how you were supposed to meet Dara and her family. I wanted to sit you down, share with you the good news once we knew everything was okay." His shoulders are high, and his entire body is poised to strike. His face is a mask of frustration and anger.

"And is the baby okay?" Darlene asks.

"Yes!" He runs a hand through his close-cropped hair and closes his eyes. "Can we talk about this later? I'm so angry, and I need to take care of Dara. Whitney said some seriously hurtful things, none of them true. Christ! Lil' mama, I'm sorry." He turns to me, both hands on the back of his head, his eyes wild and torn. He doesn't know whether to stay and fight, cut and run, or fling me over his shoulder and take me away from here. None of which will make the problem go away.

I make the decision for him. In front of everyone. My mother. His mother. Even his misguided, mean sister.

Walking the handful of steps, leaving the comfort and safety of my mother's arms, I walk over to him, reach up, and grab both of his wrists where he was holding his head. I bring his hands to my chest, where I dip my head to kiss his fingertips one at a time, watching while the tension seeps out of him with each press of my lips. A single touch is all he needs. Beautiful.

"Just us three. Me, you, and our baby. Remember? We can handle anything as long as we stay strong."

He closes his eyes, releases my hands, and pulls me into his arms.

"I love you, Dara. Baby, I fuckin' love you," he admits for the first time.

Our matching green auras merge, and it feels like sunlight bursting through the thick fog, his anger dissipating along with my sadness.

Silas finds my lips and takes my mouth in the softest, most life-altering kiss ever. I can taste the truth in his words, even though he didn't seem ready to say them. I can feel his heart pounding against my chest. See the despair and need in his eyes for me to accept him.

Love him.

Want him.

I hold both of his cheeks and stare into his eyes. "You're all I've ever wanted. I love you, Silas. And it will be okay. This too shall pass, and in its wake, we'll still be three."

He shakes his head, kisses me hard, and then runs his lips down my neck, kissing me everywhere he can as he goes. My cheeks, neck, collarbone, between my clothed breasts, down to my belly, which I knew was his destination.

"Nope. Not just three. Watch out, my queen. After this one, we're trying again. Right away. Want a handful of your children, with caramel-toned skin and blue eyes." He rubs his chin and face over my bump. "Love you too, lil' one." He kisses the bump once more before standing up and hugging me. Hard. So hard I never want to leave his arms.

"And she's free," Darlene whispers, but Silas's arms lock around me, and he stuffs his head into the crook of my neck as his mother continues to speak. "Sarah is finally free to move on because she knows you're loved, protected, and living your life as you're meant to. Happy and free."

CHAPTER SIXTEEN

Seeing your own aura: Sit in front of a mirror. Make sure the background behind you is a light, neutral color. Then focus on the outline of your body. Your life energy will be visible in a blurred-out, clear-type haze. Use all of your focus on just the outline. After a few minutes, a color will present itself. That's the color of your aura at that time.

SILAS

"Dr. Hart, I swear to God, I don't know if I can ever talk to Whitney again. The shit she spewed to Dara..." I shake my head and pace behind the couch.

As usual, Dr. Hart is sitting primly and properly in her chair, watching me fret. One of her hands resting over her very pregnant belly. She's got to be due any day now. Sarah was seven months along when she died, and her belly was not that large.

"Silas, I understand that you're hurt and angry, but you have to keep in mind, Whitney was presented with a replacement of her best friend."

"But she's the one who told me to move on! Helped me do it!"

Dr. Hart nods. "Yes, but she was doing so in the figurative sense. The physical stuff, like donating her clothes, packing up her things. Her heart hadn't let her go either. Probably because none of you dealt with Sarah's death completely before being presented with the death of your father. That's a lot for one family to handle. It's easier to sweep those feelings of grief under the rug and focus on other things, such as your company and one another."

I stop behind the couch and brace both hands on the back, curving my shoulders and dropping my head forward. "Whit and I are tight, doc. This is a blow. I want her happy about Dara and the baby, but I'm afraid she hates her."

"She doesn't hate her. Whitney doesn't know Dara. Give it a bit of time. She will learn to accept Dara into the fold, but she has to let go of her own upset over her best friend dying, her brother moving on with another woman and having a family that isn't Sarah's. You've accepted this, and it took some time for that to happen."

"I still miss her. Every day. But I love Dara and our baby too." My skin itches, feeling prickly and clammy with the admission.

"And you're allowed to. What you feel for Dara and your unborn child doesn't replace what you had with Sarah. Different women."

"I'll say. Sarah was so white she glowed in the dark." I grin. "Dara's caramel-colored skin, though, her insanely blue eyes against that skin tone, her body. Doc..." I suck in a breath between my teeth and bite back the desire to gnaw on my knuckle. Dara's beautiful stacked little body makes me crazy. Her rounding out more with my child, I'm hard all the time. All I have to do is be near her, and I'm fighting off a raging erection.

Dr. Hart laughs. "I'm glad you're attracted to your woman, especially in pregnancy. That, I can relate to." She rubs her bump in a big circle.

"When are you due again? I know you told me when we started. I'm sorry I don't remember."

"I think you've had a bit on your mind." She grins. "Two weeks, which is part of what I need to discuss with you today. I'll be heading out on maternity leave next week. I'm having a good friend and exceptional therapist see the clients who need to continue therapy in my absence."

I purse my lips and think about spewing all my shit to a new person. As much as I still think about Sarah and miss her, I'm not sure I need to continue therapy over her loss. Dara is giving me something to look forward to in our baby. Prior to entering my session, my Realtor called, stating they found a house that will go on the market in two weeks, only two streets over from the bakery. He's sending me the images and information on pricing.

"You know, doc, I have a lot of good in my life right now. I'm feeling lighter. I have a new lease on life, and I'm focusing on the future."

Dr. Hart smiles widely, her almond-shaped black eyes sparkling with happiness. She stands up, leading with her belly, and opens her arms. "I want to hug you. I don't care if it's unprofessional. Blame it on the pregnancy hormones!" She laughs. "I'm so happy for you, Silas."

I walk into her arms and hold her small body and laugh when her belly jolts and I feel a kick against my stomach. Without thinking, I place my hand over the bump and wait. The baby kicks me again, and we both laugh out loud. Dr. Hart is a beautiful soul, and I'm so glad I met her.

"You know, we're going to be seeing more of one another now that Atlas knows you're my doctor."

"No longer your doctor, Silas." She puts her hand over mine on her belly. The baby rolls, and she grins. "Now I'm your friend."

A loud scream comes from beyond the door where the waiting room is. My blood chills in my veins, and I grip Dr. Hart's shoulder as the door flies open.

Mallory stands in the open doorway, eyes entirely black, no color left to be seen. Only that's not what has me quaking; it's the shiny metal gun in her hand, finger right on the trigger.

Her other hand comes up and pulls at her wild blond mane, which has seen better days, way better. Normally, her outfit is styled to perfection. Now she stands before us in a pair of ratty-looking jeans and a filthy green tank. Most of a pink lace bra is peeking out from the scoop neck, and her chest is heaving, her fake tits at risk of falling out the top.

"Another fucking woman! Silas, baby! This is ridiculous!" she screeches at the top of her lungs and lifts the gun.

Immediately, I push Dr. Hart behind me. She tries to come around and address the whackjob client of mine. "Miss, I'm not sure who you are or what you think this is, but I'm not Silas's woman."

Mallory takes two steps in. Through the door, I can see

Dr. Hart's receptionist with a phone to her ear, ducking behind her desk and out of view. She's obviously calling the cops. Good. All I have to do is keep Mallory calm until they get here.

"I saw him holding you. Touching your stomach. Do you know he has another pregnant black bitch on the hook? And now an Asian cunt! Silas, seriously, baby, what are you trying to do? Repopulate the earth with mixed babies? You're supposed to be mine! Having babies with me!" She waves the gun around.

"This is not his baby," Dr. Hart attempts again.

"Shut up, bitch!" Mallory aims the gun to the side wall and fires off a round. It crashes through one of the doctor's pictures, scattering shattered glass into the air.

Dr. Hart's body jerks, and she folds over in front of me. "Oh no..." Her voice comes out as a whisper.

I chance a glance behind me and see a puddle of what looks like spilled water seeping into the beige carpet. *Fuck!*

"Mallory, I need to get Dr. Hart to the hospital." I raise my hands in a gesture of surrender.

Her entire body flails like one of those inflatable tube men you see on the side of the road. She cackles out a bout of laugher before lifting the gun and pointing it. "You have got to be kidding me! We're not going anywhere until you admit you love me and I get rid of every one of your pregnant bitches in the process."

A ripple of dread slithers down my spine as I realize this is not going to end well. Dr. Hart's nails sink into my waist as a painful-sounding moan rips from her lungs. "Silas...baby's coming," she grits through her teeth.

Fuck! Fuck! *Fuck!*

"Mallory, baby." I try a different tactic. "You know I love

you," I lie through my teeth.

Her eyes narrow into slits.

"This woman is not mine. She's my doctor. You're in a therapist's office. I was uh...trying to get over my desire to be with you," I say, doubling my first lie.

Her face brightens and she smiles. "Really?"

I take a step closer, and she reacts by lifting the gun again and pointing it at me.

Shaking my hands, I take another step. Dr. Hart cries out behind me. Mallory's gaze shifts from mine and narrows on the doctor.

"Help me..." Dr. Hart leans against the back of the couch, gripping her belly with both hands.

A vile expression crosses Mallory's face. "I'll fucking help you, bitch. Help you go straight to hell for taking my man from me!" She shifts to the side, gun poised and ready.

"No!" I fly forward toward Mallory, making sure the gun is aimed at me and not Dr. Hart. The gun goes off, the sound deafening in my ears.

A blinding, piercing pain rips into the right side of my chest as I barrel into Mallory. The gun goes flying out of her hand as she locks her limbs around me. "Silas, baby!" I hear her cry out as I land on top of her.

I blink back the pain, feeling my body jerking around until I'm flat on my back. My eyes start to roll around, but before I lose touch with my body, I see the boys in blue dashing into the room. Mallory is suddenly pulled off me.

Dr. Hart's receptionist cries out for the cops to get to Dr. Hart.

"I love you, Silas. I love you, baby! I did it all for you. For us. I'm sorry! Baby, I'm sorry!" Mallory cries, her arms behind her back.

Right before I lose consciousness, I see paramedics entering with a stretcher. Then it all goes black.

★ ★ ★

Fire. Nothing but fire burns across my chest. I try to move, but I can't. My body is heavy, so heavy I can't even feel my feet.

A peaceful sensation presses against my hand. The smell of sugar enters my nose.

"Dara..." I whisper through dry lips.

"I'm here, baby. Never leaving." Her beautiful voice enters my mind, and I hold on to it as the black takes over once more.

★ ★ ★

Voices. Voices jolt me from a beautiful dream I was having of Dara holding our baby. A beautiful baby boy. Skin darker than his mother's, more like my father, but with stunning blue eyes.

"I'm not leaving him."

"Child, you need to rest. For the baby."

"No. He needs me here."

The blackness swirls, and I reach for the tiny speck of light at the end of my vision. I'm in a tunnel, the voices loud around me, almost like a train speeding by and echoing all around. Except I know those voices.

"Dara, you're carrying my son's baby. He'd want you to rest."

"Go away. I'm not leaving him."

Then the sunlight sensation hits my hand and my cheek. The scent of raspberry and sugar fills my nose, and I can feel my body seeping into the blackness, only this time with the lightness of my woman's essence all around me.

★ ★ ★

"Silas, you need to wake up." A voice I haven't heard in years whistles through my mind. The blackness is still all around except a light is getting brighter. It grows with every breath I take, becoming blinding.

And then she's there.

Sarah.

Her blonde hair is flowing, a white dress covering every inch of her body. She looks like an angel.

"Sarah," I whisper, not believing my eyes.

Sarah speaks, but it's not what I expect her to say.

"You need to wake up. She's waiting for you. Scared. Alone."

I shake my head, trying to understand. "But you're here. I don't want to leave you. Honey, it's been so long."

Sarah smiles, her pink lips like a cherub's. Her brown eyes glowing with happiness. "I'm happy you found her."

"Honey..." I choke on the word, knowing she's talking about Dara. "But I love you..."

"And you love her. And that's perfect." She holds her hands over her heart. "I wanted her for you. I want you happy, Silas."

"Sarah..." I reach out, but she's too far away. Her form and body slowly glide back, getting smaller.

She shakes her head. "I have to go now, but just know Dara and your baby, they are meant for you. I'm happy here, and one day, when you're old and gray, I'll be waiting to see you again. Until then...be happy, my love."

"No!" I try to reach out again, but my arms are heavy,

weighted down.

"Dara and your daughter, they are your destiny. Now, wake up, Silas. Wake up to your new life and be free."

"I love you, Sarah," I call out because there's nothing else I can do.

"I love you." Her voice is but a whisper on the wind.

As she goes, the darkness surrounding my body lessens, and there's nothing but pain. Bone-cutting agony rippling through my entire form.

★ ★ ★

My eyes are heavy as I blink. When I can finally manage to open them, a giant blond guy is standing three feet from my bed, leaning up against the wall, arms crossed over his big chest. His lips are a flat, serious-looking slash across his face.

The warm sensation I know well is covering my hand. I glance down and see my woman. Her face plastered against my hand, mouth open, fast asleep. Dark circles ring around her eyes, even in sleep.

I try to speak, but it comes out in a cracked whisper, my throat coated in dust bunnies. The big man I don't know but think I've seen before gets the pink cup on a side table and brings the straw to my mouth. I suck greedily from it, allowing the cool water to dispel the dryness in my throat.

"Who are you?" I croak.

The man's blue eyes are sharp when they come to mine. "I'm the man who owes you everything."

I frown.

"Clayton Hart. My wife is Dr. Monet Hart. And you saved her life and that of our son. Owe you. Huge. Plan to pay up, soon as you're well." His voice is deep but filled with gratitude.

Before I can say anything, my girl blinks awake, her sleepy blues coming to mine. "Silas..." she gasps, tears filling those orbs and falling down her face. "Baby."

She comes forward and puts her mouth to mine. "You're okay. You're awake. Baby," she whispers again, this time choked up with emotion, tears falling in a stream down her cheeks.

I lift my good arm and cup her cheek. "Never leaving you." It comes out as a promise.

"No." She shakes her head.

"No," I repeat.

She sighs and rests her forehead on mine. I hear movement—the big blond guy leaving the room.

"Dr. Hart?" I say, my voice still scratchy.

"Fine. She's fine. Perfect, baby. You saved her life." Dara caresses my face as if she can't stop touching me.

"Her baby?" I mutter, needing to know everything went okay with her child.

"Beautiful boy. All ten fingers and ten toes. Because of you they're breathing and alive in the maternity ward."

I swallow around the lump of cotton and fear in my throat. "What happened after I blacked out?"

Dara leans back and eases onto the side of my bed. Instantly, I put my hand to her belly, feeling our baby. She smiles and clasps her hand over mine before speaking.

"Mallory apparently had been following you around. Saw you and me together, and then she saw you waving goodbye to Dr. Hart one day after a session. Saw she was pregnant too and snapped. Bought a gun, came to the office, and threatened the receptionist before coming in. Didn't think to do anything about the people or receptionist. Her focus was on you and the doctor."

"Fuck!"

"Yeah. They called the cops, but it was too late for you. She'd already fired when you jumped at her to save Moe."

"Moe?"

"Dr. Hart. Her name is Monet. Best friends with Mila and Atlas. Atlas is also best friends with Clayton. I'm shocked you didn't know him."

"Didn't spend a lot of time with people outside of work."

She rubs my hand over her belly. "Nope, you didn't. Though one night you did." She grins. "And I'm so happy you did."

"Lil' mama. You okay?" I rub her belly. "Baby good?"

She nods quickly. "Now that you're awake, the bullet's been removed, and my man is going to be fine, we're all good."

"I love you, baby." I kiss her soft cheek.

"I love you too."

"You didn't leave my side." It isn't a question, because even in my drugged haze, I knew she was there, every second.

Dara shakes her head. "Never leavin' my man, especially when he needs me right where I am. Holding his hand. Praying for him to wake up and be with me and our baby."

"Come here." I tip my head.

She comes down and snuggles against my side. Then she says something that hits me right in the chest, more painfully than the freakin' bullet.

"I was scared, Silas. We just got you, and I thought maybe I'd lost you, and you never got to meet our baby."

I lock my good arm around her and do my best to move my other one, which jolts my wound. I grit my teeth but know she needs my hold more. "Told you, woman. Never leaving you."

"Yeah," she whispers and then nuzzles in.

"Rest, my queen. You need it."

"'K." Her voice is low and then her weight presses my side. She's fast asleep against me within minutes. The poor thing is exhausted.

I can't even imagine what this was like for her. Hearing that I got shot. Worrying about losing me. Our baby. *Fuck.* I grit my teeth and hold her close, planting my nose in her hair. That sugary bakery smell I love still wafts through her locks. With her scent in my nose, my good arm around her, my woman and baby nuzzled up to my side, I fall back asleep. Peacefully.

★ ★ ★

The next time I wake, Dara is whispering at the door. "He's not awake yet."

"I have to see him."

I hear Dr. Hart's voice as I blink my eyes open and attempt to sit up with a groan.

"Moe, beautiful, he needs some time," a male rumble answers.

"Just a minute," Dr. Hart tries again.

"Let the woman in!" I rasp from the bed, taking in my surroundings. Flower vases are positioned all over the room on every possible flat surface; the place looks like a flower shop. Dara, standing at the door to my room, glances my way and smiles softly.

God, I love this woman. Her smile could light up any darkness.

"I want to see him too!" a voice I recognize as my brother Russell yells.

"Yeah, let us in!" Kevin, my baby bro, complains.

"Dara, now I know you're protective, but his family needs to see him." My mama's voice rings through, and she pushes her way in. "Baby boy. How you doin'?"

I smile. "Got a hole in my chest but a beautiful woman who's havin' my baby watching over me. Can't complain." I mean every word.

"Mmmhmm. Just as I thought. Crackin' jokes and raisin' hell, just like your father," she mumbles, grinning.

Dara walks over to my side. "How you feelin', baby? You need anything?"

"Besides you and a gallon of water?" I grip her hip and run my hand down to her ass and give it a little welcome squeeze.

She smirks and gets the cup, putting it into my hand. I suck back more heaven while watching my family shuffle in. Russell, Kevin, Whitney, and Chantal line up around my bed, speaking all at once.

I lift my hand, cock my head to the side, and notice there's someone sitting in a wheelchair behind them, a giant blond guy I now know as Clayton Hart standing behind the chair.

"Guys, move over. I wanna see my doctor." I wave my hand to the side, and then I see her.

Dr. Hart is holding a small bundle wrapped in blue in her arms. The sibs move to one side of the room and quiet down as Clayton pushes his wife through.

"Far enough," she says to her husband and stands, holding the bundle in her arms and walking to my side.

"I don't mean to intrude, but I had to thank you..." Tears fill her pretty dark eyes and slide down her cheeks.

"Dr. Hart, no need." I reach for her hand.

"Monet," she corrects.

"Monet. I brought crazy to your office. I didn't know I was doin' it, but it still happened. I'm the one who's sorry."

She swallows and nods. More tears falling down her face. "Crazy always finds me. Part of the business." She winks, cracking up at her own joke.

I chuckle but stop when she pushes down the blanket and shows me her child's round face. "I just wanted you to see what you took a bullet for."

"Jesus!" I whisper, eyes on the tiny newborn.

"Meet Knight Atlas Hart. Knight after the hero who saved his life and mine."

Chills ripple all over my body, goosebumps rising. "Monet..." I gasp and swallow, eyes glued to the perfect little boy with blackish hair. He opens his eyes, and they're bright blue. Sky blue.

"Honored," I rumble out, emotion closing off my throat.

Monet leans forward and kisses my forehead. I lock my hand around her neck, keeping her there while she whispers, "Thank you, Silas. Soon. We'll talk soon."

"Yeah. Soon." I let her go, her jasmine scent filling me with peace.

She smiles softly and hands the baby to Dara, who's eagerly waiting to snuggle him.

My girl looks down at the little one, holding him close to her chest. "Knight. We're going to love you and be the best auntie and uncle you ever had. You're going to have a new cousin in our baby too. And last, I'm gonna make you so many treats." She coos to the baby in her arms, and I just lean my head back and smile.

I may have a hole in my chest, but I no longer have a hole in my heart. That space is filled with Dara, our baby, my family, friends, and a new adopted clan I just got in the Harts. Sarah was right. I'm free, and so is she.

CHAPTER SEVENTEEN

THIRD EYE
CHAKRA

A couple connected through the third eye chakra is a very rare relationship. It's built on mutual love and respect for all things and all people. These people live for others in their world, not for themselves. In a relationship, this couple lives solely to make their mate happy. This in turn provides an endless harmony in the home. There is an ease to the relationship not found in any other chakra couple.

SILAS

"Easy, my prince. Easy," Dara scolds me for the hundredth time in two weeks. She's the one who's closing in on nineteen weeks pregnant, and she's treating me like I'm spun glass.

Delicate.

Not a man's man.

I'm fuckin' done.

"Babe, I said I got this," I growl, working my fingers to button up my own goddamned shirt. The woman has been dressing me for damn near two weeks, and I'm tired of it. "I'm not an invalid. Gettin' better every day. Doc says I'm healing faster than anyone he's had on his table before."

Dara scowls and places her hands on her hips, baby bump proudly displayed in a skintight tank and a pair of yoga pants. She's mouthwateringly sexy, and she hasn't let me in *there* in two weeks. My balls are so blue I'm sure they are days away from fallin' off.

I grip her with my stronger side and tug her body to me. She lifts her head and melts right before my eyes. Woman can't stay mad at me for long. Thank Christ, because there is a lot I do that could easily piss her off. She just has this ease about her that other women I've been around don't have. She's comfortable in her skin, her environment, and hopefully now, she's comfortable in us.

Hopefully, because I'm taking her to the house I bought for us right under her nose. First thing I did when I got out of the hospital was call my Realtor and ask him to send me pictures of the home he had an early drop on. House cost a fuckin' mint, but nothing compared to the ease it will give me knowin' my lil' mama won't have to walk but two blocks in a good neighborhood to get to work.

No cars.

Perfect in my opinion. Dara confided in me that she doesn't even have a driver's license. This I found out when we got out of the hospital and my woman couldn't drive us home. Vanessa Jackson did that. Seems Mrs. Jackson hasn't made any effort in getting her daughter trained on how to drive either. Looks like we both share a bit of fear when it comes to Dara being safe. I've since promised her I would be teaching her how to drive, but I wasn't eager for her to have her own set of wheels. She didn't seem concerned either way since there's always someone at the bakery or the yoga studio in the event of an emergency.

Dara being Dara just goes with the flow. No worries. She likes her life. Woman loves her bakery and her work at the Lotus House. Now she loves me and our baby. According to her, she's got all she needs.

Not true.

Woman needs a home, not a studio apartment busting at the seams with my shit in boxes taking up a full twenty percent of the space and a baby on the way.

"Where are we walking anyway?" she asks, lifting up onto her toes and kissing the underside of my jaw.

I lean forward and nuzzle her cheek, taking in her fresh bakery scent. Today's flavor must be cinnamon, because my girl is covered in the scent of cinnamon buns.

Inhaling full and deep, I have to grit my teeth when an arrow of pain steals through my chest, reminding me I'm not one hundred percent.

Dara, knowing everything, notices my reaction. She cups my cheeks and frowns. "You gotta be careful. You've only been out two weeks, and I want you one hundred percent when the baby comes so you can hold your child without pain."

I sigh and nod. "You're right. I'll take it easy."

She gifts me a brilliant smile. "A walk?"

I grin, spin my girl around by the shoulders, and nudge her toward the door. When we get there, she shoves her feet into one of the ten pairs of flip-flops she has lined up by the door. My girl hates covering her feet. Around the house, she's barefoot. Always. In bed, she frees her pretty feet so they can get fresh air. Says when her feet are cool, the rest of her is cool. Whatever floats her boat.

We hit the stairs and walk through the back of the bakery. I don't want her going through the front to the street because we'll never get out of there, and I'm on a mission. Well, two missions. One, to show my girl our new home. Two, to ask her to marry me. This will probably come as more of a surprise than the home since we haven't known one another more than four months. Still, with a baby on the way and having taken a bullet to the chest, I was slammed with the fact that life is short and I need to make the most of it. No delays. A person never knows what lies beyond, and I'm not wasting a minute of my time with Dara.

Dara intermingles our fingers and lets our arms sway as we walk along the tree-lined streets of Berkeley. I've always loved this area of California. Berkeley is mostly known for being a college town, but in reality, the town shuts down at night and you're left with the local residents moseying around and the college kids in their frat houses.

My girl sighs as the sun starts to fade into the horizon and the night chill comes upon us. "It's beautiful here. I love this area." She says exactly what I was thinking.

Proof.

We're connected in more ways than one.

"Me too."

As we walk, we get closer to a street filled with homes that are tucked back away from the street by lush greenery and intricate fencing.

"Wow. I didn't even know this neighborhood was here,"

she exclaims, smiling, her eyes wide, taking in the beauty before us.

I walk past three more homes and to the driveway of the one I want her to see. There is no For Sale sign on it because I picked it up before it ever hit the market. The residents had movers finish up packing just two days ago. They were eager to get to the East Coast, and I was happy for my good fortune. Means I was able to rush the paperwork, and while it's going through escrow, the homeowner gave me the keys.

Dara tries to walk ahead, but I stop her with a tug of my hand. "We're going to look at this one."

She glances from side to side and all around. "Baby, I don't think people will take too kindly to people walking up to their doors and peering into their windows."

I grin, pull at her hand, and press on up the walk. The home is tucked back away from the street like many of the others, but once we get around the long drive, we see the quaint-looking, rather large two-story home. Quaint because it's reminiscent of a fairy home or small castle-type cottage. It's a brilliant white with pointed rooftops in a brick color, skinny windows with red trim painted around them, and a single, matching, wooden red door. Instead of grass, there's a cobblestone patio that reaches up to the door, where a small wrought-iron table set is sitting off to the side. The owners threw it in as a present when I told them how much I liked it there and planned to get one of my own.

Vanessa Jackson, being a strong-willed mama of an only child, knew what I was up to and had already scoped out the house. She brought over a couple of huge terracotta pots to frame the door and filled them with flowers. Bursts of red, purple, yellow, and orange complemented the white background, giving the doorway a more welcoming vibe.

"Si, we're going to get into trouble," Dara warns, squeezing my hand.

I stop at the door. "Trust me, baby?"

The worry in her expression fades, and she offers me a crooked smile. "Yes."

I pull out the key to the house from my pocket and insert it into the lock.

Dara gasps but doesn't say anything.

When we walk in, the place is empty, but the window shutters are open, allowing maximum light.

Dara enters the main room, her flip-flops smacking on the adobe-style tiled floor. She spins in a circle. "It's magnificent."

"Welcome home, lil' mama."

Her eyes widen so much I fear they might bug out of her head. "This is ours? This magical giant cottage on a hillside in Berkeley?" She repeats herself as if I don't know where we are or the fact that I paid a cool one and a half million to secure it.

"It's ours. Yours, mine, and lil' one, and any future babies we bring home."

Dara covers her mouth as she walks over and peers into the kitchen. "Oh, my God. It's got a double fridge, double oven, double *eve-re-thang*!" She spins around on one foot. "Do you know how much I'm going to cook in this kitchen!" Her voice rises with her excitement.

"Hopefully every meal, babe, because you know I can't cook worth a shit!" I laugh, enjoying every second of watching her walk through our home. I've already seen it, but seeing it through her eyes is so much better.

She keeps walking and yells out, "A huge dining room! We can fit sixteen at least if we get a big enough table! Your family, my family, and the Harts!"

Dara has decided in the short two weeks since our ordeal with Mallory that Monet, Clayton, Lily, and baby Knight are family. Turns out, while spending healing time hanging out with Monet and the baby, we found out Monet, like Dara, has very little family. Atlas, Mila, and their baby Aria are pretty much the only family she claims, and they are not blood.

In those two weeks, I've seen the Harts four times. They come to visit, check on me, bring me things to read, spend time chatting, but mostly I think it's because Clayton doesn't know how to thank me. Every time he visits, he leaves, holding my shoulder, looking me in the eye, and saying one word: Gratitude.

I figure naming their child Knight after me, which is a kickass first name if I do say so myself, was beyond thoughtful. Besides, the second they arrive, Monet puts the baby right in my arms so I can bond. Says she wants her baby to know his hero personally. Me, I love it. Gives me a little practice before my own bundle comes. Not to mention, their daughter, Lily, is a hoot. The funny shit that comes out of that little girl's mouth would bring a grown-ass man to tears with laughter. And the little one loves Dara. She wants Auntie Dara to take her right down to that bakery and show her how to make something. Of course, Dara does it because she's a pushover for a pretty face. Then again, so am I.

Back to pretty faces, Dara comes running into the room. "We have a pool!" she screeches. "I love pools!"

Now that I didn't know because I've never seen her swim, nor is it the time of year to swim, but I'm happy she's happy.

Dara grabs my hand and starts lugging me up the stairs. "Be careful, baby, but I gotta see what's upstairs!" She's squealing like a little girl.

While she opens each door, nods her head, smiles, and makes a comment about something she likes, I just watch her. Making her happy, knowing she loves the home I bought for our family is all I need.

Then we make it to the master. Her hands drop to her side, she lifts her head to the ceiling, and calls out, "Thank you, Jesus, God, in heaven above. I am so home!"

I snicker and come up behind her, wrapping my arms around her. One on our child, the other across her chest to her shoulder. "How's about you thank me, since I'm the one who dropped a mint on it?"

She giggles, reaches her hands back behind her, arching her sexy body. I run my hand up to one of her big tits and swipe the nipple with my thumb.

"I'm thinking a little gratitude with your sexy-as-fuck mouth would do wonders, lil' mama. My dick is hard and aching for you after two weeks of nothing but blue balls."

She laughs but spins around and takes my mouth with hers. Our tongues tangle, and I can tell by the little mewl she makes in the back of her throat she's getting hot for it.

With shaking fingers, so excited to get my hands, mouth, hell, *anything* on my woman, I lift her tank and push it over her head. Instantly, she puts her hands behind her back, unlatches her bra, and frees her beautiful tits.

"Fuck!" I suck in a breath through my teeth. I cup both globes in my hands and circle her nipples with my thumbs. "They're not only getting bigger, baby, but your nipples are fat and round. Fuck, I want these tits in my mouth." I groan and lean over to take a tip.

Before I can get my mouth on it, she backs up and shakes

her head. "Nuh-uh, big man. I've got some gratitude to show."

I quirk an eyebrow and watch as she kicks off her flip-flops, puts her fingers in the sides of her yoga pants, and presses them and her underwear down her toned thighs. Her belly is protruding a lot now, which only makes her look like a fertile goddess.

With effort, I grip both hands into fists, forcing myself not to reach out, but my dick has other plans. The second he nudged up against her ass from behind, he got excited.

My girl, bare-ass naked, looks me up and down. I lift my arms and unbutton my shirt. Thank Christ she doesn't try to do it for me. I need to feel a little in charge here, even though she's in total control. Her hands run up her body, and she lifts and molds her own breasts, tweaking the nipples between two fingers.

A heat hits my entire body, and a mist of sweat tingles at the back of my neck as I watch my woman touch herself. She runs one of her hands down her side and between her thighs. I know the second she finds her hot button and spins two fingers around it.

She cries out and tips her head back. The image of sex and desire incarnate.

I hiss out my need through my teeth, and she opens her eyes and licks her lips. Then she walks up to me with those same two fingers she had between her legs, and my woman puts them up to my mouth. I grab her wrist and hold it in front of my face, sucking her fingers between my lips like a starving man. She moans while I suck.

"Want you sitting on my face. Right here, right now."

"Okay, but only if I get to suck on you at the same time."

She mewls as I unbutton my pants, kick off my shoes, not

bothering with my socks, and push down my pants.

Dara scrambles to her knees, where she eases my underwear down and helps me get them off. Her mouth is on my cock before I can even take a knee to the floor.

"Fuck!" I hiss and grip her hair, letting her know how very, very much I love her mouth.

Her blue gaze lifts to meet mine as she laps at the underside of my dick, swirls her tongue around the crown, and takes me deep. All the way to the back of her throat.

Now I put both hands in her hair and fuck her mouth. She takes it all, deeper than any woman has ever been able to before. World-class head. The best.

"Want my mouth on your cunt," I growl and grip her hair at the roots so it will sting but not hurt.

She moans around my cock, and it jerks inside her mouth, pre-cum at the tip. She laps it up, flicking the tip before she gives it a little kiss.

A fucking *kiss*. On the tip of my dick. Cute and silly. My girl.

Finally, she releases me, her eyes darkened with lust as I get to my knees and ease down on my back in the middle of our brand-new master bedroom, no furniture in sight, just an empty room and a wall of windows to light our way.

The second I'm flat, she straddles me, and I grip her hips. At first, she's timid, always is when her belly is hovering, but I shift her ass toward my head, grip her butt cheeks, and bring her succulent pussy right down on my mouth, dipping my tongue deep right off the bat. She moans out her pleasure, sitting up, letting me get a good, deep drink of her. She's wet as fuck, and my hips jerk of their own accord.

That move seems to bring her back into action, falling

over my body, putting her mouth right where I want it. The second her lips wrap around my tip, I thrust up, forcing her to take more. She pays me back by grinding her cunt into my face. I love it, groaning, lapping her up, licking, kissing, and flicking her clit.

Her body trembles on top of mine, and I push her hips up. "Fuck, babe, already. I barely got my mouth on you and you're going to come?"

She moans as I suck her clit hard, her body jerking as she fucks my face. "Can't help it." Her voice comes in labored pants.

I lift her up again. "Gonna make you come, and then you're gonna ride my dick. And don't you dare question my ability. I'm so fucking gone right now. Your taste on my tongue, your mouth on my cock after two fucking weeks of nuthin', woman... fuck!" Her coconut and earthy scent hits my nostrils like a smoke trail. I press her legs wider, forcing her open more, her belly resting on my chest, arms to the floor beside us holding her up.

"Si."

She gasps when I grind my two-day stubble into her tender flesh.

"Baby."

Dara jerks, more moisture coating my tongue. Fucking delicious. I can't get enough.

"I'm coming, Si. Baby, I'm coming." She fucks my face, moving her hips like a madwoman as I try to keep up. Then her entire body goes rigid, and I gorge on her cream, licking up every drop of her release until she's shaking, her head having fallen to my thighs, my dick still hard and weeping.

"Turn around and hop on my dick, babe. Now!" I growl.

"Need you, baby."

She lifts her head, does an interesting twirl, straddles my lower half, lines up her slit with my angry dick, and slams home.

Her entire body arches, hands flying to her hair.

"Jesus Christ, you're magnificent." I lift my left hand to her breast so I can play with her nipple. The right, where the bullet wound is still healing in the right side of my chest, I rest on her hip. "Ride my dick, Dara. Take it there again."

Her body bounces on top of mine, and I thank the good Lord above that I got this chance to see my woman riding my cock, her belly swollen with my baby, her expression showing nothing but the pleasure I'm giving her. Pleasure she's taking from my body.

"Fuckin' beautiful," I gasp on one of her powerful thrusts down.

Every time she lifts up, she moans like it hurts her to leave our connection, until she bottoms out, totally filled to the root, where she digs her fingers into my abdomen and sighs, like there's no place like home. Home, with me rooted deep inside her. I get it. I totally get it, because when we're connected like this, there's nothing I could ever want more. No place in the world more peaceful.

Watching her taking me, getting herself off, my body reacts...powerfully. An ache builds in my balls I can't ignore. Ribbons of sheer pleasure ripple out from where we're connected all through my body. My heart starts to pound, and my dick gets impossibly harder, balls drawing up ready to go off.

"Get there!" I groan, lifting my hips up and forcing her down hard on my cock.

She cries out and picks up her pace, bobbing up and down so fast her big tits are slapping against her skin, the nipples dark red, ripe as fuck.

Licking my thumb, I bring it down to where we're connected and spin circles around her hot little button of nerves.

"Si, Si, Si," she starts to chant, a dead giveaway she's going to come and do it hard.

"Fuck yeah!" I roar, digging my other hand into her hips so that every time she comes down, I get as far up into my woman as possible. Until it's too much. Her body locks down around mine, her pussy a vise around my dick, and finally, fucking finally, I let go.

Pumping up into her as she stills, the wave coming over her, the world exploding around me as I go off inside her. She takes it. Everything I've got until she can't any more and loses herself, coming over me in a heap of sexy, sweat-misted skin.

I hold her, ease us sideways so she's more comfortable and our baby isn't squashed but we're still connected. She keeps a leg wrapped around me as though she doesn't want to let go.

"Missed you, baby." I kiss her lips, her cheek, neck, nipples, chest, and back up. Then I bury my nose against her hair where her scent is strongest and lick behind her ear, sighing as another part of my woman's body hits my tongue.

"Love you, Silas, and I love our new home."

I hum against her skin, kissing her some more, licking her neck, just keeping our connection going for as long as possible, not wanting this bubble to break.

"You'll be happy here?"

This time she hums, kisses my neck, my chest over the bullet hole, and then back up to my lips. When she pulls away, her eyes are endless oceans of Caribbean blue. "I'll be happy wherever you and our baby are. It doesn't matter, as long as we're there together."

"How's about forever?" I ask.

Dara frowns as if she doesn't understand the question.

Staying connected, I reach out and grab my pants, digging inside the pocket and pulling out the ring box. Her head is tucked against my chest so she can't see that I pull out the ring and leave the box.

"Give me your hand."

She lifts her right hand.

I laugh. "Give me your left hand, my queen."

Her eyebrows rise up as she shimmies half over me and lifts her left hand.

I grab her hand, look into the eyes I want our baby to have, and lay it out. "Marry me, Dara. Live here as my wife, my woman, the mother of my children. Forever."

"Really? You want me forever?" Her body trembles in my arms. She told me before how hard it was to accept she was wanted by the Jacksons all those years ago. Told me in the quiet of the night her biggest fear was not being wanted.

"Baby, I wanted you the day I laid eyes on you. Then I got a taste of all that is you and knew with my whole soul, you were worth living for. Hell yes, I want you forever. The question is, do you want me forever?"

A tiny prickle of nervous energy flickers around my body as she bites her lip and then smiles huge. "Yeah, I want you forever. This life. You as my husband. Our babies. I want it all, Silas McKnight."

CHAPTER EIGHTEEN

The third eye chakra is often associated with a dark purple or indigo type color. When focusing on the aura, the energy surrounding the body may appear as a translucent purple or bluish white.

DARA

"Let me see the ring again!" Luna reaches for my hand and swoons over my rock for the third time in as many minutes.

I glance down at the perfect, oval-shaped diamond with two triangle ones hugging its sides. It's stunning. Without realizing it, I'm holding it up, allowing the light to glint off its glory.

A sigh leaves my lips, and I rub my bump. Baby is fluttering around my belly. The first time I felt the butterfly wings, I jumped up, grabbed Silas's hand, and pressed it over our baby. Unfortunately, he couldn't feel a thing, much to our disappointment. The book says he'll be able to feel the rolling and kicks sometime after the twentieth week. Which I'm finally at!

I cannot wait for our doctor's appointment, where we get the big ultrasound and find out what we're having. Silas, on the other hand, is dreading it. He keeps trying to talk me into waiting until the baby is born to find out what we've having, but I simply can't. I must know. And since he loves me and doesn't want me to be let down, he's caving to my wishes.

Secretly, I keep hoping and praying it's a boy. A son to carry on the McKnight name, the first in the family so far.

"It's so incredible, Dara," Luna shares while we walk through the largest home store known to man. At least it feels that way as I carry my extra weight around with me.

"What is?" I run my hands over a dark royal-blue couch. I've already got Silas painting the living room a smoky gray to accent the white crown molding. I've found a huge area rug that has white, gray, and a burnt-orange color and is currently on the floor of our bare living room.

"Your love story. A one-night stand turned forever." She shakes her head. "I've given up on finding Mr. Right. All I've ever found is Mr. Wrong and Mr. Right Now. There's only so much a girl can take."

"Luna, girl, you're only a year older than me. Twenty-six is not old, and you've not left the yoga studio enough. You need to get out there, see what's available."

She puckers her lips. "Been there, done that, and got the broken heart to prove it. Besides, with Mom and Crystal stepping down, I'm it. Like the bakery is for you, Lotus House is my home. It's always been my dream to run the studio. Heck, it's been my dream to run several of them up and down California. It's the reason I got the stupid business degree while teaching all these years."

I finger the price tag on the cushy sectional. Well within my price range. "Yeah, I get you. Running the bakery is tough, but finding the right help is key. Plus, you need to find some relief. You can't be the only one doing all the work all the time. You're gonna burn out."

Luna sits on the sofa and sighs and rubs her hands along the microfiber, making the dark blue turn midnight. "Oh, this is really nice."

Following her lead, I sit on the couch and decide right then. "This is so my couch!" I tell her.

She laughs and nods. The salesman must have radar on women with money to burn, because he appears out of nowhere.

"See something you ladies like?" A balding man smiles toothily and waggles his furry eyebrows with his double entendre.

Eew. Gross.

Not into overly fluffy men with bellies hanging over their belts and a mustache in need of a serious trim. My mind wanders to my fiancé and all that is Silas McKnight and his beautiful self. Nope, I'm into brothers with abs I can play tic-tac-toe on who can also lift me and my "preggo" ass and toss me on the bed like I weigh as much as a feather.

"Why? You gonna give me a deal?" I raise my eyebrows and rub my baby belly.

He rolls back onto his heels and then forward. "I could probably score you fifteen percent off if you open up an account and finance the purchase. No interest if you pay it off in six months."

"Deal!" I rub my hands together, knowing I'll pay that sucker in cash when the bill arrives, but fifteen percent on a three-thousand-dollar sectional is nothing to sneeze at. "Will it be fifteen percent off my entire purchase if I buy more stuff?" I bat my eyelashes prettily.

His cheeks pinken.

Aw, he's so easy. Now I kind of feel bad for thinking poorly of his potbelly, thinning hair, and bad facial hair.

"For you, pretty lady, of course." He rubs his hands together.

"Come on, Luna girl. I've got an entire house to furnish!"

She stands up and claps her hands. "Right!"

My cell phone rings, and I pull it out of my pocket. Ricky's name is on the display.

"Yo, bro!" I say in greeting.

"Hey, cupcake. Was wondering what you are up to. Esteban is snoozing because I tired his ass out...literally."

"Ricky..." I warn, not wanting to hear about his sexual escapades with his new beau.

"Anyway, spoilsport, was wondering what you are up to."

"Shopping."

"Ooh, what for? Baby stuff?" His tone rises in interest.

"Nope, home furnishings."

"You already buying stuff for your new pad? That place is bea-u-ti-ful!"

Luna walks ahead and scopes out an amazing armoire, which would go perfect in the guest bedroom.

"Luna, that is sa-weet! Price that, girl." I point to the armoire.

"Luna? Thought you'd be with Mr. Hotpants-baby-daddy-soon-to-be-hubby?" Ricky queries.

"Yeah, he doesn't care much for home design." I shrug to myself, checking out a cool-as-heck vase, which would look great on the sixteen-seater dining room table I've been scoping out online.

"Really? And he's letting you shop. What? Did he give you carte blanche with his AmEx Black? Please tell me he did. Thinking about it makes me so damn hot." I imagine Ricky in his house, sitting in his chair fanning himself.

I laugh at the image he makes. "No. I'm paying for the furnishings." Pride leaks out in my tone.

"Say what? How the hell did you manage that with alpha badass Silas McKnight?"

"Not without a lot of convincing." My voice drops, remembering how I teased my man, took him in my mouth until he'd agreed to anything.

"I'll bet. But sex agreements can only go so far. I know that from experience."

"True, but I also told him I'd been working in the bakery all my life and saving my money since I graduated high school. I don't pay rent, have no school loans, and I've lived simply. Not a big spender, so I've been socking my money away for years."

Ricardo whistles sharply, and I have to pull the phone away from my ear. "Damn, I should have borrowed money from you instead of taking a loan from the bank for my car. Those bastards are charging me eight percent!"

I chuckle at how he brings my situation right back to him. "That's because you charge up your credit cards with stupid shit. The day you learn is the day your percentages start going down."

"Hmmm. Fair enough. Still surprised he caved."

"Me too, but I'm damn good with my mouth." I cluck my tongue for emphasis.

"Wow wee. I'll just bet you are, seeing as you're carrying his baby and about to become his wife."

"Don't I know it!" I say with glee. "It's crazy, Ricky. Five years ago, hell, one year ago, I would never have thought I'd be shopping for my home in the Berkeley hills with the owner of Knight & Day Productions and be head over heels in love with him. It's surreal." I shake my head and follow the tile between the rooms to the next setup.

Ricky sighs his own dreamy one through the phone. "Yeah it is, but deserved. You make him happy, he'll make you happy, and everyone is happy. End of story. No need to write any more words."

"This is true. Do you want to meet up later for drinks and appetizers?"

"Because you're going to have an alcoholic beverage?"

"No, silly, but Luna might want one after a day of me dragging her around home stores!"

"Sounds good. What time?"

"Shoot for six?"

"Okay. High Point Bar & Grill? It's got a great view and happy hour runs from five to eight," Ricky offers.

"Rockin'. See you there at six."

Hanging up, I move toward the most beautiful bedroom set I've ever seen. The wood isn't dark, but it isn't light either. It's right in the middle. The sign on the end of one dresser says *Brazilian Cherry* on the tag.

"Wow." I run my hand along the dresser. It's taller than normal dressers but still fat and wide. Nice, deep drawers.

There's a matching headboard that's tall and high up the wall. This bed is queen-sized, but I've promised my man a California King. He says he wants to be able to roll all over the bed with his woman as well as fit all of his children in his bed for Sunday morning cuddle time.

I can't wait for Sunday morning cuddle times with my man and kids. Having had no family in my early years to then having just my two adoptive parents, I've wanted a big family. Silas comes from one, as did his mother and father. He is not averse to expanding our brood beyond this one. Still, since I know he lost several babies with Sarah, this one is very important to him. The man just wants to hold his own child in his arms.

While thinking of Silas, I note he's been acting so strange the last week. Not in a way that's unloving, just more protective, a little nervous. I thought maybe it had to do with the twenty-week check coming up in two days, but he hasn't said anything.

All I know is every night we go to bed in my tiny apartment, he makes slow love to me, taking his time and being extra careful. I know he's worried about the baby, but I keep telling him every day I feel the baby moving, and I'm confident he/she is okay. The one thing I haven't mentioned is I can already see the baby's aura. He now knows I can read auras, thinks it's a neat party trick, but reading the baby's?

It's a secret I haven't shared with anyone because I didn't know it was even possible. My aura is usually indigo. I've always been driven by the third eye chakra, but my own colors change along with my moods just like anyone else. However, when studying myself in the mirror, I noted my aura color was an orangey silver that's often seen in pregnant women. That wasn't the strange part. The strangeness occurred when I noticed my entire belly was a startling yellow circular shape, reminiscent of a sun. Same as Silas's resting aura.

Seeing the yellow halo around my belly has given me great peace. It means my baby is going to be like his or her father, and seeing that yellow glow makes me a hundred percent confident the baby is okay. If it wasn't there, I'd worry.

Luna comes up behind me and oohs and ahhs over the bedroom set. I agree with her that Silas will love it and it will look perfect in our new home.

After several rounds in a host of home stores, I've purchased a bedroom set, sectional, armoire, vases, lamps, another rug, a couple of chairs for a reading space, and some other pictures.

"Luna, I'm done, and Ricky wants us to meet him at High Point for drinks and apps. I'm starving, and baby needs to eat. Plus, I think my ankles are the size of paint cans!"

She chuckles, hooks my arm, and we head outside to her cherry red Ford Fusion. We both buckle up and head out of San Francisco and toward Berkeley. The traffic is a crush, so we turn up the music and sing along to the latest Gwen Stefani album.

"Don't you think Genevieve Fox looks like Gwen Stefani?" I mention our friend who only teaches two nights a week and cuts hair and hangs with her family the rest of the time.

"Totally!" Luna tips her head back and laughs, her arm coming out and knocking over her purse that she'd teetered on the console between us. Some of the items scatter down in front of me, the others under her feet.

Me being too round to do anything about the items in front of me, I just laugh at our predicament.

Luna glances at the road and then down, reaching for things and shoving them into her purse on her lap. Then someone cuts her off, and she moves to hit the brakes, only her glasses case had rolled under the brake pad and the car isn't stopping.

"Oh my God, Dara!" Luna screams and puts her arm out across my chest.

It all happens in slow motion, the red hood of a car barreling into the line of parked cars in front of us as we wait to take the onramp toward Berkeley.

The sound of metal crunching against metal rips through my ears, the airbags go off, and I'm slammed back into the seat and immediately lose consciousness.

★ ★ ★

Sirens are blaring, and my body is being lifted out of the crushed vehicle. I come to and shake off the grogginess. Pain ricochets up my neck, but I still crane to see Luna as the paramedics strap my head down tight. "Ma'am, don't move your head or your body. We need to see to your injuries."

Except before they did that, I saw Luna's motionless body, still in the car, blood pouring down the side of her head, her form slumped over the passenger's seat where she tried to protect the baby and me.

"The baby!" I call out.

"I got a heartbeat, but there's blood between your thighs. We need to get you to the hospital stat!"

No. No, please God, no. You can't do this to us.

"My baby," I whisper. "Luna!" I cry out and lose consciousness once again.

★ ★ ★

I wake in a large white and pink room. My face is hurting like mad, and not a single soul is there to greet me. A horrible sense of loneliness rips through my chest, and I grab for my belly. Gadgets are hooked up to my abdomen. One is a square that's pressing tightly against my bump. A *whoosh*ing sound is filling the room.

An instant calm comes over me at the sound. It's just like what we heard at our twelve-week checkup: our baby's heartbeat.

I glance around the room. I'm hooked up to an IV, a machine to my right is keeping track of something, and the *whoosh* noise continues. Just as I see a red button dangling from a white box hanging over the arm rail, a nurse enters the room.

A short-haired blonde with kind eyes and a cheery complexion comes over and takes my pulse. "How are you feeling, honey?" she asks.

"Um, my head hurts, my belly is uncomfortable, and there's a tightness in my chest," I answer.

"Yeah, you took quite a punch by the airbag. We're monitoring the baby's heart rate and levels. Baby was stressed when you came in, and there was some vaginal bleeding."

Vaginal bleeding. Baby stressed.

Tears fill my eyes, and I cover my baby protectively. "Where's Silas?"

"Silas?"

"My fiancé. Has he been called?"

"Sweetheart, you didn't have a thing on you. I just received a call from the police onsite who gave us your name of Dara

Jackson. No other information."

"How's my friend, Luna?"

"Pretty redhead?"

"Yeah, she was driving."

"Banged up. We patched her up, but she's still unconscious."

"Can I see her?" I ask, my heart hurting.

The nurse shakes her head. "No, honey, we're monitoring the baby. You're in this bed for at least twenty-four hours until we know for sure the fetus is okay. We're setting you up for an ultrasound. I'll send the doctor in now. You rest that head. You took quite a beating yourself."

"I need to call my fiancé. He'll be worried. And my mom."

The nurse brings the phone over to my side and leaves the room.

The phone rings once before he answers with a ragged, "Dara!"

"Silas," I whisper, my throat clogging up, my forehead pounding.

"Baby, where are you?"

"Hospital."

"God, no. Which one? I'm on my way now. Fuck! Ricardo called an hour ago. A fucking hour, saying he was worried because you and Luna didn't show for drinks and dinner. Baby, tell me you're okay?"

I start to tremble, the shock of being in a car accident, being strapped up to this machinery, the baby undergoing stress tests, and the nurse mentioning vaginal bleeding hitting me all at the same time. Big, heaping tears fall down my face. "I'm scared. The nurse is monitoring the baby for stress, and there was bleeding, Silas..."

"Fuck! Fuck! No. Baby, no. It's going to be okay. I'm here. Tell me where you are."

"Same hospital you were in."

"Okay, just stay with me. You're on speaker, and I'm in the car right now."

"You have to call my mama." I swallow, knowing how this will freak her out.

"Not letting you go, lil' mama. Staying with you until I can see you. Shit, you're by yourself. I'm sorry."

"Luna got hurt," I whisper through my tears.

"What happened? Do you remember?"

I sniff and wipe at my running nose with my gown. "Car accident."

Silas goes silent.

"And Luna was hurt, babe. She was hurt bad. I saw her unconscious, bleeding from her head. The nurse won't let me see her. Says I need to stay where I am because of the baby. And I'm scared. I'm so fucking scared!" The sobs tear through me one after another.

"Dara, you listen to me."

"She's still unconscious. What if she doesn't wake up? What if something is wrong with our baby? The nurse said I had vaginal bleeding..." I choke on my next heave. Some alarms start blaring, and I gasp, looking around the room.

The nurse runs into the room followed by a man in a white lab coat.

"Dara!" Silas's voice careens through the phone, but I'm not paying attention. I'm lost in the swirl of fear and desperation.

Suddenly the phone is taken from my hand, and the doctor's got his scope on the baby. "Miss, you need to calm down. Baby's heart rate has gone up. We're going to need an ultrasound room, stat," he says to the nurse before moving around the bed to the other side.

The doctor reviews the machine that's hooked up to my belly.

The blonde nurse hangs up the phone, and I want to howl, my connection to Silas gone. She grabs my hand.

"Dara, I need you to take deep breaths in and out slowly with me, okay? Calm down. Your heart rate is too high. You relax, the baby will likely follow."

I follow along with her breathing, which is essentially the meditation breathing I do normally, so I close my eyes and start my routine. Chanting in my head, sending love, light, and healing to my baby in waves of energy and intention. I hum a Bob Marley tune called "Three Little Birds" low in my throat and send that peace to my baby.

"That's it," I hear the nurse's voice, but it sounds faded and far away. "Good, Dara. Baby's heartbeat is closer to normal. Just keep breathing."

When I've finished the fourth run-through of the song, my own heartbeat has leveled out, I'm much calmer, and I can feel my baby rolling around. I open my eyes and see the yellow halo brighter than ever around my belly.

A relief so strong it almost makes me weak hits my heart.

Baby is going to be okay. I just know it.

CHAPTER NINETEEN

*The symbol most commonly used for the third eye chakra is
the two elements associated with wisdom, a lotus flower, and
an upside down triangle.*

SILAS

I know there is a God because I've witnessed the beauty he brings to this world. Most specifically in Sarah, my lost love, and in Dara, *my everything.*

"God, you wouldn't give me Dara and our baby if you were meaning to take them away... There is no way you could be that cruel. You're merciful. Kind. Please don't take away our baby, and protect its mama. I am in your debt, please." I beg and pray out loud in the car because I don't have any other option.

Traffic is slow, but I'm blazing my way to the hospital.

After parking at the entrance, I fling my door open, not caring if it gets towed. I have to get to Dara.

Right as I get out, Vanessa and Darren Jackson are rushing forward.

"I'll park the car, son. You see to my baby and yours." His rumbled voice is more of a roar than a statement.

I nod, toss him the keys, and grab Vanessa Jackson's hand so we can beat feet inside.

"Dara Jackson, Maternity!" I slap my hand down on the desk for information.

The individual gets the details, and we are motoring three floors up to room 343.

Even though my pace is a step below running, Mrs. Jackson is keeping up, just as eager to see her child. She's going to be an amazing grandmother. God willing our baby is okay.

The instant we get off the elevator, I see the sign toward her row of room numbers and head that direction.

I open the door, and there she is, hooked up to a couple machines, her eyes wide with fear, hair a wild mess of waves, color ashen. A doctor and a nurse are by her side, pushing her bed, wheeling her toward the door.

"Silas!" she cries out, her hand reaching out for me.

I take it and stop the bed. "What's going on?"

"Ultrasound. They need to make sure the baby is fine internally." She's squeezing my hand in a death grip.

"You the father?" the doctor queries.

"This is my fiancée, and yes, I'm the father," I answer on autopilot, squeezing my girl's hand and kissing her fingertips.

"Well, come on. No time to waste," the doctor grumbles.

"Mama!" Dara notices Mrs. Jackson.

"You go. I'll be right here with your daddy when you get

back."

Dara nods and pulls my hand to her chest. "I'm so glad you're here."

"It's going to be okay."

Tears slide down her cheeks as the doctor and nurse wheel the bed down the hallway.

"What if it's not?"

I close my eyes but keep walking, dread, fear, and anger warring for top bidding in my chest. I tamp down those feelings and force positivity into my heart. She needs this. I need this.

"It will be. Because it's us three. Together." My throat is raw, and my eyes fill with tears I can no longer hold back.

Please, God, don't make me a liar. I send one final prayer to the Big Guy upstairs in the hopes he will grant this one request.

She's wheeled into the room, next to a machine. This one is far more high-tech than the smaller ones we've seen in the gynecologist's office. There's a giant flat TV screen on the wall in front of us, another to the left of the machine.

The nurse lifts Dara's hospital gown and removes the contraptions strapped to her stomach. A reddened stripe about two inches thick crosses over her baby mound at a slant.

"What the fuck is that?" I ask, pointing to the red skin.

"Seat belt bruise," the doctor says before squirting gel on her belly and rubbing it around.

I wrap my arm around Dara's head and kiss the crown over and over. "It's going to be okay, baby."

She nods, but her body is trembling. I hate that she's scared, but I'm scared too. All we can do is brave it together. Sarah and I made it to this point last time, so I know when the doctor moves the handheld tool around it's going to produce images on the screen.

I wait with bated breath while the doctor takes over, presses the item to her belly, and flicks a button. The screen in front of us lights up, and our baby is there.

The doctor focuses the images on the baby's head, hits a bunch of buttons, and takes his time studying the skull.

I can't breathe. I'm stuck in a holding pattern with a weight on my chest the size of Texas. Nothing matters right now, nothing but that small rounded head and the doctor's assessment. Sweat breaks out at my hairline as we wait for what seems like hours but is probably only a single minute.

"Looks perfectly intact. I don't see anything to worry about on baby's head." The doctor punches more buttons. "Head measures correctly for twenty weeks along. Now let's focus on the spine."

Again, the doctor does his wiggle around the belly thing with the tool. I watch with extreme fascination as he clicks the image and looks intently at the entire line of our baby's spine, one vertebra at a time.

"Is the spine okay?" Dara asks, her voice cracking.

Doctor nods. "Yep. No problems."

She lifts my hand and holds it to her chest and face. Her lips rest on my fingertips. Every few seconds, I can feel wetness on the top of my hand from her tears.

"Baby's head and spine are good," I whisper in her ear. "So far everything is fine. Stay strong."

She swallows, and her body shudders with a large exhalation. I can sense her body relaxing, the stress leaving her with every image that pops on the screen.

Perfect head.

Perfect spine.

Perfect legs.

Perfect arms.

"Now I'm going to do the internal organs. You'll get to see the baby's heart pumping and the blood and oxygen in red and blue on the screen."

"No way!" I stare at the screen like it's the second coming of Jesus Christ Himself.

The doctor offers a small smile but flicks switches that show the heart pumping. "It's fast, probably because Mom is stressed but also because of the trauma. The heart is great. Nothing to report. Your daughter will relax inside the womb when Mom relaxes outside of the womb." This time he offers an out-and-out smile. "Everything is great. No problems. Your daughter is fine."

Daughter.

A girl.

We're having a girl.

Dara's hands squeeze mine so tight I can feel the blood pounding in my hand.

"Daughter? We're having a girl?" Her voice cracks.

The doctor turns his head. "I'm sorry. Did I ruin the surprise? You're twenty weeks. I assumed you already had this test."

Dara shakes her head. "Scheduled for tomorrow."

"Well, I...yes, you're having a girl." He moves the wand to the baby's bottom. "See right there?" He points to the space between a triangle shape. "No penis or testicles."

"We're having a baby girl. Silas?" Dara turns her head to me right as I sway backward and fall to my knees.

A girl.

I'm getting a second chance. A second chance at everything I've ever wanted.

"Thank you, God." My entire body quakes.

"Thank you," I whisper to Sarah and the baby we lost. Shivers race up and down my spine, goosebumps firing on my flesh.

"Thank you, Dara." I lean back on my heels, look up to the ceiling, and close my eyes. Ribbons of happiness replace the shaking, trembling, and nerves in a giant wave, coating all the sadness, fear, and grief, replacing it with life, love, and joy.

"I'm going to be a father. It's going to happen this time. I just know it!" I laugh and put my hands behind my head.

"You okay, son?" The doctor stands before me, holding out his hand. "Thought you were going down for the count there a minute ago."

I grip his hand, and he helps me to my feet. If gravity wasn't holding me down, I'd float away with the lightness filling my heart, body, and soul.

"Silas..." Dara reaches for me with both hands, and I go to her, resting my face right into her neck. As always, her sugary scent envelopes me.

She runs her fingers down my back, up my neck and over my head, forcing me to look her in the eyes. "You going to be okay?" Her words are whispered, quiet, and just for us.

I lick my lips and cup her cheeks, wiping away her tears with my thumbs. God, she's unearthly divine. "More than okay. Baby, I'm going to be a father to a little girl."

Her corresponding smile is one I haven't seen before. It's small, sweet, and lovely in its simplicity. "You're not sad it's a girl?" The same fear I had moments ago is plastered across her pretty face.

How could I have made her think that I wouldn't be happy about our child, whatever the gender?

Christ, I'm a fuckup.

I shake my head immediately, curl a hand around her nape, kiss her forehead, and set my other hand on her exposed belly. My child rolls under my palms, and I sigh with contentment.

"Listen to me, and hear what I'm saying." I get an inch closer so all she can see is me and all she can feel is my touch on her skin. Everything else needs to disappear so that she's encompassed by the intensity of what I feel for her and our daughter.

"I know what I've lost, Dara. Today, I also know what I've gained. This is our destiny. It's here. Right now. You, me, and our daughter."

★ ★ ★

Dara's moved back to her room and set up with the baby monitor. The nurses ask if we want the heartbeat sound turned off. We both practically scream our desire to have it blaring. Right now, we need to hear our daughter's heart beating. With every swoosh, a little of the panic and agony we just experienced fizzles away.

Just as she's settled, Vanessa and Darren Jackson enter.

"My baby!" her mother coos, arms open.

Dara sighs into her mother's embrace, and as I watch, all I can think is my woman is going to give that to our daughter. She's going to be loved and taught to love and nurture others by incredible women.

Darren holds out his hand. I grip it tight as he brings me into a hug. "Pleased you're taking care of my girl, doing the right thing."

"Nothing else I want in this world but your daughter's

hand and our baby, sir."

He claps me on the back. "Good man. We'll get along just fine, then."

"Yes, sir. I do believe we will."

"Mama, the baby is perfect. The doctor did all the tests, and guess what?" Dara has light in her eyes and excitement in her voice.

"What, baby? Should I brace for this?" Her mama holds on to the side of the hospital bed dramatically, as if a tornado is going to come crashing through the wall and take her away at any second.

"We're having a girl!" she squeals with delight.

Mrs. Jackson smiles widely, puts her hands to her chest, and looks up at the ceiling. Funny, I did the same thing when I found out but for much different reasons.

"Praise Jesus and the Lord above! My child is giving me a granddaughter!" She claps, lifts her shoulders, and hoots. "Darren, did you hear that? We're getting another baby girl!"

Darren smiles good-naturedly. "Another girl who looks like her?" He points to Dara, and then he looks at me. "Son, you're screwed. Buy a shotgun now. I had to beat the boys off with a stick and threaten them with a gun when they came sniffing around my baby, looking like a movie star since she was twelve years old. Then high school...ooo weee." He shakes his head. "Mark my words. You better have a son next so he can help...cuz you are shit outta luck, boy!" He laughs—loud and proud.

"Daddy! Our girl is going to be protected just fine. I'll teach her about boys, and her father will scare them away. I'm not worried!" Dara backs me up instantly and rubs at her belly.

Always there. Taking my back. My woman.

There's a knock on the door, and my mother opens it, peeking her head in. She must have received my frantic voice mail earlier when I was losing my shit.

"Is she okay?" I hear my brother Kevin's voice from behind her.

"Yeah, what's going on?" my baby sister Chantal says in a high-pitched whine I can hear through the door.

I'm sure the other two are behind them.

I head to the door and stop, holding up a finger to my mother. She nods and waits patiently.

I check with Dara. "Baby, you okay if my family comes in?"

She frowns. "Of course. They just want to make sure the baby is okay. Let them in, for goodness' sakes. Family is always welcome."

With that statement, my mother grins widely and opens the door, my four siblings following on her heels.

My mother comes to the bed and holds out her hand to Mrs. Jackson. "I believe we met a few weeks ago but under unpleasant circumstances."

Vanessa Jackson takes her hand. "You settle that foul-mouthed problem you had with one of your babies?" She goes right for the gusto.

My mother smiles. "Sure did. I believe my Whitney has a few things to say to your Dara. If the time is right, that is?"

"The time for apologies is always right," Mrs. Jackson confirms.

"Whit...I believe you have something to say to Dara, your brother's fiancée?" Mama reminds my sister.

Whitney plays with her long black braid, her face to the floor as she steps up. My sister must be wearing hair extensions, because her hair isn't normally that long. Still, they look real, and she rocks them well.

"It's okay. You don't have to say anything. I understand..." Dara starts. My lovely peacekeeper.

Whit cuts her off. "No, no. I was a horrible bitch, and I'm sorry. You didn't deserve the things I said, and when Mom called about you bein' in a car accident and halfway through your pregnancy, what happened to Sarah all came rushing back, but this time..." Her voice hitches, and tears slip down her cheeks. "This time I was worried I'd lost you and my niece or nephew before I ever got to know you, and those things I said were not *me*. Well, they were *me*, but so messed up, a bad side of me I never want to see again. And Dara...I'm sorry. So, so, sorry. Can you ever forgive me?" she finally rushes out, like a balloon losing all its air in one go.

"Done. Forgiven." Dara smiles genuinely, her appearance nothing but serene. Reminds me of when she's sitting before a room of clients, readying to teach meditation.

"That's it? No backlash?" Whitney frowns and bites her lip.

Dara's nose crinkles as she thinks about the question. "I don't hold grudges. Life is full of good and bad. Cause and effect. People say things they don't mean or mean them at the time but don't mean them later. Who am I to decide they aren't sorry when they've said it? I accept your apology and would very much like to get to know my future sister-in-law."

Whitney swallows, her mouth opening and closing for a second before she turns to me. "I can see now why you fell in love with her and are going to marry her."

I nudge her shoulder. "Duh!" I say, lightening the heaviness that entered the room with my sister and her drama.

At least she apologized. If Dara can move on and be the bigger person, so can I.

"I'm pretty sure it's because she's smokin' hot. Damn, bro." Kevin smirks, holding his hand up to his mouth and sucking in air between his teeth.

"Shut up. Don't look at my woman like that," I scold, narrowing my eyes.

Russell loops an arm over my shoulders. "Yeah, bro, she got a sister? I'd be all over that like Mom's fried chicken."

Dara and the women all chuckle. A fire ignites in my belly, the green-eyed monster rearing its ugly head.

"Bros, you better step off. That's my woman, who also happens to be carrying my baby girl in her belly! My ring on her finger. And no, she doesn't have any sisters!"

"A baby girl!" My mother gasps. "You're having a girl, Silas?"

I grin, go over to Dara's side, and grab her hand. She kisses the back of my hand and nods.

"Yeah, Ma, we're having a girl." I place my hand over her belly, rubbing a circle around the space where my daughter rests.

The entire room bursts out in cheers and tears equally. The guys, of course, give a bunch of "Congrats" and back slaps.

I chance a glance at my girl, and she's smiling away, sharing the pictures of our daughter the doctor gave us from the twenty-week check.

Our destiny.

CHAPTER TWENTY

It can be interpreted through many spiritual teachings and study of the seven chakras, that babies are driven by the third eye chakra from the moment they are in the womb and through the early years. A baby's motivations are based on intuition. Learning their way by touch, taste, sight, feel, and hearing. A person with a healthy third eye chakra will have an innate connection to their five senses. However, that doesn't mean the chakra will stay their primary driving source. That can change as their personalities form and they experience the beauty life offers.

DARA

Four months later...

"Seriously, Silas, if you ask if I'm okay one more time,

I'm going to throttle you!" I growl and then grunt, curling over and leaning against the railing at our home when another contraction barrels its way through me. My abdomen tightens, and at first I hold my breath.

"Breathe, lil' mama. In for five, out for five, remember," Silas coos softly.

I nod, allowing his words to seep into my frazzled mind. For a solid minute, I breathe with my husband, standing on one of the stairs in our home, preparing to head to the hospital.

After the car accident, Silas made quick work of getting me to the altar. He did not care that I was six months pregnant. We married in the backyard of our new home, a total of sixty people present. Guests were family and very close friends. I wore a silky white sundress and a crown of flowers around my head. We both wore flip-flops, mine with white sparkly beads, Silas's a deep brown. We encouraged friends and family to bring their swimsuits and provided beach towels as the giveaway with our names and wedding date embroidered on them. We had a local meat company come and grill out on a large BBQ, offered a full bar, and told everyone to dress casually. My father gave me away. Luna and Ricky stood up as my attendants, and on Silas's side, he had Atlas and Monet. We didn't care that we were mixing up the traditions because we're about making our own.

It was by far the best day of my life.

Now I think I'm going to have a new day that will take that position. The day I meet my daughter for the first time.

Silas opens the car door, his hand shaking as he does.

"Want me to drive?" I smirk and then wince when another contraction hits. "Oooooweeeee." I clench my teeth and wait until it stops before getting in the car.

Silas ignores my joke but runs around his BMW, gets in, puts the car in gear, and then jams out the drive and toward the hospital. We have a solid twenty-minute drive, but I hope it takes less than that. The baby seems to want out. Contractions are coming every three minutes, leading me to believe this is not going to be a long labor and delivery.

"Still keeping the name you want a secret?" I ask, trying to change the subject away from the agony starting at my back and rolling around to my abdomen.

Baby kicks, shoving her foot up into my ribcage. I grit through that annoyance and rub her little foot through my skin, trying to push it down. Poor thing is already upside down, and her head is smashed between my pelvic bones. She can't be enjoying this.

Silas purses his lips. "I'll know it for sure when I see her."

"Baby, what if I hate it?" I pout.

He grins at me briefly and puts one of his hands over my giant belly. "You won't. If it's meant to be, it will be. I can't force it on you, and vice versa."

"But I already told you mine." I frown and then grip the "oh shit" bar in preparation for another round of pain.

"Vanessa is your mother's name."

"Yeah, and it's a good name. A beautiful name, from a beautiful namesake. People name their children after their grandparents all the time."

"Then we should name her Vanessa Darlene," he quips.

I shrug. "If that's what you want." I'm willing to make any concession if I get to have Vanessa in my child's name.

He groans and rubs at the back of his neck, eyes focused on the road. "Baby, I don't. I just need to see our daughter before I commit. Okay?"

Another contraction barrels down on me, this one far stronger than any of the ones before.

"Shit, babe, only two minutes twenty seconds on that one. They are already progressing. Fuck!" He slams his hand down on the steering wheel.

I breathe and chant internally, willing my baby to wait until we get to the hospital. "It will be okay." I reach over and grab Silas's hand. "We've gotten this far. We'll get to the finish line too. Us three, safe and sound, remember?"

He sucks in a huge breath of air and lets it out. "Just us three."

"Until you knock me up again. But we agreed, baby has to be a full year old before we try again!" I remind him.

He grins and waggles his eyebrows.

"Nuh-uh, no way! I know that look, Mr. McKnight. You are not knocking me up six weeks after we have this one. I want some time with our daughter before we try. Close to two years apart. You agreed!"

Silas lifts my hand and kisses each of my fingers. "Whatever you wish is my command, my queen."

I roll my eyes. He's going to try to get me pregnant again right away. I just know it.

★ ★ ★

"One last push and you're done!" my doctor calls out. "Bear down, Dara. Let's meet your daughter!"

Both Silas and my mother have one of my thighs pushed back, and I'm spread wide. I take in as much air as I can, bear down with all my might, and then she's here.

My daughter.

On my belly. The nurses clean up my girl, wiping her off, revealing perfectly pink skin, lighter than both Silas and me, as well as wisps of dark-chocolate hair.

When she's clean, the nurse pushes up and removes my paper gown, leaving my breasts out free to the breeze, and sets my naked daughter right on top of my chest. A warm blanket is then put over both of us.

"I'm going to head out and tell everyone the good news. If that's okay with you two?" my mama asks.

"Yes, please," Silas says as my mother kisses my temple.

"So proud of you. So proud," she says before leaving us private time with our baby.

"You said you wanted to try to nurse right after birth, right?" the midwife asks.

I nod, mesmerized by my daughter in my arms.

"She's so little and perfect. Our daughter." Silas kisses my forehead, leans down, and presses his mouth to our baby's head. "I love you, Destiny. I love you, lil' one."

Destiny.

Chills and gooseflesh rise up all over my skin, and the tears fall. That's her name. He's known it all along. "Destiny Vanessa McKnight," I whisper in our little huddle.

Silas smiles huge and nods. "She's always been my destiny. Just like her mother. I love you, Dara." He kisses me slowly and softly.

"I love you. And I love you, my sweet cupcake." I snuggle her up higher so I can kiss her soft skin.

"Let's get her weighed and a tag on her right away," the nurse says, reaching for my girl. I hand her off, but the nurse brings her back and puts her right on my bare chest again. "Okay, Mom, she's ready. Seven pounds even. Twenty-one inches long even."

I commit that information to memory as Destiny's mouth starts to work against the fleshy part of my breast as if she already knows what to do.

"Lift up your breast with one hand, and as the baby starts to nuzzle, make sure you get as much of your entire nipple into her mouth as you can." The midwife peeks over, reaches forward, cradling her hand around my daughter's head and urging her deeper onto my breast. "There you go. Good, Mom. Now just enjoy. When she's full, I'd suggest Dad take off his shirt and have skin-on-skin bonding time right away too."

Silas nods. "Anything my girl needs. I'm right here." He hovers over the bed and watches our daughter nurse, petting her head and sniffing her. "She smells good already. You are like your mama, lil' one." He laughs while I pet my daughter's cheek.

When I'm done nursing and the baby is sleepy, I pass her off to a now shirtless Silas. He doesn't care who is there or what is going on; he wants direct bonding time as soon as possible. We discussed this at length between us and our midwife, and so far, everything is going perfectly. Since we're breastfeeding, Silas won't be doing feedings. We decided I'd feed and he'd burp and settle her so we both have as much equal bonding time as possible.

"Just pat and rub her back," the midwife encourages as Silas adjusts the baby's head on his muscled pec, and the midwife puts the blanket over the two of them.

"How's it feel, Daddy?" I ask my man while the team of people clean me up and get me ready to move into the receiving room.

Silas smiles huge. "Right. It feels right."

The baby makes a tiny burp noise, and I can tell by the cheesy facial expression that he's pleased with himself.

"Can I have her back now?" I purse my lips and reach out my hands.

"Yeah." His tone is husky and filled with emotion. "You want your mama, lil' one? Me too. But you're going to have to share, and she's going to have to share you too, with me. All right? Good that we got that settled early on," he discusses with our sleeping baby.

He passes our daughter off to me, and then the team wheels me into the room we'll be in for the next day or two.

★ ★ ★

I have never felt so loved in my entire life. Between Silas and my daughter, my heart is filled to bursting. I never knew I could feel this way.

Silas, my husband, which is still hard to even think is reality, is leaning his bum on my bed while I hold our daughter. My parents have just come in to meet her privately, but the horde of visitors is encroaching.

"Mom, Dad, Silas and I would like to introduce you to Destiny Vanessa McKnight," I say proudly but with a little warble to my voice. I've wanted to give this gift to my mama my whole life. She gave me everything when I was eight years old, and I had nothing to give in return. And now, at twenty-five, I can give her a namesake in my child.

My mother stops by the side of my bed, lifts up both her hands to her face, and promptly bursts into tears. "I never thought I'd have this, Darren. Never," she croaks, her rounded body and bosom heaving with the effort.

"Mama, I love you. Silas and I want to honor you by giving our child your name. Give back a little of what you've given me. I chose you, the same way you chose me."

"Give me my grandbaby before I lose my mind, child." She kisses my head not once but twice. Double the love. It's her signature.

Silas lifts our daughter, walks around my bed, and places her in her grandmother's arms.

"Look, Darren. Our grandbaby. Living proof of our legacy of love," she whispers, but I can hear her. My mother has never treated me like an adopted child but rather a part of her soul because she chose it to be that way. I was never at a loss for love, and now my girl is going to have that love in them too. I couldn't be happier.

At least I thought so until an impatient knock on the door. Behind the door is not only Silas's entire family but the Hart and the Powers clans too.

I simply watch my daughter get passed around from person to person, Silas the guard, needing to watch each handoff as if he were a referee. The man cannot settle. He wants to be near Destiny and me at all times. I think he's still reeling from finally becoming a father after battling that desire for so long. Regardless, it's beautiful, and I'm not going to nag or scold him about his overprotective ways.

Over time, my guy will get used to the fact that he has a loving wife and a daughter who are alive and well. It may take a while, but I'll be there to help him find his way. My intuition is strong, and I know what he needs intimately...our Destiny, together.

EPILOGUE

Two years later...

SILAS

The sun is warm on my skin as I sit outside with the chubby bundle snuggled in my arms. Dara is in the pool, Destiny in her arms as she spins around in the shallow end. My girl loves the pool. She loves anything dangerous. My lil' one was walking at ten months and trying to dive in head first at twelve. Like Dara, she's not afraid of anything. Destiny accepts life as it comes.

I love watching my girls together. Carefree, easy, no worries. It gives me peace to see their smiles, and these two smile a lot.

Unlike my serious little man in my lap. Jackson Devon McKnight, our six-month-old. Dara pushed to wait a full year to get pregnant with our second child, but I won out in the end. Okay, I won by three months. She allowed us to try when Destiny was nine months old. Of course, we got pregnant right away.

When we went to get our twenty-week sonogram and I found out we were having a son, I responded much like I did the first time. Much to my chagrin. Having two beautiful women in the house was a blessing and a curse at the same time.

These women own my soul, control all my thoughts. I needed another man to help pick up the slack. And I got him. Boy, did I get my match. Jackson Devon, named after Dara's parents and my dad, is exactly like me so far, with one exception—he's calm like Dara. He enjoys the scenery. Never cries. Sleeps well. Eats well. Doesn't make a fuss. If he can see his mother or his sister in the vicinity, he's a happy guy. Same as me. With my girls in my direct line of sight, I feel peace. It seems he gets that too. Jackson loves just taking in the sights. Sitting on his old man's lap and chilling. He's happiest with me. I think it's because he likes to see the McKnight girls in action, not the other way around.

I watch as Dara swings Destiny around in a circle before placing her on her hip and exiting the pool. The water runs down my wife's sexy-as-hell body in the small bikini she only wears at home. The water droplets sluice over her curves in the same way I want to use my tongue.

She sets Destiny down, and my naked little girl runs over to me. "Daddy!" She holds out her wet arms, and I curve my arm around her side, allowing her to soak my polo and shorts. I don't care. I'm never going to pass up an opportunity to hug my daughter. Ever. I missed so many of those with the children I lost, I'll take advantage of every second with the ones I do have in my life. Be it my children or other children I love. They are all blessings and deserve to be treated as such.

"Did you get my text?" Dara asks, leaning forward, her long hair sending wet drops onto our baby's legs. He giggles and pats at them.

"Yeah. You said the Harts are coming to hang for dinner. Want me to grill out?"

She nods. "Laid out steaks to marinate. You know what Moe told me?"

"What?"

"They're trying for number three!"

"Seriously?"

She nods. "I'm thinking we should time it right so that we can be pregnant at the same time. That would be so fun!"

I grin. "Woman...you just had a baby six months ago, and you're telling me you want to get pregnant again? Already?"

She curves a sexy shoulder toward her chin. "Maybe I like the result?"

I waggle my eyebrows at her seductively. "I think we should start trying tonight."

"Is that right?"

"Hell yeah. No time to waste!" I raise myself out of the chair, my boy in one arm. I grab her waist with my free hand and plaster her wet body against mine. "If these kids were sleeping, I'd already have you pregnant."

She snort-laughs in the cute way that drives me wild. "Really. You think your swimmers are that good?"

"Try me. You. Just. Try. Me," I taunt.

My beautiful wife purses her lips, picks up our baby girl, and grabs a towel from the stack by the door. "You think it's your destiny to get me pregnant tonight?" She grins.

I shake my head. "No, baby. We already have our destiny, our future..." I snuggle Jackson close and kiss his sweet baby cheek. "Let's just be free."

"Free?" One of her eyebrows rises with inquiry.

"Yeah, lil' mama."

"I got you." She winks and sways her hips as she turns to bring our daughter inside and get dinner ready for our guests.

"Yeah, you do, from the moment I laid eyes on you, I knew you were special. My intuition told me," I call out as I follow her into our home. I'd follow this woman anywhere.

THE END

Want more of the Lotus House clan?
Continue on with Luna Marigold
and Grant Winters' story in:

Enlightened End
Book Seven in the *Lotus House Series*
Coming June 26th, 2018

EXCERPT FROM *ENLIGHTENED END*

A LOTUS HOUSE NOVEL (BOOK #7)

The Winters Group offices are located inside the Transamerica Building, the second-tallest skyscraper in the heart of the San Francisco financial district. What's most interesting about the building is that it's shaped like a pyramid. A friend told me there is a conference room at the top that they use to impress a big client or seal an important business deal. I'm certain I never want to set foot in it.

Interestingly enough, there's a security screening station in place. I move right over to it, my canvas wedges squeaking on the marble floor. I set my purse on the conveyer belt and head toward the officer. Without a word, probably because I didn't set off any buzzers or alarms, I'm allowed to continue through. The security guard hasn't taken his eyes off my chest or body since I walked up. Ignoring him, I make my way over to the table to await my bag.

I notice out of the corner of my eye the guard is still checking me out, only this time, it's my ass as I wait for my purse. When my purse pops out and I toss it over my shoulder, I hear him address the person who was standing behind me.

"Yeah, sir, you're going to need to give me your building ID." His voice is stern and authoritative.

Funny, he didn't ask me for my access pass. I think about telling him this fact but realize if I do, he's going to prevent me from gaining access to Grant Winters, and I *need* to see the man face-to-face. He has to look me in the eye and tell me he's destroying my life's work...my family legacy. I'll have it no other way.

Hustling to grab my purse, I spin on my wedge and head toward the directory. Apparently, five full floors are occupied by the Winters Group. I jet to the bank of elevators and pick the last floor because it has a little placard that says Winters Group Executives next to it. I want to whoop with glee at my good fortune. Then again, the people who come here are usually preapproved, and somehow my bubble-butt got me through. I'll just thank my lucky stars and hope my luck sticks.

When I exit the elevator, a woman in a tailored gray suit glances up at me from the receptionist's desk. Her dark hair is pinned back into a severe bun, her lips stained a cherry red. Her eyes are almond shaped. Interesting. Kind of like a cat's.

"May I help you?"

"Um, yeah, sure. I need to see Mr. Grant Winters, please." I smile my most genuine, cheery smile.

As the woman frowns and clicks on her keyboard, staring at a computer monitor, I'm not so sure my charming smile is going to work.

"Your name?"

"Luna Marigold. I'm the owner of Lotus House Yoga in Berkeley."

The woman's eyes narrow briefly. "And do you have an appointment with Mr. Grant?"

I shake my head and cross my arms over the high bar of the reception desk, getting comfortable. "No. He, uh, sent me this letter, and instead of calling or emailing, I figured it would be best to chat face-to-face. You know, look the man in the eyes while we do business." I pull out the letter they sent. It's crumpled and creased, definitely not flat, white, and pristine like it was when I received it.

I hand her the letter and she scans it. Her eyes widen momentarily. "I'm certain Mr. Grant would rather you email your concerns or any questions you have regarding the eviction of Lotus House Yoga. According to this document, your building is being demolished in six months. There's nothing further to discuss."

I clear my throat and inhale and exhale smoothly, calming myself down. "Excuse me, Miss. I don't mean to be rude, but this is my business. My family, my life. My studio. And your boss is going to demolish it in five months and twenty-eight days. I think I deserve the right to discuss this situation with him *directly*. This is not for you to decide. Now, if you would be so kind as to contact Mr. Grant, tell him I am here, and I'll be waiting in reception over there." I point to a grouping of white office chairs. "I'll wait as long as it takes for him to see me. I'd appreciate it." I offer my cheery smile, even though this woman does not deserve it.

Her lips pinch together, and she cocks her head. She reaches for the phone and presses a button. "Yes, Mr. Grant. I'm sorry to bother you, but a Luna Marigold of Lotus House Yoga is here without an appointment."

I narrow my eyes, but she doesn't falter. Apparently being bitchy is her norm.

"Yes, I know it's most *unusual* for a person to show up without an appointment... I can tell her to leave if..."

"I'm not leaving until you speak to me!" I say loud enough

for the person she's talking to on the phone to hear me.

The receptionist swallows. "Yes, you heard that. She'll be sitting in the reception area when you're finished with your meeting. I understand. Thank you, Mr. Grant."

Her gaze narrows to slits. "Mr. Grant has a meeting now but will call for you when he's done. You're lucky he's being so kind. It's not his usual style." She practically sneers.

"Have you ever taken yoga?" I ask, throwing off her bitchy vibe.

"What?"

"Meditation?" I continue unfettered.

"Excuse me?"

"Had your chakras realigned?"

"I don't even know what you're talking about. Yoga and meditation. Charkas. Pfft." She waves a dismissive hand like I just spoke another language.

"You'd be a lot nicer, much happier, and your face would have fewer *wrinkles* if you practiced yoga and spiritual wellness."

Her eyes widen to the size of saucers.

I dig through my purse and pull out a card. "Here's a free yoga class card. It's good for yoga, vinyasa flow, aerial, naked yoga, meditation—any class we offer, really." I shrug. "You should give it a shot. You'd feel and look so much better." This time I do offer my cheery smile again.

"Naked yoga?" she whispers.

I grin. "Totally. And it's taught by this hunk named Atlas Powers."

"A man teaches it?" She lifts a hand to her chest as if she's shocked.

"Yep, it's co-ed too. It's all about freeing your societal

restrictions. Challenging yourself to let go, release everything negative you are holding on to. Even the clothing you wear. Basically, it's designed to set you free."

"Wrinkles?" She presses her fingertips to a tiny line forming between her brows, probably from being so crabby all day at her job. "Yoga gets rid of wrinkles?"

"It can. If you are doing the right facial poses, as well as letting go of stress, getting good sleep, and drinking lots of water."

The woman shakes her head and lifts her hand to take the card from the top of her desk. "Thank you," she mumbles and looks down and away.

"No problem. *Namaste*, friend."

"Friend." She half laughs, as if me calling her friend is funny. I'm not sure why she would think it was so humorous. I'm a firm believer that anyone can turn into a friend, even if they are at first rude. Sometimes people do not realize how their actions hurt others. Everyone makes mistakes, and everyone deserves second chances. This is something I was taught by my mother and father, and I continue to live by that motto. It's served me well over the years.

"Anyway, thank you. Go ahead and take a seat until Mr. Winters calls for you."

"Sounds like a plan. I'll just be over here reading." I pull out my tattered and worn-out favorite book, *The Seven Spiritual Laws of Success* by Deepak Chopra. Every time I lose my sense of self or my path in the business world or otherwise, I start reading about each law. The lessons he teaches in this self-help book guide a person through finding their own path to enlightenment and success in all things. It's helped me a hundred times over, and I hope it does again.

Right as I finish thumbing through the section on the *Laws of Least Effort*, which refers to acceptance of a situation, taking responsibility, expending energy given through love, and keeping myself open to all points of view, the receptionist calls out to me.

"Mr. Winters will see you now." She smiles softly, stands, and heads my direction. "Through these doors."

Hey, I got the icy woman to smile, a good sign. Maybe my karma is turning around and is about to move in my favor. Though again, like Deepak teaches in his books, I have to be detached from what I want but still hopeful. If it happens, it happens. Be okay with the outcome you receive as it comes.

Right now, however, I'm not okay with any outcome other than this Mr. Winters person agreeing not to bulldoze my dream and my apartment, not to mention the bakery where I have breakfast every morning, the café where I eat my lunch or dinner every day, and the bookstore where I score all my favorites titles.

The receptionist leads me down a long hallway. We pass by a bunch of glass windows where I can see people on their phones or busily typing away on their computers. It's weird, though, because the windows are glass, but they aren't windows to see *outside*. They are windows to see the people *inside*.

A shiver ripples down my spine, and my hair stands up. It's not a good feeling. I wouldn't be able to work in a fishbowl. As it is, Lotus House is painted with murals depicting a forest, waterfall, and the ocean. I'm greeted by people who want to see me. They come just to see me and take my class and listen to my words and teachings. The thought of sitting behind a desk and being watched from the outside gives me a frightened feeling.

Silently, I send out a bit of soothing energy to the folks who work here, pushing love, light, and serenity their way.

The receptionist stops at a set of double doors at the very end of the hall. She knocks and then, without waiting, opens the door for me. "Mr. Grant. Luna Marigold," she announces but doesn't exactly introduce us. I can't even see the man until I walk past her and through the door.

The office is huge, with a seating area, a bar, and a glass desk with chrome piping. The windows are not exactly floor to ceiling, but they are slanted, so he must have an amazing view of the city. The windows are frosted over, and I don't know if this is a type of glaze or if it's like one of those super-secret type blinds like in the movies. It reminds me of the way light filters through a shoji screen. It actually gives off a very calming effect, even though the rest of the room is black, white, and chrome, lacking any personality.

The big glass desk has a chair behind it, and I can see a head of dark hair peeking over the top, but he's facing the other way.

"Okay, Father, thank you. I'll handle it." He turns fast, slams the phone into the cradle, and his eyes shoot to mine. They are the most piercing shade of sapphire blue. His hair is a dark mess of waves. His chin is slightly squared, with high cheekbones and a beautiful, strong, straight nose. His lips are what steal my attention. They are perfectly shaped with a dip on the top lip I'd like nothing more than to rest my finger against. The bottom lip is full, an elegant crescent shape, which suits his face.

In a word: Remarkable.

His eyes fill with something I can't quite name before he stands, buttons his blazer, and comes over to me. I haven't moved.

He holds out his hand. My goodness he's tall. Well over six feet. Maybe six two or three.

"Grant Winters."

I blink before extending my hand. The second our hands touch, a sizzle of energy so hot hits my palm. I jolt back a few steps and pull my hand away from his hold.

"I must have zapped you. I'm sorry." He smiles.

Sweet Shiva. His smile. Even. White. Brilliant.

"Are you going to speak?"

I open my mouth, close it, and open it again until I manage to mutter, "Um...I'm Luna."

"Luna." His voice is a clear, crisp, masculine tone. Confident. Straightforward.

"Yes. Luna Marigold from Lotus House Yoga."

He folds one arm over the other, and I watch the move as if he's just performed a special dance. Every inch of him is mesmerizing, from the tip of his shiny black shoes, up his long legs, to his broad frame and tanned neck. He's wearing a tailored navy suit, which fits him to perfection. His hair is the only thing a bit wild about him. Everything else is dialed in to the most minute detail.

"Wow," I whisper, not realizing I let it out.

He grins. "I could say the same about you. Redheads are quite unique...special, even. Did you know that fewer than two percent of people are redheads?"

The question hits my sluggish brain and rolls around until something clicks. "Um, yeah. I did know that. Same with green eyes."

Grant walks over to his desk and leans his bum against the surface. He crosses his ankles over one another while placing his hands on the top, fingers curling around the edge. Cool as a cucumber. Casual, almost approachable, definitely cocky.

"How can I help you today, Luna?"

Continue reading in:

Enlightened End
A Lotus House Novel: Book Seven
Coming June 26th, 2018

ALSO BY AUDREY CARLAN

The Calendar Girl Series

January (Book 1)
February (Book 2)
March (Book 3)
April (Book 4)
May (Book 5)
June (Book 6)

July (Book 7)
August (Book 8)
September (Book 9)
October (Book 10)
November (Book 11)
December (Book 12)

The Calendar Girl Anthologies

Volume One (Jan-Mar)
Volume Two (Apr-Jun)

Volume Three (Jul-Sep)
Volume Four (Oct-Dec)

The Falling Series

Angel Falling
London Falling
Justice Falling

The Trinity Trilogy

Body (Book 1)
Mind (Book 2)
Soul (Book 3)
Life: A Trinity Novel (Book 4)
Fate: A Trinity Novel (Book 5)

The Lotus House Series

Resisting Roots (Book 1)
Sacred Serenity (Book 2)
Divine Desire (Book 3)
Limitless Love (Book 4)
Silent Sins (Book 5)

Intimate Intuition
(Book 6)
Enlightened End
(Book 7)

ACKNOWLEDGMENTS

To my editor. **Ekatarina Sayanova** with **Red Quill Editing, LLC**...Thank you for knowing all of my bad writing habits and loving me anyway. This time I SWEAR I'll try to remember that Heaven and Hell were not capitalized in the bible so they are not capitalized in a manuscript. Of course, if I forget, I know you'll fix them. #GoTeamAC

To my Waterhouse Press editor, **Jeanne De Vita,** I adore working with you. Your spunk, sass, and smarts are such a blast. Thank you.

To my one and only pre-reader, **Ceej Chargualaf**, I hope you truly understand how much you mean to me and this process. It's been an incredible year, and with you on my team, I always know there's someone there to lift me up when I'm down. And yes, since I dedicated the book to you, Silas is yours, with the exception that you must share him with Dara. #madlove

Jeananna Goodall, thank you for always being the light when I'm dark. The dark when I'm light, and helping me to find a sense of balance. You understand me, my soul, and why I write my stories. Having you at my back is magical.

Ginelle Blanch, Anita Shofner, and Tracey Vuolo, I love the differences you bring to the beta process. From the emotional, small error finds, to the way my stories touch your heart, I can't imagine not having you as part of the process.

To the Audrey Carlan Street Team of wicked hot Angels, together we change the world. One book at a time. BESOS-4-LIFE, lovely ladies.

ABOUT AUDREY CARLAN

Audrey Carlan is a #1 *New York Times, USA Today*, and *Wall Street Journal* bestselling author. She writes wicked hot love stories that are designed to give the reader a romantic experience that's sexy, sweet, and so hot your ereader might melt. Some of her works include the wildly successful Calendar Girl Serial, Falling Series, and the Trinity Trilogy.

She lives in the California Valley where she enjoys her two children and the love of her life. When she's not writing, you can find her teaching yoga, sipping wine with her "soul sisters" or with her nose stuck in a wicked hot romance novel.

Any and all feedback is greatly appreciated and feeds the soul. You can contact Audrey below:

E-mail: carlan.audrey@gmail.com
Facebook: facebook.com/AudreyCarlan
Website: www.audreycarlan.com